"Jessica Stone is a gifted storyteller and doesn't just write–she paints on the universal canvas of love, loss, and redemption. A remarkable author to watch!"

~ Tara Johnson, author of *To Speak His Name,*
All Through the Night, Where Dandelions
Bloom, Engraved on the Heart, and others.

"This story wrecked me in the best way. It's raw, real, and so beautifully written that I felt every ounce of grief, longing, and redemption right alongside Elle. It's about love—the kind that breaks you, heals you, and changes you. It's a story of faith, forgiveness, and finding your way back to the people who matter most. If you've ever wrestled with loss, regret, or the question of whether second chances are possible, this book is for you—and it will stay with you long after the last page."

Emily Hampton, author of *Grace Like Wildflowers,*
Barefoot in Heaven and the *Barefoot in Heaven Devotional,*
Holy Shenanigans, and *Dancing Toward Forever.*

Beauty in the Bittersweet

JESSICA STONE

Dedication

To my mom,
who supported me when I made her an unanticipated grandma,
believes in me when I don't know what I'm doing,
and will never let me forget how much she loves me.

And to my girl,
who made me a mother,
yet somehow became the one I go to for life advice,
and will always be my reason for not giving up.

A mother/daughter relationship is one of the most complex, up and
down, angsty, wonderful, heart-wrenching, love-hate, beautifully
messy connections there is. Thank you both for teaching me a mother's
love—sometimes tough, always gracious, infinite and unfailing.

Saudade

/souˈdädə/

Noun: *a feeling of longing, melancholy, or nostalgia*
that is supposedly characteristic of the Portuguese or
Brazilian temperament. (Dictionary.com)

Saudade is an emotional state of nostalgic longing for someone
that you love. However, it acknowledges that longing for the past
detracts from excitement for the future. Saudade describes both happy
and sad at the same time, which is most closely translated
to the English saying 'bittersweet.' (Wikipedia)

Chapter One

$\mathcal{D}$ust floated high in the air, illuminated by midday sunshine refracting through the stained glass that drew my gaze. I focused on the particles, willing myself to rise and dance among them, leaving this heaviness behind. If only it were so simple. Instead, my fantasy was sharply disturbed by the squeal of the podium microphone as my only remaining relative adjusted it to her liking.

"Today is a day I never imagined would come. It doesn't seem possible that such a brilliant light could just be blown out like that—in an instant."

The same ubiquitous breath capable of snuffing out a life lifted the hairs from my skin, and I rubbed my arms.

"Each of you made my sister's life richer by being a part of it, whether Catherine was your counselor, a friend... your mom." Aunt Jan looked down at me in the front row before seeking out others in the pews farther back, then continued, "Despite being less than five-and-a-half feet tall, she was larger than life. Perhaps that's why she's gone so soon." There were some titters at this, mixed in with the sniffling. My aunt's attempt at levity fell flat for me, however, and I shifted my weight on the unforgiving pew.

"Catherine survived harsher tragedies than most people will ever face, although I know there are exceptions in this very room. Yet, for all her heartbreak, I still envied her, in a way. She seemed to have an innate grasp of what was truly important. She didn't hold ill will toward anyone, though she certainly could have. Instead, her pain became her purpose—her passion and motivation for helping others."

I might not have known names or faces, but I'd recognized the scattering of single-parent households as I'd passed them by on my way down the aisle. Their posture, the way they huddled, trying to somehow make up for the space between them. Partial families like mine had been—torn apart by violence.

Aunt Jan's voice thickened with unshed tears. "She may have been my baby sister—she will *always* be my baby sister—but she was also my touchstone. She wouldn't want us to spend too long mourning her. No, not Catherine. She would remind us that she is in heaven surrounded by all the love she could ever ask for, so we should pour that love into those who need it here. That's exactly what she lived to do—give love to those who didn't have enough."

As the congregation stood, the air rustled, dispersing the dust into parts unknown. And I gazed upward, wishing it would take me too.

I caught my reflection through grainy eyes in the entryway mirror as I hung my keys next to the front door. My nose was rubbed raw, and I was surprised the pounding in my head wasn't visible. But today, tears had been acceptable, and they'd flowed like the Yahara River—slow and steady—since the moment I'd entered the church.

Mom's funeral service had been referred to as "simply lovely" by those who had attended. It had been simple, just as she would have wanted. There was a time Catherine Miles kept a long list of contacts. She'd been the type to exchange numbers with anyone to whom she sensed a connection: a barista at her coffee shop, a stranger at a bookstore, even *my* friends. However, as the years added up, she clearly valued time with those closest to her over trying to hang on to five decades worth of acquaintances. I was grateful for the pared-down gathering. I'd hated mingling in the roomful of strangers almost as much as laying my mother to rest. Those I didn't know kept a respectful distance, drawn more to my aunt, who tolerated their tears and rhetorical questioning *whys*.

These moments were my first alone other than fitful sleep in almost a week. My steps slowed as I wandered through the living room, inhaling the familiar citrusy scent that lingered beneath the aroma of too many donated casseroles. Mom had always stayed mid-project, and her daily routine waited for her now: files she'd intended to look over stacked on the side table, photos with at-risk youth she'd mentored slanted against the wall to be hung, and magazines she always bought but rarely made time to read piled on the lower shelf of the coffee table.

My plan to hire an estate manager after selecting a few important mementos might have seemed practical but now struck me as unrealistic. How could I relegate my mother, who had always given so much for me, to trinkets small enough to fit into my suitcase?

Making my way to the kitchen, I avoided the avalanche of leftovers in the fridge and half-heartedly rummaged through the pantry. I knew I should eat but lacked the motivation to even transfer a no-thank-you helping to a microwave-safe dish. It's funny what a loss of this magnitude takes with it. Grief replaced so much, my appetite included.

I spotted a distinct yellow lid and reached for the jar, then shook my head at its paltry weight. My mother's deeply guilty pleasure. Despite her perpetual diet, she could never resist a few spoonsful of Biscoff Cookie Butter late at night. The sweet crunchiness brought back memories of our study sessions ten years before—me at the start of high school, her taking college courses online. Both of us lying on the carpeted floor in front of the fireplace as we alternated between catching up on that day and preparing for the next while passing the jar back and forth.

The vibration of my phone interrupted my reverie. I checked the caller ID and licked the spoon clean, taking several seconds to steel myself before answering.

"Hey."

"Hey."

So, we were being civil today.

"I just wanted to let you know I'm heading home this week. Josh is going to pick things up in Toronto."

My husband, Micah, was the tour manager for a rock band whose popularity had skyrocketed, creating the earliest links in a chain of events that led to the current precarious state of our marriage. I still wavered between sticking it out or just walking away. That's what starter marriages were for, right? But, so far, we were both holding on—if not to each other, then to the hope we'd had not so long ago.

His colleague Josh had been a godsend over the last year, but ambivalence about Micah not being in Canada when I returned home stalled my reply. I belatedly murmured, "Oh. Ok, that's good." A longer silence. We both cleared our throats. "I probably need to pack up a lot more here than I expected. You know, you never realize how much stuff there is ... " My voice trailed off.

"Yeah, I figured that might happen." His tone was low, wary. His words, like mine, sounded unnatural and cautiously chosen. We were still on eggshells, but at least we were speaking. Oddly, my mother's death had brought back a hint of our old 'I've got your six' alliance. Micah might not have been privy to how I'd pushed Mom away lately, but he knew I was not prepared to lose her. Especially not like this. So suddenly, when she'd seemed to be in the best of health.

Nostalgia provided a flash of sentimentality, and I whispered, "I missed you today," then held my breath. I almost wanted to take the words back, but not because they weren't true.

"Elle." He hesitated, and the weight of his momentary silence pushed the air from my lungs. "I'm sorry. I'll see you when you get back." The phone went dead, and I was once again alone with my thoughts, and a heart full of *what-ifs*.

Morning came early, and with it, disorientation, as remnants of loss-filled dreams tried to keep me in their clutches even as my circadian rhythm pulled me into the new day. The realization that something was wrong never came gradually. One minute, I was benignly confused—the next, sorrow slammed into my chest. Awareness filled me, hitching a ride from my heart through my veins to seep into every finger and toe.

My mother is gone.

I'm officially an orphan.

I stumbled to the bathroom and splashed my face with cold water in a futile effort to turn my mind to the tasks before me. I could have kicked myself for allowing the previous evening to pass without putting much of a dent in the lengthy to-do list I'd insisted I could complete on my own. After organizing the funeral, Aunt Jan had headed back to Illinois when it was over, mercifully taking the names of everyone who needed a thank you card with her. My mother's realtor, Vicky Miller, had become her close friend after Mom purchased this home. Vicky assured me my mother had provided her with everything she needed to take care of the listing and hopefully easy sale. The rest was up to me.

Five minutes later, my mind barely a step ahead of my feet, I trudged down the stairs to start coffee, already on the phone with the first on my list of pod-style moving companies to gather information on rates and availability.

Unlike me, my aunt was an early riser, and she'd had the coffee brewing before I'd even woken up the last several mornings. The perky voice on the other end of the call asked me to hold, and I gratefully activated the phone's speaker before setting it down. My still-bleary gaze skimmed along the countertop until it landed on the ceramic container mirthfully labeled 'Coffee-Coffee-Coffee' in tribute to one of our favorite Lorelai Gilmore lines.

The intense aroma of espresso brought life to my eyes as I scooped it into a filter. Using the pot to fill the water reservoir, I turned the faucet off just in time to hear Little Miss Bubbly inform me that the pod I needed could be delivered as early as the following evening. As she prattled off the confirmation number, I managed to bump the metal carafe against the coffee jar, knocking it over and spilling its contents.

Hurrying the young woman off the phone—and trusting that my pod was reserved without copying down the mix of numbers and letters she'd provided—my eyes followed the wasted trail of finely-ground beans. They streamed from the tipped container to the counter, trickling to the floor. With a heavy sigh, I righted the canister. At least today's pot was salvaged. That's when I saw the white shard on the tile, nearly eclipsed by the pile of squandered dark roast.

The lip of the ceramic jar had hit the edge of the granite just right, not only busting off a V-shaped fragment but leaving a crack that ran nearly to its base. I'd made my mom that coffee canister years ago in a school pottery class, anticipating the laugh she'd get from the *Gilmore Girls* reference. I stifled the wave of despair that rose in my chest and threatened to push me to my knees. She would have said, "It had a good run," while shooing me away so she could clean up my mess.

Good thing I'd gotten used to cleaning up after myself lately. Even if it was my own fault for rejecting the help I knew she would have offered. Skirting the pile, I went to find her broom.

By early afternoon, I had a system as I sorted through Mom's downstairs possessions: general donations, items her church could use, anything with monetary (but not sentimental) value to post online, and things I would need to ship to relatives or friends. In an ever-growing offshoot box near the last group were various personal effects I might not keep for myself but needed a moment to touch, smell, and remember once more. Things liable to make me cry, but I couldn't—*wouldn't*—take time for that today.

A couple of hours later, I took a break from packing to check my work voicemail. As the licensing assistant at a small media publishing house, part of a team promoting music for film and television, I'd aspired to make myself indispensable over the last two years. Over my mild protestations, Henry, my boss, had offered two weeks of leave when my mother died. I was grateful for his generosity, but the time away was both a blessing and a curse. What details might slip through the cracks? Or worse, who else might they pull in to fill my absence?

Satisfied that my work life was in order, I hung up and assembled another cardboard box for the built-in shelves I'd been clearing. Amidst the books and keepsakes, a silver hinged frame caught my attention.

My parents on their wedding day in one side. Micah and me on ours in the other. Both days filled with such promise for the years ahead. Promises that had been broken for all of us.

Micah and I first met three and a half years earlier, when I was twenty-one, during an internship for my final semester at Belmont University, where I obtained my BBA in Music Business. Nashville can be a small town, and after our initial meeting, our paths crossed a few times in the following months, both of us eventually confiding we had begun to seek the other out.

I remembered calling my mom to tell her about him.

Me: Guess what! I'm going on a date with the guy I told you about...
Mom: Oh? Malachi, right?
Me: No, Micah! Micah Reed.
Mom: Oh yes. I knew it was one of those minor prophets.
Me, glad she couldn't see my eyes roll: Ugh ... Mom!
Mom: What are your plans?
Me: I don't know yet—he said he's taking me somewhere in Nashville he's sure I've never been before. It's on Friday night, and it's supposed to be super nice out. Help me pick what to wear!

She suggested a dress I'd worn a hundred times, like I knew she would. And I didn't wear it, like she probably knew I wouldn't. But until recently, she'd always been the first person I called to share any news. The shoulder I cried on when Micah and I had our first disagreement. The first to know we had confessed our love to each other. Our first trip together was to visit her. She welcomed him with open arms, then promptly put him to work on a pile of chores she had saved up. I was mortified, but it became obvious he didn't *just* want to make a great impression.

The two of them were thick as thieves in no time, and Mom joked that his easygoing personality might tone down my Type A tendencies. Later, I overheard her telling Micah how much my father would have loved meeting him. She shared this like a secret, waiting until I'd left the room. It was one of the rare times she brought her late husband up, and I was surprised she revealed even this much to my new boyfriend.

I barely remember my dad, John, though I sometimes dream of a voice I imagine was his fighting its way back from my unconscious while I sleep. I was in second grade when he died, the victim of a panicked young mugger while away on a business trip, and for a while, it was as if both my parents were lost. But our fractured family survived. Time was a kind healer for me, and faith, a healer for my mother.

Satisfied that my work life was in order, I selected an apple from the fruit basket someone had sent and decided I needed a change of scenery—or at least a move to the second floor. I climbed the stairs to my mom's office, considering what to do with her computer, printer, and other electronics. The small room appeared neat, but I knew my mother, and I anticipated drawers and shelves that stashed everything from coloring kits to scientific calculators. Grabbing an empty plastic tub, I decided to start in the closet.

Ten minutes later, with the extra school supplies now packed away, I came upon an unlabeled banker's box on the floor. Opening it, I had a cloudy recollection of much of the contents. For as long as I could remember, the Bible on my mother's nightstand had been accompanied by some sort of pretty notebook, replaced every so often with a new one. I'd never even seen her writing in them, but here they were by the dozens, worn spines lined up.

I reached for one with a dainty floral cover. It was small but thick, and I opened it near the center. My mother's handwriting, a mix of print and cursive, always started out loose but became tighter and less consistent the more she wrote.

> *"I remain confident of this: I will see the goodness of the Lord in the land of the living. Wait for the Lord; be strong and take heart and wait for the Lord. Psalm 27:13-14"*
>
> *This has not been the life I signed up for. So much pain and heartbreak. There was no way for Elle to understand. I know she didn't mean what she said, but I didn't know how to explain. I only want God's best for her. I wish she could see that mere human love won't be enough to build the kind of marriage God intends for her. A cord of three strands is not easily broken.*

The entry, dated about eight months prior, continued to the next page. I closed the book, mindful of intruding on something intensely personal. I reached for another notebook in the box, not reading, just opening to verify that these were indeed an accumulation of journals kept by my mother. Flipping through without processing the content, I saw scripture references, sometimes short lines, often paragraphs. On many pages, the ink blurred and ran together, and I pressed my hand against what I instinctively knew were my mother's tears.

I slowly replaced the two books and pulled the box out of the closet. Pushing to my feet, I headed for the one room I hadn't gone into since the day it had been necessary to select a dress to take to the funeral home. My mother had always considered her bedroom to be her sanctuary, and she kept it altogether clutter-free. Sitting on the edge of the mattress, I closed my eyes, trying to remember the last time we curled up here to watch movies.

I couldn't stop myself from sinking into the memories any more than I could fight the softness of the plush floral bedding pulling me down. I pressed my nose into the place she'd last laid her head, where the scent of her rosemary shampoo lingered in the silk pillowcase, nearly convincing me she wasn't truly gone.

Even still, I wouldn't cry.

At last, I reached toward the nightstand and found what I knew would be waiting. The current journal had a pale gray cover with a soft ribbon marking her last entry scarcely a third of the way into the book, and as I held it to my chest, the tears I had not built into today's schedule finally broke free.

Chapter Two

Clasping my arms behind my back, I extended my elbows in an attempt to feel something—anything—crack in relief. Four solid days of packing, hauling, selling, and shipping had left my back begging for a break. I had just scheduled the final donation pick-up when the professional cleaners arrived, and I gave them a quick rundown before driving my mom's bright yellow Honda to a nearby café. My laptop and planner were in the passenger seat, and the box of journals was wedged into the cavity of the floorboard. I didn't plan to read them in public with her loss so raw, but I'd kept the collection with me rather than relegating it to the pod that had already been picked up and would be deposited in my own driveway on the mover's timetable.

I sipped a refreshing iced latte while scrolling through the condolences that had flooded my social media over the last few days. It had been unusually warm for late September in Wisconsin and despite my view of the parking lot, sitting at the small metal table outside was good for my soul. I subconsciously kept moving Micah's name to the bottom on the list of messages that needed a reply. We hadn't spoken on the phone since the night of the funeral, communicating only in brief texts a couple of days later:

Micah: Hey. Hope things are going well. Any idea where the credit card bills ended up?

Me: I don't know, did you check the basket

Micah: First place I looked.

Me: Can't it wait until I get back

Micah: If we want to waste money on late fees …

His use of proper punctuation meant he was annoyed.

Me, several minutes later: I think they're in my brown purse on the coat rack. Or maybe the blue bag in the closet. I can't remember which one I used last.

Micah, even more minutes later: Found them.

Micah again: Two hundred bucks at Ulta??

Double punctuation was even worse.

Me: Do I have an allowance now? Going to give me a curfew too? I'll pay the bill, Micah.

I didn't know whether to be proud of my snark or embarrassed. Throwing his name on the end was a not-so-subtle way of getting *my* increased irritation across.

The three dots popped up immediately but a reply never materialized. However, he had called this morning while I was showering. The one step forward and two steps back was getting old, but what if our most recent bickering had pushed things to the brink? I wasn't eager for him to make a unilateral decision about our marriage, even if I was still figuring out if there was any grass left to water on this side of the fence.

With no other messages to respond to but not ready to talk to Micah, I hit the unlock button on the car's key fob and jogged to the passenger side. The writings in these books contained my mom's innermost thoughts, although I didn't feel worthy of knowing them. Perhaps I'd given up that right. But they continued to beckon me during the more monotonous tasks as I boxed up sheet sets, towels, and Tupperware. I'd been able to resist their invitation so far only because weariness overtook me at the end of each long day.

Mom and I had always been close, but our argument at the beginning of this year had changed our relationship and brought out hidden heartaches from both sides. I couldn't even justify *my* spitefulness. I had taken things out on her that had nothing to do with her, leaving my mom hurt and confused. While we had begun to talk by phone more frequently in the months before she died, there were still so many things left unsaid and apologies unfinished.

"You always think you have time," someone said to me as they clasped my hands at the wake. That one sentence had run through my head an infinite number of times on that day and continued to taunt me. An accusation, reminding me that when I'd needed my mother most, I had pushed her away. And now, after seeing the one entry dated only days after our fight, I realized her pain ran as deeply as mine.

I chose an older journal at random, not yet ready to confront what I would find in either of this year's books. In addition to the black and white striped notebook, I lifted her well-loved Bible from the box. It had absorbed the scent of lavender from her room after years of being kept next to the bed. Gripping my selections carefully, I settled back into my seat. Leaving the journal closed, I ran my hand over the embossed Bible cover.

Lord, please, let this be okay. I just need to feel close to my mom. I don't know how to grieve her loss after the way I treated her. I can't imagine how I'll ever heal—or if I even deserve to. I'm so angry with myself for letting things get this out of control—I faltered, then admitted—*and angry with You for taking her like that, before we could work things out. Before she could help me figure out what to do about my marriage . . . .*

Tears welled behind my eyes. I couldn't recall the last time I'd prayed, other than the dazed, *"No God please no,"* through numbed lips over and over when I got the phone call from my mother's neighbor, Mae. She'd gone by to share root balls from the peonies she was transferring and found my mom slumped over on her porch swing in the backyard. There was no need for the ambulance that arrived less than seven minutes later. A ruptured brain aneurysm had taken her, seemingly swiftly and, I tried to believe, without pain.

With a deep breath, I reached for the journal. It began eleven years earlier, the summer before I started high school. Mom had been contending with the idea of going to college herself. After losing my father, she felt her calling was to help others in similar circumstances. She had worked at least two, sometimes three jobs at a time since my dad died. She stretched herself beyond measure to make sure we could stay in our home, I could continue my piano lessons, and there would be options for my future education. I was becoming more independent, and I worked to earn my own spending money. Yet, Mom feared the commitment of obtaining the degrees required to be a licensed grief counselor. As I read this journal entry, I realized she had struggled with the choice for other reasons as well.

Eight years ago, I despised the idea of grief counseling. After the shock wore off, I just wanted to forge ahead. Keep my memories safely boxed up, untainted by the fear and anger I'd locked in their own boxes. And I was terrified to open any of them.

Coming to understand they are all part of the same package and don't need to be avoided was the hardest part. It still is. But maybe that package is also a gift.

I never wanted the distinction of being an expert on loss. And, truthfully, I still feel unqualified when it comes to healing. I pasted on a smile for Elle's sake, and she adjusted well, but what if she never learns how to mend from inevitable hurt because I taught her to just press on?

Since John's passing, I've often felt lonely, but Elle never seemed ready to share our lives with anyone new. Whether I go back to school or start dating, it will be an adjustment for both of us. I just don't want Elle to worry about losing me too.

Even if my heart is in the right place, big changes are scary and feel a bit selfish. How do I know Your will?

Reading my mother's words, I could still hear the tenuous uncertainty in her voice as we talked about how I would need to help out more around the house if she pursued her degree. I also recalled her exhilaration when she told me she had cut back her hours as a hotel manager, turned in notice for her part-time office job, and would be starting with fifteen credits that fall at UW Madison.

While the transition challenged us and we had to adjust our routine with the start of each new semester, Mom believed God could redeem our loss for His purpose. It just took a leap of faith—so much easier said than done.

I leaned back in my seat, my mind a million miles away. Actually, more like six hundred miles, to Micah in Tennessee.

When he'd first confessed, the word 'divorce' was on the tip of my tongue. Only fear of its permanency left it stuck there like peanut butter. Instead, I'd wielded my anger like a dagger, jabbing at him when he got too close, whenever he tried to explain. After all, there was no excuse. No way to justify the way he'd betrayed our marriage.

But in truth, I didn't want to hear the *why*. I knew it already. I hadn't been enough. Not good enough. Not attractive or attentive enough. I didn't need him to spell out my shortcomings. He begged for my forgiveness, but I couldn't admit how distorted that felt. My mortification was over my failings more than his.

Eventually, the tumult simmered under a cool façade, weighted in place by the responsibilities I piled on top of it. In that way, I *was* like my mom—boxing up everything I didn't want to deal with. But if I could do one thing well, it was my job. I had a career to worry about. Bosses with expectations—though none higher than the ones I placed on myself. There were ladders to climb and dreams to catch. And, outside of that, a best friend who needed me, now more than ever.

I'd spent a lot of time focusing on what I wanted out of life. I wondered when I'd stopped considering God's will.

I picked up my phone, absently turning the screen on, then off again. I looked around and discovered I was alone on the outdoor patio. I didn't know what to expect from this call with Micah, but we'd had our fair share of shouting matches in the last year. For the first time in too long, I decided to sincerely listen—to him, and to whatever God might be telling me.

My flight home left Madison on Sunday afternoon. Attempting to get comfortable in the window seat, I felt my stomach tighten with nervous energy. Micah would be picking me up at the airport, which was what he'd been calling to confirm on Friday.

I hadn't yet sent him my flight information, and he sounded relieved when I accepted his offer instead of taking an Uber home.

Fortunately, it had occurred to me to rescue one of my mom's colorful carry-on bags from the giveaway pile. The collection of journals was safely wedged into the compartment above my head as the sudsy clouds receded below. Memories of this view swirled in a kaleidoscope, obscuring the foggy window. Bright green at the start of summer to blinding white in winter—every trip home since I moved away for college had been bookended by an eagerness to spend time with Mom and a mirrored impatience to get back to my fast-paced schedule. Knowing there wouldn't be a reason to make this familiar journey after the house sold cast a poignancy over the scenery. The renovated bungalow with its wrap-around porch was in an established neighborhood and had been well cared for in the six years my mom owned it. Vicky was confident that this time of year—with school having begun—wouldn't be a deterrent for an area that didn't cater to families with young children. *As long as it sells before Wisconsin winter hits,* I thought, while doubting the likelihood.

My mother's car would be delivered on Wednesday, separate from the storage pod of furniture and boxes arriving later in the week. Henry expected my return to work that same day, but with Micah back from Canada, he could be home to accept the CR-V and figure out where to park it in our shallow, garage-less driveway.

As the plane flew south, I could feel the pull back into my world of pitches and deals. Guilt stirred my conscience. Over the years, my mother often brought up my tendency to throw myself into work to avoid controversies in other areas of my life. Now I knew why she recognized that behavior. Say what you will, but the last ten months would have been a lot messier if I'd

BEAUTY IN THE BITTERSWEET

let my emotions continue to run loose. Instead, I had worked with such dedication that my name had been batted around as a replacement for one of the licensing reps who'd announced she was accepting a position with one of the "big three" in music publishing.

Getting this promotion would provide a salary increase that would either give Micah and me some breathing room, or would make divorce more feasible. It would also give me professional clout that had been difficult to come by organically. For an industry where most people were vying for the microphone, I stood out by avoiding it, and the crowds it drew.

The flight was only ninety minutes, but the stress and emotional exhaustion of the previous two weeks—added to the past year—dragged me into a deep sleep. I bounced awake when the wheels hit the tarmac, and I let most of the plane empty before I scooted from my seat. Micah would be waiting, in all likelihood being shooed from the pickup area if he sat there a minute too long. But I didn't rush. The tightness in my chest had turned to full-on anxiety at the thought of the half-hour ride home. There were only so many topics we could bring up that wouldn't ultimately lead us back to what he'd been doing during our time apart.

Micah's pewter gray truck was at the curb when I rolled my scuffed black suitcase through the sliding doors. The wheel they'd broken between Madison and home tried to pull me to the right every half a foot, adding irritation to my anxiety. Ever the gentleman, Micah appeared around the tailgate and effortlessly tossed my bag into the backseat, doing the same with my mom's borrowed carry-on before I could ask him to be gentle with it.

I climbed in and took my time fastening my seat belt while he eased back into the traffic pattern exiting the pickup area of the terminal. We had become increasingly adept at keeping our attention fixed on virtually anything except for each other in the last eight months as the fighting became too draining for either of us to initiate. As we took the ramp to the series of interstates from I-40 to I-24 to US-31 toward our modest home in East Nashville, I decided to be the one to speak over the too-loud country music filling the cab of the truck. "Paul came to the funeral," I ventured.

Micah reached to turn the volume down without looking at me. "Oh, really." Not questioning and not giving me much to work with.

I fiddled with the buckle on my purse, pushing it almost open before pulling it a little too tightly again. "Yeah. He looked like he wasn't taking it well."

Paul Spencer and his wife Alison were my mom's friends from church in Monona, but Mom had known Paul when we still lived in Madison, where I grew up. Tall and broad-shouldered, it took me aback to see the tears flow unchecked down his cheeks when he bowed his head to offer quiet sympathy on the day of the funeral. I had hoped to speak to him again, but my next view of him was his dark blue suit jacket and salt-and-pepper hair disappearing through the heavy wooden doors of the church.

"His wife wasn't with him?" Micah's question was one I hadn't considered until now.

"She wasn't. I didn't really get much of a chance to talk to him."

Silence again. I tugged the visor down against a sunset that wasn't really in my eyes, then tentatively asked, "Do you want to just order in?"

I couldn't question him about work or friends. I had nothing to say about my own job or other mundane topics. He didn't ask about my flight or even how my week had gone. And he knew better than to bring up how I was feeling after losing my mom. His wasn't the comfort I needed. The only safety was in the here and now, and that left us with choosing dinner.

Our two-bedroom, one-bath, robin egg blue single-story with less than 1500 square feet of living space was the perfect home when we'd found it two years ago, only weeks before our mid-October wedding. We had been riding high on youth and new love, together for fourteen months and engaged for the last four. This house, freshly on the market and right at the top of our budget, became ours the Tuesday before our Saturday ceremony. We put our honeymoon off indefinitely and used our meager savings for the down payment, furnishing with the best of what each of us had to offer and immensely thankful for a heavily picked-over bridal registry.

As the first year of our marriage came to an end, the walls had shifted closer together. The lack of privacy began to grate on both of us, and the string of show dates for Micah's up-and-coming band having fewer gaps between them and keeping him on the road appeared to be a blessing.

Until it wasn't.

Chapter Three

The next morning, Micah left before I even got out of bed. I'd heard him rise an hour before, peeking one eye open to watch him vanish with his clothes in hand to the bath down the hall. At one time, he would have come back into our room with his blond hair still dripping from the shower, shaking his head to cascade cold water on my face, playfully waking me up. I lay there for a few minutes, mourning the loss of the future I'd expected. Mourning the lost time with my mom and the now irreparable friction in the easy relationship we'd had for so long. Slipping on my house shoes, I realized what I needed to get me through today.

My best friend, Carrie Stephenson, lived twelve minutes away. She'd been my college roommate and my maid of honor, and it was doubly hard to hold myself together over the last two weeks without her by my side. Earlier this summer, Carrie had begun to experience inexplicable shortness of breath, and within a few days, noticed a lump in the side of her neck. As she navigated a series of tests, I went with her to each of them. However, my shock as she received the diagnosis of Hodgkin's lymphoma kept me from being much help as we clutched each other's hands in an office at Vanderbilt University Medical Center. I don't recall much besides the dark blue-green shade of the walls that closed around us like a dark pit and the cloying antiseptic scent that must be pumped through hospital vents. The doctor spoke succinctly, and we both sat in silence. I'm sure he realized any additional information he tried to share right then wouldn't penetrate our numb minds.

Carrie's prognosis was optimistic. She'd wasted no time in seeking answers, and we found the best oncologist we could hope for. Classic Hodgkin's disease caught in stage one has a promising cure rate, but classic spreads faster than other variants. Carrie's third and hopefully last round of chemo would start in a couple of weeks, likely followed by radiation. Despite this, my closest friend always let me know she was thinking of me. She called at least once a day during the time I was in Wisconsin, and I was eager to see for myself how she was doing.

I sent a text to let Carrie know I'd be by around lunchtime and brought my mug of steaming coffee back to the bedroom. After emptying my luggage of laundry and toiletries, I stowed the now broken suitcase in the spare room closet before turning to the carry-on I'd snagged to bring the journals home. I had intentionally tucked it into the corner last night, eager to unpack it as soon as possible but not ready to share my find with Micah.

Gingerly unzipping, I slid my index finger around to make sure no bindings or pages were caught in the teeth and opened the bag. The puffy jacket I hadn't needed with the nice weather was wedged into the soft-sided case, and it had assisted in keeping the journals fairly neatly stacked one on top of another, despite Micah's hurling it into the backseat.

The contents were the most important things I had left of my mother, and it was both fitting and inappropriate they had made the journey in a bag covered in multicolored smiley faces. I had chosen it out of practicality, but no matter what size I needed, I would have never found a solid-colored or basic piece of luggage in her house. We were so alike when I was younger, or at least it had seemed that way. Now I stayed too busy—or too stressed—to be playful.

I gently laid the journals across my bed, opening the front covers to note the dates she'd scripted diagonally inside, and arranged them accordingly. They spanned almost thirty years, beginning around the time she married my dad. There were thirty-eight books in total, plus her Bible, which I now rested on my own nightstand.

It struck me as almost irreverent to see my mom's entire life displayed like this. The highs, lows, and everything in between were quite literally spelled out in front of me and mine for the taking. I'd thought I understood my mom so well but now realized that was only Catherine, the mother. My memories were filtered through the limited understanding of an egocentric child. Only as I reached adulthood had I even begun to understand her as a multifaceted woman with a life before and outside of me.

We had developed a friendship I acknowledged as special and not to be taken for granted as I got older. Still, our time together was filled with conversations about *my* friends and *my* plans for *my* life, and she always supported and encouraged me. I only became aware she had goals of her own when she broached going back to school herself. Even then, I recalled, she'd planned her schedule around mine, and I realized it was no coincidence our graduation dates coincided.

With a few hours until I needed to leave, I reached for the first book. Once a deep purple, it was now faded with age. The cover, stamped with the words 'My Dreams,' had chips of golden paint flaking off. My mom would have been twenty-four at the time. The writing started in a flurry of excitement. Her wedding was upcoming!

Mom gave me this diary so I'll always remember this time in my life. She says that one day it will just be a blur, but I can't imagine forgetting how exciting it all is! John and I are finally getting married! The last four years with him were so wonderful, and I absolutely cannot wait to be his wife! Only three more weeks!

The next entry was dated two and a half weeks later:

Who has time to <u>write</u> about life when I've been so busy <u>living</u> it? All the details are coming together. Two more days until we say 'I do' and the reality is setting in. Dad prayed over us tonight before John went home.

He quoted Ephesians 4:2-3, 'Be completely humble and gentle; be patient, bearing with one another in love. Make every effort to keep the unity of the Spirit through the bond of peace.'

I can't imagine John and me not loving each other. Not that we haven't had our challenges. He was really disappointed when I decided not to go away to college with him. We fought for weeks. He was convinced that one day, I'd have regrets. But I found a job I like, and besides, it's not like I can't go back later, if I want. Lots of moms take classes when their kids are older. And I don't need a degree to be John's wife. This is all I've ever wanted!

I leaned against the headboard, thinking of the explanation my mom had given for why she'd not continued with her schooling then. At the time, the tuition would have drained my grandparents' finances, as they were already paying for Aunt Jan's pre-law degree. My mom claimed she hadn't known what she wanted to do, so why waste money? But, in the end, she was convinced it had all worked out the way it was supposed to. The families she'd guided through their own losses would surely agree.

Her naïveté matched the girly flourish of her pen as she continued:

Now that John has finished school and we'll be married, I'll keep working for the agency, and maybe one day they'll let me move up from being a receptionist. Of course, I don't want much more responsibility because I'm praying there are going to be at least three little ones running around to keep me busy. Two girls and a boy?! God, You're so good to us!

Tears sprung to my eyes as I reflected on the miscarriage my mom had suffered a week after my dad was killed on a chilly September morning in Queens. My little sister, named Brianne as a match to my full name, Brielle, would have been born in December of that year. Tragically, the stress of her husband being shot over an eighty-dollar withdrawal was too much for Mom's body to handle. The loss of my dad and then her growing baby turned my mom into someone I didn't recognize. She moved like a shadow through the house, hollow-eyed, tending to my basic needs with dispassion and, increasingly, only after being reminded. When her sister tried to check on her daily, she rarely engaged in the conversation.

One day while Mom slept, Aunt Jan called and I picked up the phone. Every one of my seven-year-old fears came spilling out, and the next thing I knew, I was settling into the back of my aunt's minivan for the two-hour drive to her home in Aurora, Illinois. I stayed there for several weeks, giving my mother the time she needed to make it through her initial grief. My aunt brought me home the day before Thanksgiving and kept an eye on us through the holiday weekend to make sure we could adjust to some semblance of normalcy. Mom greeted me with a weary smile, but I sensed the difference in her looking *at* me instead of *through* me, and even my young child's mind recognized we would be alright.

Cross-legged on my bed, I thumbed to the end of this particular journal, catching glimpses of newlywed love jumping off the pages with bright pink hearts sketched next to entries about her days as a new wife. The scripted lines were punctuated with multiple exclamation points, whether she was frustrated with her husband or joyous over making up with him. The passion she had with my dad was evident in the doodles and the smudges from tears. I realized my feelings for Micah hadn't been strong enough to elicit more than annoyance in quite a while. When did I stop caring enough to bother getting upset?

Two hours later, I headed to Carrie's house. I drove a few minutes out of the way to the nearby grocery store to pick up some of her favorite foods. Her appetite wasn't what it used to be, but I was sure I could tempt her. Soon, I was heading back to my car with a tote filled with avocados, the Australian yoghurt we both loved, and a variety of soups from the deli. In case the healthier options didn't do it, I also had a box of her favorite gingersnaps, presuming the spice would help ease the nausea she'd been battling.

When I arrived, only the screen door stood in my way, so I didn't need my copy of the key to her house. I found Carrie lying on the couch wearing a hooded sweatshirt with a blanket tucked under her chin. I checked to make sure her toes were covered, alarmed at the way the afghan enveloped her. Her eyes, which had been closed, now watched me through sparsely remaining lashes, and she offered me a weary smile.

"Ellie, I'm so sorry I couldn't be there for your mom's service." Her voice, once melodic, croaked the words, and entire syllables sounded as though they were missing.

"Oh, Carr, don't say that. I know you were with me in spirit. I'm sorry you had to go so long without me here to help!" I fluffed her pillows. "How are you doing today? Better or worse than yesterday?"

As my best friend and I caught up, I realized her responses were taking too much out of her and assured her chitchat wasn't necessary. I convinced Carrie to try eating a bit and brought a washcloth for her face while the container of Italian wedding soup heated. She winced as I helped her sit upright, and I pulled one of the stools from the breakfast counter over, perching on it to help her eat.

A scant two months prior, Carrie had been a dreamer, full of hope. Receiving the diagnosis was taking the expected toll on her body, although her sweet spirit never wavered. But she'd ceased talking about her future. *When* had been replaced by *if* in her vocabulary.

It seemed unfair to indulge in my grief or vent about Micah—Lord knew Carrie had heard enough of that—but I did want to tell her about the journals. I needed to know if she thought it was wrong of me to be reading them with my mother now gone.

When Carrie asked for a break from her lunch after only four bites of mostly broth, I put the mug on the television tray near her and reached for my bag on the other side of the stool. "Hey, I want to show you something I found. When I cleared out my mom's house, I came across these journals."

Sharing with her how I hoped my mom's diaries could give me insight into the facets of her that I hadn't gotten to know, a lump began to form in my throat. "I really can't forgive myself for the things I said to her in January. She knew I was avoiding telling her something big, but I didn't want her to know about Micah. I didn't want her to be right." My best friend was the only person I'd been able to trust with the secret of Micah's affair. She was also the only one who knew how I'd pulled away from my mom...and the reason I'd thrown away so many precious months with her.

"I started reading her older journals, but I've been skipping over what she wrote this year." My breath hitched. "We never completely made up, and it's all my fault!"

As I fought back the tears, Carrie reached for my hand, squeezing with what little strength she could gather. Her froggy voice full of empathy, she reassured me, "You know your mom never stopped loving you, and anything she wrote will attest to that. I think it's a gift from God that she kept these journals, and they can help you. Think of it as the guidance she'd give you if she were here."

A few minutes later as I tidied up the dishes, I found myself hesitantly praying again. *God, if you're there, please give us a miracle and take this cancer away. I feel so lost already without Mom and Micah.* I propped myself against the doorframe, only able to see the wisps of sandy hair across the top of the pillow where Carrie lay. She had started to drift off before I slipped silently into the kitchen, and her last words ran through my head again.

"Elle, forgive yourself. Our weaknesses magnify His power."

Arriving home later that evening, I stood in my narrow closet facing the double-hung rows of blouses and slacks. I tried to generate my usual enthusiasm for returning to work the next morning as I pulled down my favorite striped blouse and a blazer to fight the morning chill. In one respect, I was eager for the distraction, and there'd be plenty to keep me busy.

But one of my mom's—and Micah's—frequent accusations was that I got so wrapped up in my job that other things were neglected. For my mom, 'other things' meant having babies. She had wanted most to start having kids, and lots of them, right away. I'd stabbed her in the heart with my retort that it wasn't my obligation to give her the family she'd been unable to have herself. I regretted the words the second they escaped, but it was too late to explain. It wasn't that I didn't want to give her grand-children *one* day; I simply wanted to climb the ladder while I had opportunities. You win the music industry game by making connections—and not the kind you make in the PTA.

For Micah, success came with much less effort. He didn't understand that the competitive nature of my career required me to be accessible. If that meant I had to cancel plans every once in a while, or if I got busy and didn't show up to an event with him, it was because *my* success rode on securing the next deal.

He, on the other hand, lucked into a band whose second release hit the number four spot on the charts, catapulting them to instantaneous stardom and taking him along for the ride. The lead singer, Martine Vaughn, and I first met a year and a half before. One of her sultry-voiced songs landed on my desk, and

I worked a deal that got it featured in the romantic comedy of the year.

When I introduced Martine to Micah that spring, it appeared providential that her band, Still Waters, was set to release their debut album mid-summer and hadn't found a tour manager yet. Promoting the album started locally, but the soundtrack hit "Take Me Away" broadened their visibility, and soon Still Waters had gigs booked across the country. Micah went from being gone three days a week to three weeks at a time, but I tried to be available when he was home.

Evidently, my efforts didn't compete with the time Martine made for him while they were on the road.

Time he was still unwilling to give up.

Chapter Four

Micah got home shortly after five that evening—early for the rare days he worked in town. I was chopping vegetables for pasta primavera, tossing in extra so I could share leftovers with Carrie, when I heard the front door's telling creak. Our kitchen was at the back of the house, and he slipped down the hall to the bedroom without greeting me. A few minutes later, he stepped in behind me as the fragrance of sautéing zucchini and garlic filled the air.

"I have bad news."

I turned slowly, avoiding meeting his eyes at first. But why should I be the one cowering? Micah owed *me,* not the other way around. I raised a defiant stare.

"Josh can't stay for Winnipeg, so I need to go up tomorrow."

My lips tightened, trying to hold in the sarcastic reply I so badly wanted to hurl at him. But I caved as I returned to the stove, mumbling, "I'm sure *the band* will be glad to have you back."

He swore under his breath. "Elle, geez! It's my job!" He heaved a thick sigh and I spun, the roiling pasta water forgotten. Micah ran his hands through his hair, leaving it standing on end. His eyes and tone softened. "We're almost done with this circuit. There are only four weeks left. I'll come home in between if I can."

"*If* you can. Sure." My temper flared, and it occurred to me how oddly satisfying it was to get angry instead of pushing this argument to the side or accepting his false deference. Without pausing to figure out if I was really going to miss him or just needed a target for the shards of my broken heart, I let my voice rise.

"Micah, you do realize now I'll have to empty the pod by myself? *And* I'm going to have to take off on Wednesday to be here when the car is delivered?" Now that I'd begun, I couldn't hold back. "You not being at the funeral was bad enough! I had to explain to everyone that you'd chosen your band over *me*! Just because Josh couldn't fill in for you … why do you still choose *her*?" I gasped back a sob, aware I was scratching at freshly scabbed over wounds.

When he didn't say anything, I pushed the pan off the burner. Overheated from my outburst, I irritably scrunched the hair curling around my face into a knot on top of my head. I turned back to him with a deep breath to slow my heart rate. "Please tell me," I pleaded softly, "Did anything happen while I was gone?"

I first found out about my husband's dalliance with the smoky-voiced, blue-haired singer quite by accident. The previous Halloween, just weeks after our first anniversary, Still Waters' management hosted their annual costume party. Regrettably, I got caught up in negotiations for a deal I was putting together and didn't realize how late it had gotten. By the time I called Micah to tell him I didn't feel like getting dressed up for what would only be an hour or two, he didn't answer his phone. A few days later, one of the roadies I met in passing complimented me on my peacock costume at the party. She said she figured out it was me because she saw Micah and me kissing outside the back door of the venue.

Micah didn't deny it when I confronted him but insisted Martine had propositioned him, and he had pushed her away. Still, he'd passed the buck with startling speed. And with every rationalization, heat billowed in my chest.

"If you'd just shown up for once … " He stopped short, the rest of the implication hovering like a thundercloud that threatened to burst with whatever he had pent up inside.

"So, you went and found the next pair of available lips?"

"Elle, it wasn't like that. Martine was drunk. I don't think she even knew what she was doing. You know how she is."

The thing was, I hadn't known. Months on the road with her, and he'd never thought to mention that I'd sent him off with a woman who tended to get frisky after a drink or two.

I managed to furiously dissect every sentence he used to defend himself but still couldn't hear him over my own insecurities. Yet, what choice did I have but to give him the benefit of the doubt? Now, almost a year later, I was still struggling with that choice.

We spent that Thanksgiving with my mom in Monona, enjoying the snowy weather, delicious feasts, and time with her neighbors and friends who dropped in. Mom and I dragged Micah along for Black Friday shopping, and he appeared surprisingly understanding when I needed to spend several hours Saturday afternoon on work calls. Besides, he was texting on his phone every time I glanced over.

It was the middle of December, as we were finalizing our schedules for the holidays, when I grew suspicious again. He fumbled over an innocuous question about our plans for the week between Christmas and New Year's, and I pushed back in my chair. "You told me you'd be with the band from the 26th through the 28th, but home by the weekend. Why is New Orleans on your calendar for the 28th and 29th?"

The deer caught in the headlights look said it all, but I waited for a reason that made sense. *Let it be a surprise trip for us,* I wished fervently. Instead, he shamefully covered his mouth.

Now, Micah covered my hand with his. "Brielle, nothing has happened. Not since last winter."

It still astounded me how he'd gotten drawn into the affair, especially after I found out about the kiss. That December night, he admitted he'd gone to bed with Martine after a show in New York the previous week. I canceled our Christmas plans with my mom but waited until the last minute to do so. I told myself it was because I didn't want to ruin my mom's holiday, but in the end, I decided it was easier to live the lie if we weren't face-to-face.

The past nine months since Micah's confession had been filled with promises, accusations, and discussions alternating between separation and tentative reconciliation. The tour kept him away, so building any genuine trust was difficult. He promised it was just a one-night stand, and a mistake, at that. He'd never been sure about meeting Martine in New Orleans but hadn't figured out how to break it to her. Like his fluster over getting caught would give *that* defense any weight.

To be fair, he began to come home more frequently, but I couldn't even look at Micah without picturing *her.* There was nothing new we could say to each other. Any mention of the tour inevitably brought up my lack of trust. Any time I needed to work from home, he blamed me for our lack of closeness. We battled over events I refused to attend because Martine was on the guestlist, and I'd end up furious when he'd go without me. He swore he'd conveyed to her that their relationship had to remain professional, and she'd been publicly dating a drummer from another band for most of the year. But the rift between Micah and me stretched wide and unbreachable.

When I'd received the call two weeks before about my mom's death, Micah took the next flight home but arrived with no luggage and informed me with a pained expression he'd be heading to Montreal the next day. He was certain he could make it to Wisconsin for the funeral with Josh stepping in for him.

Despite my trepidation regarding his schedule, that evening was the closest we'd been in a long time—certainly since before he got involved with Martine. He held me when I cried and comforted me with memories from when things were untainted between Mom and me. Many of those stories with her included him, and I was grateful for his presence. He drove me to Carrie's house so I could tell her in person and loitered nearby with a helpless expression while Carrie stroked my hair as I broke down in her lap.

… Which was why I got so angry when I awoke to a text the day before the service saying he wasn't coming.

That night, Micah and I lay in bed in sullen silence. Dinner had turned into rubbery pasta and soggy vegetables eaten at a table the size of an ocean between us. Micah swore he would return at least once before the tour wrapped the following month, and I could only shrug. It wasn't worth arguing over. Even when we were together, we meshed about as well as a misaligned zipper and grated on each other just as badly.

The next morning, I woke up before he did and lay still as I watched him sleep. It had been forever since I'd seen him like this, and I tried to view him in the same light I used to. The blond hair falling across his forehead hadn't darkened much since the photos I'd seen of him as a towheaded toddler. His straight nose had a smattering of light freckles across it, no matter the time of year. A faint shadow of stubble roughened the cheek facing me, and permanent smile lines creased the corner of his mouth. That smile used to be all I needed to feel secure in my relationship with him, and in my life.

Then, his affair had sent me whirling like a child's spinning top. Carrie's illness brought me dangerously close to the edge. I was surprised that losing my mother hadn't made me topple. Perhaps after the shock wore off...

Before I could follow the thought any further, his face grew tense, as though in waking, he was becoming alert to the strain this day could hold. Part of me wanted to be out of bed before he opened his eyes, but it would have been too obvious, so I didn't move. When he became aware of my gaze, his eyes took on a questioning expression that melted into softness when he realized I wasn't on the attack.

"I was thinking." Micah half rolled toward me in the bed, diminishing the gap between us. "Since Josh won't be staying in Canada, maybe he can come by on Saturday to help unload the pod?" He tendered the suggestion hesitantly, as though he didn't know if I'd find a way to be offended by this proposition.

I debated briefly before responding. In truth, there weren't a lot of heavy items being delivered. The only furniture I had selected—the four-poster bed with its matching chest of drawers from my teen years—was meant to replace the Ikea set from my college apartment that was now set up in our spare room.

I remembered seeing Josh drive away in a pickup truck the last time we'd gotten together for an industry event. Although I didn't know him well, I'd appreciate the help getting the old pieces to a donation center.

"If he's available, it would be nice." My answer was received with a nod of acknowledgment, and Micah promised to reach out to Josh before heading to the airport.

As he tossed the final items into his suitcase later that morning, my thoughts retreated to February when I had confronted Martine myself. She answered her front door with a toothbrush in her mouth and wearing a half-unbuttoned flannel shirt. Neither of us spoke—she because of the foam trying to escape, and I because I wasn't prepared to find her in such a state at almost noon on a Friday. With an arched brow, she waved me in and left me standing uncertainly in her foyer while she disappeared, presumably to spit.

When she returned, she slouched onto the bench by her front door with one leg tucked under her, revealing she had not added shorts to her ensemble while she'd been gone. The sensuality that sold out venues was evident even now, with her lustrous hair tumbling around the tattooed shoulder she'd left exposed. I shrunk in her presence, my pre-rehearsed speech inadequate when confronted with the competition.

"So ...." The acerbic way she chose to break the silence put me on the defensive, and I clenched my fists at my sides, straightening my spine from its momentary crumple.

"It may not feel like a big deal to you," I began in a low voice with my eyes narrowing, "but this is my *marriage*. To you, Micah is just another in a string of men you toy with, but he knows he made a mistake with you. He loves *me*. We might've gotten off track, but you're nothing except a flash in the pan."

Martine rolled her eyes, but I hoped my rebuke chastised her. With a dismissive wave of her hand, she started to suggest I show myself out. Anticipating what she was going to say, I couldn't resist beating her to it, stopping as I pulled open the door to interrupt her with one final statement.

"As far as Micah and I are concerned, you two never happened." I took satisfaction in stressing that my husband and I were on the same page. Slamming the door behind me, I was convinced our marriage could heal with enough time and privacy.

Despite the bravado I'd feigned in Martine's doorway, I envied her innate self-confidence. Surely, that had been a part of what drew Micah's attention. Now, I watched him getting ready to head off for another four weeks with her and considered his response when I'd recently suggested he not continue as their tour manager. He'd balked, the firm set of his lips making me wonder what he was holding back. Of course, I assumed he was using his contract as an excuse to keep Martine easily accessible. He insisted there were too many moving pieces to trust the remaining shows to someone new. He'd left to rejoin Still Waters without telling me goodbye. The next time I'd seen him was when I got the call about my mother.

As long as Martine didn't make their affair public, we could put this all behind us. There would be another band needing a manager like him, and his success with Still Waters could open plenty of doors.

Perhaps this would be the one positive thing to come out of our involvement with Martine Vaughn.

Chapter Five

The next morning, I'd been at my desk for over an hour before Henry's rotund form filled the entrance to my cubicle. I held up my index finger while I completed the fifth voicemail I'd left so far. "Apparently, no one's working yet today," I grumbled, disconnecting the call and swiveling in my chair to stand and give him a brief hug.

Henry Hicks was as close to a father figure as I had in my life, and after interning for him during my final semester of school, he was now a firm but fair boss. He put me through the same interview process as other candidates, offering the job only after cautioning me against sensitivity to criticism. Ironic, since I'm my biggest critic. Maybe that's why he brought it up.

"Mistakes are only a problem if you don't learn from them, Elle." I'd tucked his advice away—right between my mother's encouragement to keep up with my six-month dental cleanings and Carrie's urgings to drink less coffee.

I thanked Henry for the generous donation he'd facilitated from our company to the adolescent grief support center my mother had devoted her spare time to. He waved away my appreciation, avoiding the sentimentality he seldom displayed. After taking a few minutes to run through the statuses of several potential deals that had come in while I was gone, he hefted himself out of the spare chair in my cubicle.

As he reached the doorway, Henry turned, his eyes squinting in his florid face. "You're doing okay, right?" This wasn't the first time he'd asked, and I suspected he'd perceived a change in me over the last year. I'd kept the difficulties in my marriage and the tension between my mom and me out of the office, but he'd noticed I was always the first to pick up any extra projects, no matter the detriment to my personal time.

With a too-bright smile, I assured him I would be fine once I got back to work.

Sighing as he backed away, he muttered, "Still my moneymaker."

The morning evaporated, and I was just starting to get back in my groove when I received the call that my mother's car would be arriving in less than an hour. I allowed a smidge of pent-up annoyance from the interference to escape as I hurried to my car and threw my blazer and handbag across the passenger seat before darting through the maze of traffic.

While I waited for the truck to arrive, I stood with my back to the glass door and faced the warmly decorated living room. Micah and I had done a beautiful job of creating a space reflecting both of our tastes. The two-seat couch in cognac leather was the only piece we had splurged on, and we hadn't gotten its worth yet in evenings wrapped up in each other's arms. We should have made more of the happy memories. It was a challenge to envision us laughing instead of yelling at each other across this room. But, before Monday night, it had been a while since we'd even bothered to argue. We had passed like ghosts when we were both at home, avoiding eye and skin contact, each of us in a waiting game as we wrestled with our thoughts on how to move forward.

The roar of the transport trailer on our narrow street brought me back to the present. I rushed outside to tap my foot impatiently as the driver navigated the machinery to release the CR-V to the only space he could access. Micah had pulled his truck as far into the driveway as he could before taking an Uber to the airport, and I pulled the vibrant SUV behind it. Still, I could tell my black Corolla wouldn't also fit without blocking the sidewalk. Leaving the matter to deal with after my return from work, I ran up to lock the front door, then maneuvered my car from in front of our mailbox.

As always, work was waiting. And as always, I was eager to get back to its unwavering stability.

That evening, I curled up in the floral-patterned chair in the corner of the living room with my MacBook and several songs I was working on placing. This was what I did—what I loved to do, but I couldn't concentrate even for the length of a four-minute recording.

My heart was unsettled, and the grief I'd managed to mostly hold at bay was now finding holes to ooze through. There were so many little things I hadn't shared with Mom over the last months. A phone call required fibs and omissions, which meant keeping track of all those lies. How had I let this happen?

My mom had understood me, often better than I understood myself. The week before I married Micah, we found time during all the pre-wedding activity to go to lunch, just the two of us.

"Mom, I know I love him. So, why do I feel like an out-of-control snowball rolling down the sledding hill in Olbrich Park?"

"Elle, you have to give yourself some grace. You have always been so concerned with staying on top of things." She patted the back of my hand, a tender reprimand. "You're about to experience the biggest life-change you've ever had! There's bound to be some uncertainty. But when you don't know what's coming, that just means anything can happen. Endless possibilities and ways that God can work good through it all."

She tried to tuck her too long bangs behind her ears, using the motion as an excuse to blot dampness from her dark eyes. I imagined her happiness for me was muddled with wistfulness. For so much of my childhood, it had been just us. Our circles stretched to include family and friends, but we came home to each other. We knew each other's moods and quirks better than anyone else. I guess that's how she could always tell when I was hiding something and why avoiding her seemed to be the only way to keep secrets. Secrets she could never forgive me for now.

After a useless hour with little progress, I stood to stretch my legs and ended up on tiptoes in my closet, reaching for the top shelf.

The journal I selected had a tandem bicycle on the sky-blue cover with the artistic rendering implying movement, although there were no riders drawn. The chorus of an old Nat King Cole song, "Daisy Bell," stirred from deep in my memory:

Daisy, Daisy, give me your answer do
I'm half crazy, all for the love of you
It won't be a stylish marriage
I can't afford a carriage
But you'll look sweet upon the seat
Of a bicycle built for two

I remembered this book from Monday when I put them in chronological order. It stood out to me because, while thinner than most of the notebooks, by the dates she'd inscribed, it covered well over a year's timespan.

Settling back into my cushioned chair, I flicked on the table-side lamp, then impulsively jumped back up to grab the box of tissues from the coffee table. The journal started with a subdued tone late in 1999.

After the difficulties we had conceiving Brielle, I thought we'd finally broken through. I started to suspect I was pregnant again last month, but I didn't even want to write about it, just in case. So, why did I let myself hope? I don't understand. Maybe this is what a crisis of faith is. 'Six weeks along,' that's what Doctor Myra said. 'Sometimes the baby simply isn't developing well.' She tried to explain, but I still don't believe it. How could a loving God decide a tiny baby doesn't deserve to live?

The entry left me stunned. I would have been slightly over two years old when my mom lost this baby, so of course, there's no way I would have remembered, but she'd never told me. During our argument and subsequent conversations, as timid as they'd been since January, she still hadn't confided she'd suffered a miscarriage before Brianne. Shame scalded my cheeks with the memory of how I'd hurled such insensitive words at my mother about not having more children herself. The journal burned my trembling palms.

I read deep into the night, several passages more than once. My parents' marriage had become turbulent after the loss of this child, with my mom's anguish bleeding through the pages. Her jagged words came from a place of fear—that God had abandoned her in her time of greatest need. She distanced herself from her husband, overwhelmed by grief and perceived inadequacy as the mother of a toddler who depended upon her. From her writing, I gathered my father had stepped in to take over my care, more so than either of them had anticipated. For a while, my mom had found me, her own child, to be a source of renewed pain rather than healing love as she mourned the death of my unborn sibling.

Gradually, her journaling displayed increased hope and acceptance, and I found references to scriptures such as Romans 8:24-25: *For in this hope we were saved. But hope that is seen is no hope at all. Who hopes for what they already have? But if we hope for what we do not yet have, we wait for it patiently.*

Her entries were fewer, shorter, and more sporadic than I expected for a year so fraught with trauma, but it explained why the narrow book covered so much time. The notations were brief, however, the emotion spilling from the pages was palpable and difficult to digest. I felt more invasive than ever before, but I couldn't tear myself away. The initial struggle between my parents to come together during that time instead of pulling away from each other was evident in the loneliness woven throughout the first several months. Eventually, the patience my father had offered shone through in entries expressing gratitude and renewed love for him.

The following year began with our move from the tiny apartment I recalled only from old photos to the home where I'd grown up. My father had started with a new advertising firm in Madison, and it sounded like he wanted to give my mother something to reinvigorate her. The house, white when they purchased it but painted sunshine yellow at my mom's request, held my earliest fuzzy memories. The journal entries were still infrequent, but the ones there were conveyed enthusiasm for the shopping and decorating that goes with having twice as much space.

There were stories about making room for the piano my father surprised her with, toddler me starting a garden, and meeting new friends in the neighborhood. Reading these pages, I wasn't sure if impressions of my dad were coming back to me or if I was simply picturing him more clearly with my mother's words bringing him to life. My third birthday party, one of my most distinct early memories, featured a dancing clown—who I now realized had been my own father. A photo of me sitting on his knee was slipped between the pages, and beneath the makeup, I could see sparkling brown eyes with flecks of orange, exactly like mine. I stared at the photo for several long minutes, unexpected tears gathering in my own eyes as snippets of that day flitted across my mind.

I turned the page, confused to see the November date. My birthday was in June, so five months had been left blank. The first line of the November 15th entry left me frozen.

I lost another baby. God, I hate you!

Chapter Six

I pounded my pillows into shape for the umpteenth time. The numbers on the digital clock kept reconfiguring themselves, cycling through minutes, then hours, as images from the most recent journal entry played in a loop on the ceiling. My mom had experienced horrible cramps one night, and when they intensified rather than abating, my father convinced her to go to the hospital. Not yet even knowing she was pregnant, she wanted to believe it was only a worse-than-usual monthly cycle. She wrote that she was more afraid of hearing the truth than she was over the copious blood loss. Reading her words all but shattered me. Her dream of a large family had been snatched from her womb twice, and she didn't even realize her heartbreak was only beginning.

The next morning, I managed to leave the house only twenty minutes behind schedule after sleeping restlessly for a couple of hours. As I pulled out of the grass where my car was angled behind the CR-V, I noticed the tread marks I was leaving behind in the soft ground. The tantalizing aroma of my take-out dinner and heavy satchel of work the previous evening had compelled me to park as close as I could, ruefully at an angle that took my front tires off the concrete. Shifting into drive, my attention rebounded to the meeting I needed to prepare for later in the afternoon and all I would have to accomplish between now and then.

Despite being back at work with my schedule full, throughout the day I was distracted by sudden flashes of a particular scripture from the previous evening. Several months after the first miscarriage, my mom had referenced Hebrews 6:19: *"We have this hope as an anchor for the soul, firm and secure."*

Her hope, and my father's, had been severely shaken rather than holding 'firm and secure' after the second miscarriage. Despite my shock at the entry declaring her hatred toward God, I could understand its origin. How had she recovered? And more so, how had she then endured my father's death, followed by losing Brianne? What had rekindled my mom's faithfulness to the God who had taken nearly everything from her?

But now, this afternoon's meeting was about to start. I shuffled my strewn notes into order, then downed the driblets of my fourth cup of coffee. Rather than sharpening my focus, I felt jittery and awkward. Throwing my office cardigan on over my sweat-stained blouse, I headed to the conference room.

Initially, my role as an assistant had been limited to finalizing details and making sure all the correct paperwork was signed. As I'd gained more experience, I was able to contribute earlier in the process. This was one of my first times presenting the pitch, and here I was fumbling my way through. I could see the waning interest in the producer's eyes.

The music selection was strong and might stand on its own, but I should have been better prepared. Especially with a promotion on the line. There might not have been another contender within our department, but that didn't mean it was a lock for me.

Swallowing the apology that wouldn't help my case, I handed over a hard copy of the proposal and escorted my guest to the elevator. As the doors slid open, an attractive dark-haired man strode out, his eyes sweeping over us dismissively before side-stepping me and heading toward the meeting room we'd just vacated. I watched him for a moment, curious.

My mind should have been on to the next task, but instead, I took the stairs to the balcony above. Hugging myself against the chill in the air, I gazed as far as I could at the town that represented the life I'd always dreamt of. Since high school, being a part of this music scene was my biggest ambition. Meeting Micah had fallen directly in line with my plans. I quickly decided he checked all the right boxes. Although my mom adored him, she had expressed discomfort at the idea of my marriage to a non-believer.

"Your lives will never go in the same direction if God isn't leading both of you. At least take some time. Marriage can wait a while longer. Get to know each other better and experience more trials together without the added pressure of being married."

She'd asked me to listen to her, but still promised her support when I forged ahead. Then the earliest stressors in my relationship began to show themselves, but I glossed over them. And in an effort to cover up Micah's affair, I flung in her face that she must not remember how hard it was to be married. But I clearly had no idea what my parents had endured.

Not long after I came in from the balcony, the sky let loose with big, fat raindrops. These were the kind of storms I loved, but driving home in the darkening evening was treacherous. By the time I turned onto my street, I dreaded the dash to the front door. Pushing the damage I was doing to the yard to the back of my mind, I pulled in once again next to the CR-V. I cringed as I felt my front tires gouging the soaking ground.

After indulging in a hot shower and pouring a glass of wine, I started a sheet pan of vegetables and chicken and slumped onto the couch. My heart, still aching from all I'd learned the previous evening, couldn't handle reading another journal entry tonight. Instead, the image of my dad I'd found tucked into last night's book made me reach for another small box from my mom's house. There would be more coming in the pod this weekend, however, one stack of photographs had made its way home with me—the box holding the picture I'd selected for my mom's funeral program.

That particular photo lay on top now. I studied it, rubbing my thumb across the deep auburn hair covering Mom's forehead as though I would be able to feel the silky texture. She'd cut bangs, wear them for a few weeks, and unfailingly start pinning them back. As soon as they were long enough to fit into her short ponytail, she'd decide it was time to have them again. Her olive complexion was the beautiful result of Portuguese heritage, and her deep brown, almost black eyes gazed into the camera as though she wanted to share a secret. As always, her lips were painted a familiar shade of pink—Cherries in the Snow by Revlon.

Setting that picture to the side, I shuffled through the heap below it. Organized, my mother was not, and the photographs encapsulated several decades: elementary school pictures when my coiled hair reached my waist, a photo with only my eyes showing between a striped wool cap and matching scarf while snow tubing with my youth group, a Christmas postcard of the two of us the only year we had them done. I flashed back on the torment in her eyes when the photographer asked if the rest of our family would arrive soon. I quickly flipped the photo over to the one beneath it and caught myself chuckling at a shot of my mom and Micah. The Revlon lipstick color was pretty, but it was not transfer-proof, and she had just kissed his forehead, leaving a fuchsia smear he wasn't aware of as he grinned.

Placing the small stack of photos on the coffee table, I closed my eyes, remembering.... Mom had engaged clients with her authenticity, and she demonstrated infallible grace for their journeys. She understood the pain of healing. And her work didn't end with her professional counseling. She'd loved the kids she'd volunteered with—children and teens who had lost a parent, often through street violence. Surely those kids had filled as big a gap for her as she had for them. She'd had so much love to give and only me to raise as her own.

I checked the meal roasting in the oven as the mouth-watering scent permeated the air, and realized I'd rescued it in the nick of time. Leaving it to rest for a few minutes, I went back to the living room to re-box the photos. As I did, I uncovered one I hadn't seen before—a younger version of my mom, no bangs this time, with a huge smile and her arms around a man it took me a few seconds to recognize. It was Paul, her old friend from Madison, with no salt in his peppery hair and a bushy mustache.

Not bushy enough to hide the Cherries in the Snow lipstick print on his cheek, though.

Chapter Seven

$\mathcal{I}$ stayed late at the office on Friday, determined to start the following week that much further ahead of schedule. I would have gone home to work from the comfort of my living room, but lately I was finding myself inordinately mindful of the empty space on the end of the couch. Pushing my pride to the side, I'd called Micah the previous evening after checking his schedule and seeing the band would be traveling to Calgary overnight.

"Hey, how's the drive?"

"Not too bumpy. What's up?"

Swirling the last sip in the bottom of my wine glass, I'd tried to formulate a reason for the call. The tour bus gave him space to sleep but he hated being on it overnight. He usually worked instead of slept, and I was interrupting.

"Just seeing what the plan is for this weekend, you know, with Josh." We'd been over it but there was no harm in checking.

Micah confirmed Josh would come by at nine on Saturday, which was about an hour after the moving crate was being dropped off. We may have sounded more like roommates than spouses, and we ended the call with a simple "talk soon," but as we disconnected, I acknowledged something I hadn't in far too long...

I missed my husband.

Micah and I met on a Saturday in February of my senior year. The music expo we were both working had over five thousand attendees, industry reps, and peons like me trying to learn the business. Overwhelmed by how many cogs were in the wheel, I stuck close to my booth, despite my supervisors' encouragement to go network.

A couple of my classmates who were also there for their internships finally pulled me around our section with them. I was studying a list of artists represented by a familiar label when my friend Claudia spun me around. One of her favorite new singers was strolling past, but rather than following her pointing finger, my eyes landed on the well-built man across from us. He was turned away, blond head bowed to listen to an older gentleman who had his attention. I only caught his profile, and then a group clogged the path, blocking my view. When the crowd dispersed, our eyes met, but my friend was yanking my arm, asking if I thought she should go try to catch up to the star to ask for her autograph.

I allowed her to drag me after the musician she was fangirling, but the singer was long gone. By the time we turned around, we were in a different aisle, and my break was ending. The rest of the afternoon flew by as I fielded questions, listened to the way my internship supervisors—Erica and Constance—responded to wanna-be singers and songwriters, and tried to keep the stacks of information packages squared along the edge of our table.

Later that night, as the crowds thinned and we broke down our booth, my eyes darted around, searching for the blond hair and navy sport coat. When Constance asked me to find a roll of packing tape to borrow, I practically skipped, knowing where my first stop would be. Nearing his booth, which was almost taken apart, my steps slowed. He was lying under the table, stripped of his jacket, and fighting with a stuck collapsible table leg. The moment I was within reaching distance, the leg gave in to his pounding, and the table toppled. I lunged to catch it at the same time he rolled from beneath it.

As he stood and dusted off his hands, I stayed coyly silent, waiting to see how he'd handle the gaffe. Shaking his hair back into place, he extended his hand in introduction.

"Tonight, the role of 'damsel in distress' will be played by Micah Reed." The cheesy line was delivered with a sheepish grin.

Mindful of the amused eyes surrounding us, I tried to remain cool as I shook his hand. "Elle Miles with Starship. Can you rescue me back by letting me borrow your tape?"

Over subsequent months, I discovered the entertainment agency Micah worked with shared several artists with my publishing house, and his name appeared periodically on contracts I handled. I would avail myself to sit in on conference calls he might be a part of and attended industry events with an eye perpetually flitting to the entrance. It still wound up being the end of April before our paths crossed again. Constance asked me to fill in for a lunch meeting in The Gulch, and Micah was reclined at our patio table, one arm draped over the empty chair next to him, reflective aviators and glossy teeth as he brought the other two guests to laughter. As I approached the table, his grin widened. "Well, if it isn't my knight in shining armor!"

Olivia Sanchez, a budding artist, was one of the others, along with Ted Elliott, who I learned was a project manager with Micah's agency. I attempted to keep a professional demeanor throughout lunch, but I wasn't oblivious to the humored glances exchanged between Olivia and Ted when Micah directed questions my way. I wished for the meeting to end, solely so the butterflies inside me could get some rest. When we stood to part ways, Micah asked if he could give me a call later in the week.

As we got to know each other, I found out Micah had relocated to Nashville only a year before. He'd grown up in North Carolina, attending UNC Greensboro, where he obtained a degree in Media Studies. After wavering a bit in school and having no clear career path, his gravitation toward the entertainment business was to the chagrin of his parents. His father was a CPA, and his mother taught high school English, and they wished he'd provide another example of stability for his younger brother.

We'd been chatting under the pretext of exchanging information regarding Olivia, who was voicing some songs for an animated movie soundtrack Starship had contracted. Our conversation flowed naturally and flirtatiously, and the butterflies swarming my middle collided with a burst of elation in my chest.

Micah asked me on a legitimate date the week before my twenty-second birthday, slyly refusing to tell me what he had planned. The sticky, early June day melted into a warm breeze as the waning sun dissolved. He charmed Carrie, who was even more bashful in those days, while he waited for me to slip on my sandals. She carried the wildflowers he'd brought to the kitchen as I closed the door behind us, on my way to what I hoped even then might be my very last 'first date' ever.

When my alarm went off at 7:30 on Saturday morning, it was only the fear of the truck arriving a few minutes earlier than scheduled that had me jumping out of bed. No matter how hard I try, I am not a morning person.

Starting the single-serve coffee maker and drumming my fingers on the counter while my cup filled, I gazed out the kitchen window at the collection of cars in the driveway. I had no excuse besides laziness for why I'd once again left the Corolla in my self-made parking spot that caused the front tires to crater into our side yard. I planned to ask Josh to follow me to Carrie's, where she was letting me leave my mom's car until I had the moving pod picked back up. Hopefully, the grass wouldn't look too bad by the time Micah returned. I had no intention of parking that way again.

After a quick shower, I moved both my Corolla and the CR-V half a block down the street to give the pod deliverer more room to operate. Still-wet curls dampened my collar as I hurried back toward my house at the same time the driver pulled onto the street behind me.

In the forty-five minutes between the truck leaving and Josh's arrival, I stripped the bedding from my old spare mattress and emptied the contents from the small dresser I was letting go. As I searched the kitchen drawer for the tools we would need to disassemble the bed frame, I heard a rap on the outer screen door, followed by Josh's gravelly "Halll-ooo?"

Josh Jenkins was the tour coordinator for an artist and aspiring actress who had been filming and was now promoting her first starring movie role. Because of this, she'd limited musical performances, allowing Josh to cover sporadically for Micah. The first time Micah had reached out to him for help was the previous December when I found out about the affair. The fallout resulted in Micah not traveling with the band for the remainder of the year. This included sold-out venues in Las Vegas and Colorado Springs, and Josh rearranged his schedule to step in without even asking why Micah would make such a request. When my mother passed away, Josh again dropped what he was doing to cover the shows he could, and I now regretted my aggravation when he'd been unable to stay for the week of the funeral. I hadn't seen Josh in person since a July 4th picnic we

BEAUTY IN THE BITTERSWEET

had all attended, and I realized as I waved him in that we had never been alone together.

The deep voice was an incongruous match to Josh's slight build. His dark, straight hair had grown past his shoulders in the months since I'd last seen him. Around thirty years of age, he had skin that showed his love of the outdoors, with green eyes cornered by premature squint lines and enough scruff on his chin to add to his attractiveness. Micah and Josh had been friends for a few years but were not extraordinarily close, and I wasn't sure if Josh had deciphered Micah's history with Martine. Did he guess I hadn't been enough to keep my husband's attention?

I covered the sudden wash of humiliation with a varnish of efficiency. "Thanks for coming. I don't think this will take long at all."

"Elle, I was so sorry to hear about your mom. I hope Micah told you I sent my condolences."

The sincerity of his words touched me. "Of course he did. Thank you so much." In truth, I was pretty certain Micah hadn't passed along any message since most conversations between us were cursory, but I pushed the thought away.

Josh declined an offer of coffee, so we grabbed the key to the storage crate and headed outside. The only bulky item that had been difficult to let go was the piano. One of the few stories Mom had shared about my father was how he had researched for months to surprise her with a beautiful Queen Anne console piano because she'd always wanted to learn to play. Unfortunately, her enthusiasm had not translated to hidden talent. I'd been sitting next to her on the bench while she practiced, and when I turned five, her lessons were reassigned to me. I continued to play throughout high school, and I was quite skilled. If we could have combined her passion with my ability, we might have really had something. But after moving away for college, I didn't miss playing, and I hardly dabbled when I was home for summers and holidays.

When I ran my fingers over the keys in the days after her passing, all it brought was regret. More regret, always regret. Closing the fallboard for the last time, I told Aunt Jan I didn't have any room in my small home for a piano, and unless she wanted it for herself, I would be fine selling it. By the time I flew back to Tennessee, it sat alone in the home that had once been filled with my mother. Her life, her voice, her warmth and grace. All that remained was the one thing she'd loved that hadn't quite loved her back.

Vicky, Mom's realtor, offered to meet potential buyers for the instrument while she got the house ready to list, so I'd posted it on a few online sites. The majority of items in the storage crate were some of her knickknacks, jewelry, dishes, photos, and personal files. Alongside these boxes were four others from her attic. They were labeled with my father's name and sealed shut with tape so old it was feeble and cracked. One day they could tell me more about the man my father had been.

Other than the furniture Josh was helping me with, I planned to spend the remainder of the weekend bringing boxes in one at a time while finding homes for the contents. However, the items I needed Josh to move had been loaded into the crate first. Since we had to pull out several containers to get to them, Josh carried the heaviest into the house for me. We worked expeditiously, aiming to finish before the predicted mid-day storm rolled through.

Before hauling the bed frame and chest of drawers across the yard, we headed to the spare room to bring the Ikea pieces to Josh's truck. As he disassembled the bed, I thanked him again for his help getting these donations to the Rescue Mission and dropping the extra car at Carrie's. Of course, I was grateful, but what I really wanted was to broach the subject of Still Waters.

"So, um, how was working with the band?" Inwardly, I rolled my eyes at the transparent cue. If Josh knew anything about Micah and Martine, this was a pitiful ploy to get information.

He trained sympathetic eyes on me as he continued to rotate the screw counterclockwise. "The band performs well. Martine is too much work."

Well, I guess we weren't beating around the bush.

With a nervous laugh, I decided to leave pretense aside. "I honestly don't know what to do here. I mean, I know this is a dream opportunity for Micah, having such a successful tour to manage while starting out in his career. But I feel like we were just getting used to marriage and then he was gone for months on end."

I faltered in a moment of clarity. I could hear my mom's voice urging me not to rush into marriage with a man who didn't share my beliefs...to see how we'd handle challenges before being joined together for the rest of our lives.

Josh's questioning look caused me to shake my head. "I'm sorry. I shouldn't be venting to you about our problems."

He continued to unscrew the bed frame as the thoughts I'd before now only verbalized to Carrie floated between us. Then he stood, bracing his shoulder against the wall to face me. I wiped my palms on my jeans, unsure of how he'd respond to my unleashing such personal information on him when he'd only come to move furniture.

"Martine seems like an opportunist, and Micah is too smart to fall for it again. He knows your relationship is more valuable than any successful band tour." Josh's raspy voice softened, smoothed by compassion that reached almost palpably across the room. "I have learned that God doesn't allow anything He can't redeem. No matter how messy it might get."

My eyes widened, then I blinked and looked away. I hadn't been aware Josh was a Christian, and this turn in the conversation

surprised me. He must have sensed I needed some time to process his perspective, and with an easy movement, he bound bed
slats in one hand and gave me the neat little package to carry to
his truck. Before I could return for another load, he'd followed
me out with the head and footboards under one arm and the rails
in the other.

After tying the small dresser down in the back of his truck
and covering it with a tarp, Josh made quick work of setting up
the new pieces in their place. I ran my palm over a spindle of the
four-poster bed that I had cocooned in from my 'tween years up
through my most recent trip home. It was a solid piece, crafted
to withstand time and generations. The drawers of the chest had
concealed love notes from my sixth-grade boyfriend and e-ciga-
rettes during my amusingly short-lived rebellious stage (I didn't
even know I was supposed to inhale). They had been emptied to
make space for Micah's boxers and t-shirts when we'd visited as
husband and wife during our first, mostly blissful, year of marriage. It was comforting to have these pieces here now.

The last thing I needed from Josh was to follow me to
Carrie's so I could park the CR-V in her driveway, and then
give me a ride back home. I shot off a quick text to let her know
I was on the way, then grabbed a baseball cap to protect my
frizzing hair from the developing rain. Passing Josh's truck as
I headed to the vehicle parked a few houses down, I hollered
to him that it was less than a fifteen-minute drive to my best
friend's house.

While I used the fob to lock the car after pulling in behind
Carrie's Jeep, I motioned to him to crack his window. "Give me
a minute. I'm going to check on her real quick, and I'll be right
back!"

I was relieved I'd grabbed my full set of keys because her
door was locked when I tried the knob. "Care-Bear, it's me!" I

called out, making sure to wipe my sneakers well before stepping off the entry rug.

At first, I thought she'd simply left her afghan in a discarded pile on the floor. It wasn't until I drew nearer that I realized the slight mound of swirling chevron print disguised Carrie's body.

A moment later, I was screaming from the porch. "Josh! Help! She's not breathing!"

Chapter Eight

When the ambulance arrived, I was sitting in tears on the floor next to Carrie. Josh had dashed inside so fast he'd left his truck door open, but he reassured me she was breathing, although unconscious. Fine hair clung to her perspiring forehead, and she didn't respond to my voice or panicked shakes. Josh gently pulled me away as the EMTs checked her vital signs. Their voices exchanged information so rapidly I didn't know how they could follow what the other was saying.

As they lifted her into the ambulance, I wrung my hands, debating between riding with her or following in the CR-V so I would have a way to get home, whenever that was. Josh took the decision away from me by steering me toward the step up into the back of the ambulance. "Stay with her! I'll be right behind you."

Without watching for my acknowledgment, he dashed through the drizzle toward his truck. I waited long enough to see him swipe the rain that must have accumulated on his seat to the floorboard before he jumped in.

What felt like an hour later, but in truth was less than half that, we were guided to a corner of the Emergency Department by a somber, ebony-skinned woman in silver-framed glasses and a crisp white coat. "She's going to be fine," she began, alleviating my panic. "You found her on the floor?"

I nodded, not yet trusting myself to speak.

"Patients with certain cancers can experience something called syncope when they stand too quickly or for too long. I'm telling you this term in case you hear it again or read it in her discharge paperwork. Basically, her blood pressure dropped, and she fainted. I know it's scary, but right now, I think the most important thing is for you to know she is alright, although we might need to discuss arranging someone to stay with her for a while. Why don't you come and see her?"

As I started to follow the woman, whose nametag read Dr. Yolanda Wright, Josh tugged my elbow back. "Elle, I can stay right here so you know where to find me...."

He'd probably caught a whiff of my anxious perspiration but I begged him anyway, "Come with me, please." Reluctantly, he followed me through the filmy curtain as Dr. Wright parted it.

Carrie was reclined in the narrow bed with her eyes half-open. I rushed to her side, exhaling as though I'd been holding my breath since discovering her. I pressed her pale hand to my cheek, battling a mix of fear and relief.

"Carr, I'm so sorry! I should have been there sooner. I shouldn't have left you alone!" The words didn't make sense, but my guilt was overwhelming. My circumstances had consumed me over the last year, but Carrie was fighting for her life, and the reminder left me irrepressibly ashamed. Not only could I not relieve her, but I'd piled on my own issues, drawing strength from her when she had none to spare.

She granted me a weak smile, too exhausted to speak. Her eyes slid questioningly to the corner where Josh waited, trying to make himself invisible. I glanced behind me, motioning with my head for him to come closer. "Carrie, Josh was with me when I found you. He's Micah's friend." Reflecting on the day we'd shared, I corrected myself. "Mine, too."

Josh rested his hands on the end of the cot, behaving self-consciously in the space, but his voice was steady as he smiled at her. "I'm sorry we're meeting under these conditions, but I thank God the doctor said this wasn't too serious." I glanced back and forth between the two of them, realizing Carrie had reached up to smooth her hair and was offering him a shy smile in return.

Right then, a nurse slipped between the folds of the privacy curtain, tugging it closed behind her. "Hi there. I'm Bridget. We're going to keep Miss Carrie here overnight to be sure she's okay before sending her home. Don't worry—it's only a precaution." She turned her attention to Carrie. "We've called your oncologist, and she agrees. She'll come by to see you soon."

Josh and I determined with Carrie out of danger and in the process of being moved to a room, he could run me home, and I would return with my own car. Giving Carrie a gentle hug, I whispered in her ear, "I noticed you noticing him noticing you!"

Her ears turned pink but she giggled in return.

With a wave, I promised to be back as soon as possible, and Josh bid her goodbye. As he turned to go, he paused and offered, "I'll be praying for you." It was evident he meant it.

Carrie was soundly asleep when I tiptoed into her fifth-floor room later that afternoon. The storm clouds persisted, and the space was dim with little sunlight, but I quietly pulled a chair as close to the window as I could rather than turning on a light. I carried a sandwich I had thrown together along with some snacks in a bag to get me through until visiting hours were over. I'd also grabbed two journals covering the year scribbled on the back of the photo of Mom and Paul.

I riffled through the first book, which started the previous August, stopping to listen once more for the depth of Carrie's quiet breathing before leaning back into the uncomfortable vinyl.

My mom started working overnight at a hotel when I turned eleven, and she was promoted to manager within two years. She'd been comfortable having our twenty-three-year-old neighbor sleep over four nights a week while she worked her eleven PM to seven AM shift. She would come home in time to get me off to school, sleep until early afternoon, then worked another part-time office job for a furniture store from two until six. On those evenings, I would start an easy dinner that she'd finish when she arrived home, and we'd catch up with each other over my homework. During the Christmas season, Mom added in retail work on the weekends. The entry I now read from the December when I was twelve made it clear she was exhausted but also grateful.

I haven't had a day off in almost two weeks, and I feel it. Half the time, I don't know if it's morning or night, however, I thank you, God, for health and for enough energy to keep going.

"For I know the plans I have for you," declares the Lord, "plans to prosper you and not to harm you, plans to give you hope and a future." Jeremiah 29:11"

This verse has been heavy on my heart lately. Being a single mom, even to a daughter like Elle, isn't easy. We stay afloat, but Elle needs time to just be a kid. She's so dependable, almost to a fault, but I never expected my life would turn out this way. If only John was still here.

The entry continued with my mom listing financial concerns, including tuition for my piano lessons and the phone I was begging for as a Christmas gift. These appeals were not presented as worries but prayerful requests to an omniscient God who would provide in whatever manner He deemed necessary for our growth. The entry closed with a reminder.

2 Corinthians 9:8 says He will give me what I need to be able to honor Him.

Hearing Carrie begin to stir, I made note to look that particular verse up later and left the journal on the windowsill above the room's climate control unit. Carefully lifting the wooden chair, I carried it to her bedside. Carrie's eyes fluttered open, glazed at first, then sweeping from the tubing taped to her arm to the metal pole standing sentry-like next to her. She sighed in resignation.

"Hello, Sunshine," I murmured in the quiet room. "Are you feeling any better?"

Her voice was stronger when she moaned. "All this I.V. fluid has me filled to overflowing. Can you grab the bedpan?"

With that business concluded, Carrie sighed. "The last thing I remember is trying to get to the bathroom, desperate to brush my teeth. Her nose wrinkled. "And after all this, I still haven't gotten to brush them!"

I called for a nurse to come and check her out, afraid to help her up if it might cause the dizziness to return. With our assistance, Carrie sat at the edge of the bed for a couple of minutes, using a flimsy hospital toothbrush and spit tray. When we were alone again, Carrie raised her eyebrows. "What about that first impression I made on your friend Josh?" She pouted playfully. "Some warning woulda been nice!"

"Yes, speaking of," I countered, "can you warn *me* the next time you're going to take a nap on the floor, so I don't go into a panic? I thought you'd checked out on me!"

After a few minutes of teasing, I brought Josh back into the conversation. "So, speaking of Josh, who you might remember has filled in for Micah a few times, it turns out he knows exactly what kind of person Martine is." My lips pinched. "I've been stuck between mad and hurt ever since this whole thing started. I can't continue to live this way. Neither of us can. Avoiding each other and letting it simmer between us—it's gone on long enough. When Micah comes back, we are going to have to ... " my voice trailed off.

"Get to fishing?" Carrie filled in for me.

"Or cut bait." I spoke the words with my mouth set in a grim line.

By the time Carrie's oncologist, Dr. Greer, made it to the room, Carrie had eaten a few bites of her dinner and gone back to sleep. I had attended enough appointments with her over the summer for the doctor to remember me by name. She gravely explained the risk of additional episodes of syncope, as well as other misgivings she held regarding Carrie living alone. With the next round of chemo scheduled to start Monday, Dr. Greer recommended Carrie remain admitted and have an aide for the three recovery weeks following. I assured the oncologist I'd look into options for round-the-clock assistance to keep Carrie safe and cared for.

After she left, I lay with my head on the edge of Carrie's bed, covering her cool hand with my own. Tears flowed down my cheeks, soaking the sheet under my face. The room grew darker, the faint murmur of voices ebbing and flowing in the hall the only clue my friend and I weren't utterly abandoned in our separate but joined miserable states. I felt hollow and void of thought, with no hope in reserve.

Carrie's parents had her late in life, a surprise daughter after three boys. They divorced when she was a teenager, and her father and his new wife now lived in Florida. He called sometimes, but Carrie never answered when I was around. She hadn't seen him in years. Her mother lived in a suburb of Knoxville near two of her three sons. Both men were married with kids of their own, and Carrie's mother provided childcare while the parents worked. She'd come for several days after Carrie's diagnosis, but there had only been one short weekend trip since. I suspected it would be difficult for all of them to make arrangements that would allow Ms. Stephenson to come help with her daughter's care. Carrie had often reminded me that the connection I shared with my mother was a precious gift, and I knew it was because she did not enjoy the same relationship with either of her parents.

I awoke with a start when Carrie's fingers lifted the brim of the hat I still wore. Visiting hours had ended, and although the staff did not intrude on our time, I needed to get home. Before leaving, I scouted out graham crackers and juice from the nurse's station and set Carrie up with the remote control and a sitcom. Despite it only being 8:30 and Carrie sleeping most of her day away, I suspected she wouldn't be awake for long. Still, I hated to abandon her now that she was fully alert. I dallied by the bedside, then urged her to call me if she couldn't sleep.

As I rode down in the elevator, I sent Micah a text to let him know where I'd been all day. We had gotten out of the habit of checking in with each other. The downfall of our relationship could be placed squarely on his shoulders, but we both shared culpability for its current state and how we would move forward. He'd given an inch a time or two. Now it was my turn.

I was practically home before I heard the faint chime of a return message. Parking my car at the curb this time, I fumbled in my purse for my phone and house key as I stepped around the dark silhouette of the storage crate in the driveway.

Hate to hear about Carrie, Micah's text read. *Thank God you happened to stop by when you did.*

I hadn't considered what might have happened had I not needed to go to her house this afternoon. The prospect made me double over. I thought I was dried out from the earlier tears, yet this new revelation left me awash with fresh sorrow. Yes— thank God! My mother would have knowingly proclaimed He'd orchestrated the events today. Surely, Carrie was under His protection.

Earlier, with my attention split between the bustle of the Emergency Department and desperation to see Carrie, I'd started to reach for my phone with the thought I should let my mom know what was going on. It wasn't the first time that had happened since her death.

Reading her journals had threaded a gossamer connection between us as I saw our history from her perspective. I had a better understanding of the difficulties she'd loved me through. She'd journaled about faking her smile, but in my eyes, she'd been strong even when her own heart was broken. Despite being sapped of energy and hours in the day, she'd never left me feeling neglected. She'd always made time for another bedtime story, another hug and kiss.

Collapsing onto the couch, I dropped the bag from the hospital onto the cushion. The wrapped half-eaten sandwich slid onto the seat, and I looked at it with disinterest. I lived in a state of almost perpetual drive. Sometimes it manifested as laser-focused energy for work, and other times as edginess, but it eventually left me dry.

I wanted a hot shower and my bed, but instead, I curled into a ball propped up by the rounded arm of the couch and let the vestiges of the day trickle away.

Chapter Nine

A stiff neck woke me early Sunday morning, and I stumbled to the shower. Only after the hot water had run out did I wrap up in my fleece robe and take coffee and my mom's Bible out to the back patio. We'd furnished the small slab of concrete with a freestanding Adirondack-style glider that had gotten little use in the last year. Most recently, when I needed some space from Micah after an argument—an argument over the growing chasm between us, no less. I'd tried to explain I was busy with work. He'd called me out for not making our relationship a priority. I swayed for hours that night, only going back inside when the mosquitoes and my conscience became unbearable company.

Stretching my bare legs down the slats of the seat, I rested my head against the faux-wood backrest and pushed the glider into gentle motion. The emptiness held on from the night before. I wasn't just alone, but lonely. I pulled my robe tighter around me, wishing it could bring warmth to the chill in my heart.

My last conversation with my mom had been on a Sunday morning like this one. She'd called as I was straightening my hair—as always, endeavoring to smooth out the curls that had a mind of their own. I'd seen the notification register but decided to call her back when I was finished. The cramped bathroom and 1800-watt dryer were hardly an endurable combination, and I was in a hurry to put this chore behind me.

As I unloaded the clean dishwasher, the speakerphone resounded the trill of waiting for a connection. Mom answered, out of breath, "Hi, Elle ... I was calling to check in, but now I'm walking into church." I tried to let her go, but she interjected. "No, I have a minute. You know everyone is going to stand around and socialize for a bit. How's your weekend? Any update on Carrie?"

I assured her I had nothing to report, and a moment later she called out, "Alison! Paul! Honey, let me let you go. I want to chat with the Spencers for a minute. Love you!"

With that, she was gone. The entire conversation seemed so insignificant then, but two days later, she was *gone*. From my life, from this world, no warning—just gone. The glider continued to glide, even without urging. The world went on as though her death wasn't a disruption. She used to say, "God is still on His throne," when things didn't go according to plan. She'd said it a lot. But God never explained Himself. He didn't make it all make sense. He kept sitting on His throne, and nothing ever changed for Him. When my world was shaken, nothing changed for Him. Like my mother dying and my husband cheating and my best friend battling cancer despite being only a quarter-of-a-century old didn't even matter to Him. *He just sat there.*

The eruption of such volatile thoughts reminded me of my mother's journal entries after the second miscarriage. I had yet to read anything from the years directly following the autumn we lost my dad. I had avoided those journals—a red one, a paisley one, and a black and white composition notebook—more studiously than I'd avoided the books from *this* year. Inserting myself into her heart and thoughts as she coped with her husband dying and the loss of her so-close-to-being-born, already-knew-her-name baby daughter seemed beyond intrusive. It seemed disrespectful and insolent. But finding out how she'd managed, how she'd survived, and how she'd forgiven God was the draw. My pain was harsh, but hers was unfathomable. If prayer had healed her, I needed to understand how.

In addition to the Bible, my phone rested in my lap, tucked into the pocket of a cream-colored robe. Fumbling to extract it, I had a sudden flash of the lemony yellow nightgown covered with oversized tropical flowers I'd come across as I did a last-minute check of my mom's home. The donation boxes had been taped shut, and I'd groaned when I realized her gown was still hanging from the hook on the inside of her closet door. Relenting, but also relishing the evocative scent of my mother, I'd folded the brightly colored fabric into my suitcase. It wasn't my style, way too much—everything, but it was sacred in its own way. Catherine chose yellow paint and yellow vehicles and yellow clothing, and they all conveyed her signature joy. She chose joy.

Ignoring the trickle of emails that had come in from work since Friday, I found where I'd typed the scripture reference from the journal entry the previous afternoon. As I leafed through the Bible in my lap, I was awed by the extent of highlighting and margin notes my mom had added. It was apparent God spoke clearly to her when she read His word. I'd had glimpses of this type of relationship with Him when I was younger, but feeling it deep in my soul was still elusive. As I landed on 2 Corinthians 9:8, I closed my eyes, yearning to know I wasn't forsaken.

"And God is able to make all grace abound to you, so that having all sufficiency in all things at all times, you may abound in every good work."

I read and then reread the words. My mom's journal entry was a reminder of this—that He would provide for her needs so she could continue to glorify Him with her deeds. We had always had enough to get us through, even during the leanest times. But I sensed it wasn't primarily the physical needs God met that caused my mother to cling to this verse. 'Sufficiency' was the word that stopped me. In my mind, I compared it to 'abundance.' Surely there were times my mom had barely been holding on. Not only in regard to bills being paid on time and Christmas wishes fulfilled, but getting enough sleep through it all. Things hadn't been easy, and although I'd been aware, I hadn't agonized over our financial state. It occurred to me perhaps that was my mom's comfort as well. I trusted her to provide for us, just as she'd trusted God. And He had given her enough to keep going, yet not enough to keep her from depending on Him.

I thought about what Catherine had endured: three lost babies, becoming a young widow, and the difficulties of single motherhood. God must have provided abundantly for her spiritual needs, or she would not have been the strong, faith-filled mother I'd known. She might have remained heart-shattered and bitter. She could have turned from Him. Instead, she had accepted His grace and allowed it to change her.

When I'd first found out about Micah's infidelity, I'd been as angry with God as I was with my husband. The perfect marriage and future I'd planned were falling apart, and all I had left was my career. It became *my* saving grace, and I relied on it. Work was the one thing I could control.

My parents had dreams and plans too, and there was no way for me to understand why they hadn't been blessed with more children or why my father had to be at *that* particular ATM that day. Catherine never entered into another relationship—not one I'd known of—and I'd asked her once if she was happy with her life. Her answer hadn't made sense then but it stuck with me. She'd replied, "It isn't about chasing happiness. It's about chasing holiness."

At the time, I took it to mean our only mission was to follow God's rules. Wasn't that what holiness meant? Mom's words might have made it seem like a choice between one or the other, but the way she lived didn't. Her spirit—both joyful and pure—had drawn her into the confidences of the families she worked with, and for most of my life, kept me pointed in the right direction.

"And God is able to make all grace abound to you, so that having all sufficiency in all things at all times, you may abound in every good work."

I focused on the beginning. *"And God is able to make all grace abound to you."* At the center of it all, God had provided an abundance of grace. And when my mother was overfilled with it, it flowed out of her, touching everything she held dear, allowing the good she did to also multiply in abundance across all the lives she touched.

I contemplated that verse throughout the morning. After calling the hospital to check on Carrie and assuring her I'd visit soon, I sat with my computer to make sure nothing urgent had come in from Starship. I noticed our shared work calendar had been updated to reflect an extension to our weekly meeting. Perhaps we'd landed a major contract that would level us up. One could dream.

Repacking the small tote bag to take to the hospital again, I made sure I had the same two journals from the previous day stowed inside. I was still curious to find out the nature of my mom's relationship with Paul, and I was sure the answer was there.

Carrie was eager for distraction after a full day confined to her hospital bed. I pulled the journals out of my bag and told her what we were looking for. "Paul was part of my mom's friend group when I was young. I remember him from Sundays after church, when the adults all stood around chatting for *ages* before finally deciding to just go to lunch together."

Years later, when Mom moved to Monona, Paul and his wife Alison already lived there, and they invited her to their new church, where she soon became a member. The previous Thanksgiving when Micah and I visited my mom, they provided the turkey for the meal that included my mom's neighbor Mae and her husband, as well as another widow from across the street.

Carrie and I each took a journal and skimmed through them, seeking any reference to Paul from the years I was twelve and thirteen, around the time he appeared in my mom's life.

It was Carrie who first found his name. I took the book and paged back for context. In an entry a few weeks earlier, I found Paul's name again. Before reading it, I slipped my finger between the pages like a bookmark and laughingly prayed aloud, "Lord, please forgive us for snooping on my mom's love life!"

After murmuring the preamble under my breath, I read her introduction of him out loud.

At work tonight, a guest came strolling through the lobby in the middle of the night. His name is Paul Spencer, and he had insomnia. He's in town for business, and we ended up talking for over an hour. He lives upstate but might be moving down here if his business meeting goes well. It's been a really long time since I enjoyed talking to a man. He's good-looking and quite clever, with a great sense of humor. He's staying another night. He didn't suggest it, but I hope I get to see him again.

The idea of my mom crushing on a man amused me, but correlating that with the image of Paul was even more perplexing. He'd been in the picture for over a decade, and I remembered when he married Alison. We'd attended their wedding the summer before my senior year of high school.

I jumped forward to the page Carrie had originally come across, which was almost two months later. I could tell right away I'd missed some of the story by skipping ahead, but I caught the gist by reading this entry.

It's been a month since our first date, and every day I like Paul more. I could see myself falling in love with him. But I'm not sure if the timing is right. Elle hasn't been herself lately. All the hours I work, plus trying to find time to spend with friends (and Paul) might be leaving her feeling neglected. She's growing up, but she still needs me. She thinks I don't know she's experimenting with vaping—that will be a hard conversation this weekend. But not as tough as trying to introduce Paul might be. I haven't been seriously interested in anyone since John. Even though I went out on a few dates over the years, Paul is the only man I've been able to envision a future with. Elle and I have been on our own for so long. What if she's not ready for everything to change? What if I'm not?

The cringe on Carrie's face mirrored my own, but she tried to comfort me. "Teenage girls put their mothers through grief. It's a rite of passage."

I lamented, "I was certain she didn't understand *anything* back then, and there she was, falling in love behind my back. She was more than a mother. She was a woman. How could I still not see that? Why was I so afraid tell her about Micah's affair?"

Carrie begged me to look at the situation differently. "Elle, you're learning a lot about your mother, but your journey is yours, and hers was hers. She didn't blame you for the way her relationship with Paul ended up. She was only trying to be the best mom she could be."

That afternoon, I shared with Carrie the poignant discoveries I'd made in the previous journals. Even as she teared up over the losses of the other babies, she reminded me my mom was reunited with them now in heaven.

As I tenderly brushed her thinning hair and helped her change into a new gown before I left, I considered how blessed I was by this friendship. Despite the doctor's cautious assurances, I knew I could still lose her.

I could still lose everything.

Just like my mom had.

Chapter Ten

Each Monday at noon, my department would order lunch and review all current and upcoming projects. Aside from myself, our staff included four others: the two licensing representatives, Constance Pelton and Erica Morgan, the contract writer, Shawn Beauford, and our boss, Henry Hicks.

Today's meeting was the first time I'd gotten to catch up with the whole team since my return the previous week. I was the assistant to both licensing reps, but with Constance's expected resignation, I was awaiting a promotion to her position. She and Erica had been increasing my responsibilities, and I was confident about stepping into the role.

As we filled our plates with hot chicken and sides from Hattie B's, I thanked my co-workers for the sympathy card they'd left on my desk, and for the lovely plant, which I'd taken home. My cubicle in the center of our crowded space didn't provide even the minimal natural light the peace lily needed to thrive.

We were assembling around the small conference table, trying to keep our greasy fingers away from our meeting notes, when Henry appeared, followed by the same chiseled-face man I'd encountered near the elevator the previous week. My stomach lurched, like it knew something I didn't.

"Good afternoon, everyone. I trust you enjoyed lunch." Henry had never been one to miss a meal, so I could only assume this mysterious stranger was more important than Hattie B. "I'd like to introduce Donovan Archer. He'll be joining our team and bringing some great experience and connections. Donovan, anything you'd like to share?"

"Hey, y'all. Good to be here." His drawl was affected, like he'd picked it up imitating Andy Griffith reruns.

This guy got Constance's job? In such a small group, I had nowhere to hide. I covered my shock with a napkin under the guise of wiping stray hot sauce from my lips.

Donovan clapped Henry on the back like they were old friends. "You know, I was having drinks with Tim and Kenny the other day and they had nothing but good things to say about you, Henry."

Ugh. A name-dropper.

"I'm excited to be here and have no doubt—with some hard work—we can make a real name for Starship." Donovan tossed his gelled hair. It didn't even budge.

I'd been passed up for a guy as pretentious as his own name. *Does he think we don't work hard?* I twisted the cap from my water bottle and tried to swallow my disappointment along with the tepid beverage while everyone else murmured welcomes to the interloper. My throat constricted, the mouthful of liquid nearly ejecting in a choking cough. No one paid me any attention.

As our meeting wrapped, Henry's boss, the head of Starship Publishing, slipped into the back of the room. Henry's brows barely raised at Lorna Mackenzie's entrance. She made occasional forays to our floor, and the infrequent interactions we'd had over the years had left me in awe of her. Taller than Henry in her expensive black and gold heels, she reflected an almost regal elegance, and her short cap of silvery hair distinguished rather than aged her.

She stepped gracefully to the side as Donovan, followed by Erica, Constance, and Shawn filed out of the conference room.

As the assistant, each Monday I would stay behind to package up any remaining lunch and take it to the minuscule kitchen we shared at the end of the hall. Neither Henry nor Ms. Mackenzie left as I tossed the boxes of leftover chicken and macaroni into the paper bag they'd been delivered in. I was keenly aware they were in a gratuitous discussion until Ms. Mackenzie walked toward me with her arms outstretched.

"Brielle," she clasped my hands as I let go of the food bag. "I was so sorry to hear of your mother's passing." She spoke in a softly lilting voice that belied her striking appearance.

I thanked her with a murmur. This entire day was catching me off guard. Blindsided by losing the promotion I'd been gunning for and now an impromptu meeting with the president of our publishing house, who was going out of her way to greet me. Taking a breath, I spoke again. "Thank you, Ms. Mackenzie. It was completely unexpected, and I appreciate Henry granting me so much time off."

She waved her hand. "Please, it's Lorna. That time was imperative and the least we could do for you." She paused, then glanced over her shoulder at Henry, who moved to stand next to her.

He shoved his hands into his pockets. "Elle, I know I'd suggested you gear up to take Constance's place when she left, and I'm sure the news today must have been a bit of a letdown in regard to that."

I pressed my lips together, latching onto the gruffness in his voice, even though I knew it disguised a kindhearted nature. I hadn't even been told they were looking outside the company. Henry must have known I would be more than let down. I'd done my best during the remainder of the meeting to push my thoughts aside but it wasn't easy with Donovan Archer sitting next to me, a polished Gucci loafer propped on his opposing knee, taking up more space than he should have been allotted on my side of the table.

Unless...maybe there was room in the budget for a third licensing rep. I waited expectantly, wondering if I'd proven myself enough for them to give me the opportunity after all.

Instead, Lorna explained another opening in Talent Acquisitions. The opportunity would be in a parallel division of Starship. Instead of moving up into a licensing representative position, Henry and Lorna had discussed starting me as an A&R rep, which would entail discovering and developing new talent for publishing. I knew this also meant I would spend most of my time in crowded honky-tonks and glad-handing at events.

The idea petrified me.

After hearing them out and agreeing to give their offer some thought, I headed to my office with my eyes fixed on the slightly scuffed tips of my discount pumps. As I sank onto my seat, I could hear the annoying squeal of the chair I'd swapped from the desk on the other side of mine. A moment later, Donovan's lowered voice penetrated my space. *Oh great.* He must have been assigned the neighboring cubicle until Constance's office was free.

"Yeah, man. Starship is small potatoes compared to what I'm used to, but no surprise with who they have running the joint. At least I'm here to show them how it's done. Then Warner will realize letting me go was a mistake."

Working for this guy might be worse than schmoozing for a living.

Aside from benign texts exchanged since Micah left, we hadn't spoken much since his return to Canada. That wasn't uncommon for us this year. When I was in *a mood,* being able to reword messages as many times as necessary helped keep our conversations placid. But I was also never sure if he was alone, as he claimed, or if Martine was running her talons through his hair while he sent me the obligatory *'just checking in'* text.

After looking over his schedule for the week, I decided this evening should be a good time to catch Micah for a phone call. I wanted to tell him about the conversation with Henry and Lorna, and the predicament I now faced. I also wanted to ask if he'd considered not continuing with Still Waters after the tour ended in three weeks. But I didn't want to do either via text. This was too important to risk misconstrued intentions.

After throwing on leggings and a raglan sleeve shirt, I sat at the kitchen table with my phone. Changing my mind, I moved to the cozy leather couch. The phone rang five times before his outgoing greeting began. Did he not want me to know he was ignoring my call, or was he occupied with Martine? It was easy to ignore the possibility he was legitimately busy.

"Hi, Micah." My voice came out unnaturally high, and I cleared my throat before continuing with a less forced tone. "Listen, I have some news I wanted to talk over with you. It's sort of time-critical." I rushed to add, "I mean, it's not an emergency. Anyway, call me tonight if you can. Thanks."

Biting my lip, I sat with the phone in my lap for a couple of minutes, mulling over my options. Moving into talent acquisition seemed further and further outside of my comfort zone the more I considered it. But working under Donovan Archer held little appeal either. Next to none, as a matter of fact.

I was getting to my feet to start a simple dinner when my phone vibrated.

"Hey, Elle. How are you?" He nonchalantly disregarded a commotion in the background.

"You sound busy." I raised my voice over the noise. This was a mistake. I didn't want to talk about my career or our marriage while he was out partying.

"No, it's fine. I'm on my balcony at the hotel, and there's an event going on downstairs. How *are* you?" He repeated the question patiently, and I remembered this is how spouses are supposed to talk to each other. Not hurrying to pass along the most abbreviated information and end the conversation.

I relaxed into the couch and closed my eyes, picturing his smile that used to instantaneously calm any anxiety. "I'm ok. It was a Monday, ya know...how are you? You're in British Columbia, right?"

Listening to him describe how beautiful Kelowna was, I imagined traveling with him. We hadn't gone on many trips during our time together. Visiting each of our parents, mine more so than his, was pretty much the extent of it. Our one Christmas with his family in North Carolina seemed much longer than the thirty-six hours it actually lasted. And we had given up our honeymoon to make the down payment on the house. We hadn't minded at the time, but now I wondered if that had been one more chance to connect that we'd bypassed.

Micah concluded by reminding me of his schedule for the rest of the week, and a boulder thudded in my gut. What would living with him day in and day out look like after all that had transpired? I'd told Carrie when Micah came back, we would have to agree one way or the other about what came next for us. The tour ending meant no more procrastination.

"Well, I wanted to tell you about something going on at work," I began. "It turns out they hired someone else for Constance's position, so if I want to move up, I have to leave the department. They want me in A&R, of all places."

"That doesn't interest you, I suppose. What happens if you don't take it?"

"I could also stay where I am for now, but this new guy…" I paused, unsure of how to summarize everything I didn't like about Donovan Archer. "Well, I think he's going to be…challenging as a supervisor." *Challenging* was not the first word that had come to mind.

"You're such a hard worker, you'd win him over. But I think you work just as hard at avoiding situations you're uncomfortable with. I think you should give it a shot."

"Maybe you're right and he won't be that bad."

"Who won't? I meant A&R."

I closed my eyes. Was I really leaning toward staying in Licensing with that arrogant chauvinist Donovan? Talk about choosing the lesser of two evils. But A&R bundled all of my biggest fears into one terrifying package.

Selling Starship to potential artists should be easy. Lorna Mackenzie's company was modest only because it was discriminating. But selling myself and what I could do for fledgling talent was a different story. It didn't matter if they were the one on stage. When it came down to it, their spotlight would be on me when I made their dreams come true or popped them like an overinflated gum bubble.

My husband loved to be the center of attention, and the bigger the circle he could regale, the better. But I hated people watching me, waiting for me to screw up. It was why I didn't stick with piano. I dreaded hearing the words, *"Play something!"* at every gathering my mother hosted. To me, one wrong strike all but negated the rest. Too many mistakes, and people walked away.

At the very least, their attention strayed.

Micah and I tried to have some honest conversations earlier this year. I wanted to understand why he'd cheated with Martine.

We had gone so far as trying marriage counseling. However, because of his tour schedule, there was no way to achieve the consistency we needed to make much progress. One of our sessions had provided a breakthrough, though.

"When I first met Elle, I was impressed with her dedication, despite still being an intern. She stayed on top of things, and it was clear doing well was important to her. But now, she uses work to avoid the parties and events I'm invited to, and I'm always making excuses for why she's not with me. She thinks if she doesn't 100% commit to something when I first mention it, then she's not standing me up when she doesn't come. And she loves to wait until it's go-time before she lets me know she's tied up."

Micah's openness with the marriage counselor left me stunned, but I couldn't find fault in what he'd said. The fact that he'd tried to use my work ethic as an excuse for sleeping with another woman, though—that just made me furious.

"I love Elle. I don't want our marriage to be over. But I was so frustrated when she waited until I was already at the Halloween party to bother telling me she wasn't coming. That's part of why I kissed that woman. Yes, Martine started it, but I didn't stop it. I'd slipped one day when she asked what Elle does to occupy herself with me gone so much. I vented that Elle might not even noticed me leaving. I didn't exactly mean that Elle wasn't attentive, but the way Martine started acting gave me something I'd been missing. I didn't intend for it to get physical. I regretted kissing her, even more so after the way Elle found out. I never wanted to hurt her. Then, when we were with Catherine for Thanksgiving, Elle spent the entire Saturday working. She didn't even seem to notice how annoyed I was about it."

Now, as we discussed whether I should stay where I was or accept the new position, something else niggled the back of my mind. I still wanted to know if Micah would consider finding a new band, and if he wouldn't, what that said about the value of our relationship to him. Although this topic was one of the reasons I'd called, now I was afraid to ask.

Instead, I timidly suggested, "Since our anniversary is next weekend, is there any chance you can come home?"

His response warmed me. "I was planning to."

Chapter Eleven

Henry had assured me I could take time to make a decision about the position, and he would still need to find a replacement for me if I accepted the new job. The lessened pressure to provide a quick answer allowed me to focus on the projects I'd been given during Monday's lunch meeting. My only distraction was the anticipation of Micah coming home to celebrate our anniversary.

Well, Micah and my new supervisor. He wasn't even official yet—he and Constance were overlapping for a few days while he got settled—but the man seemed to hold me accountable for all our lost contracts, going back to the beginning of time.

"Can you explain why this deal didn't happen?"

"What could you have done differently?"

"Tell me how you'd pitch me on this if you had to do it right now."

He had it out for me, and I didn't know why.

On Monday, I'd only spent a few minutes with Carrie since she was sleeping hard after her first dose of this week's chemo. I stopped by again Tuesday to see if she could answer some questions that would help me hire aides for after her discharge.

It was the dinner hour when I let myself into her room, but she wasn't even making a charade of eating. The tray on the hospital table was still covered at the side of her bed. Carrie angled her head toward me, and I could see she didn't have much more energy than the evening before when she'd been asleep. Still, she welcomed me by flipping her hand over and trying to adjust her position.

"Rough stuff, huh, friend?" I hated to see her like this, baggy pajamas revealing virtually translucent papery skin. This round of chemo was proving more arduous than the last.

With an impish smile, Carrie tipped her head to direct my gaze to the nightstand. There nestled a squat bouquet of cheery Tango, Venere, and Amandine Roses filled in with fragrant eucalyptus. I recognized the various Ranunculus varieties because they'd been some of my mother's favorites in the gardens she'd tended since my childhood.

"Oh my! Well, I didn't send them! Who are they from?" I scooted around the bed.

Blushing, Carrie started to whisper, "Read the..." Before she could complete the sentence, a dry cough wracked her weak body, and I quickly stopped to roll her onto her side. Catching her breath, she assured me she was alright. I poured a cup of water from the pink pitcher sitting on the table and raised the head of her bed so she could take a sip. Once again nodding that she was fine, Carrie urged me to read the card.

'Carrie, I hope you don't mind that I called the front desk to ask if you'd been discharged. When they said you hadn't, I thought maybe some color would brighten your room and your spirits. I'm praying, Josh (Elle & Micah's friend)'

I looked from the small, folded rectangle to my friend. "Woah! That's the sweetest thing ever. You guys must have really had a moment when you were waking up in the emergency room!" Carrie laughed at my waggled eyebrows.

"I can get his number from Micah, if you want." My ethereal friend had not lost a hint of her beauty, and I was delighted over Josh's seeming attraction to her. Carrie hadn't dated much in recent years. She'd had a boyfriend during high school, but moving away ended their relationship. Then there was a guy from her church she had spent some time with for a few months during college. That ended when he continued to push for a physical relationship despite Carrie's refusals. After him, Carrie kept her focus on school and the tutoring she did on the side.

A cellist, Carrie attended Belmont School of Music, majoring in Music Performance. Hearing her play always brings me to tears. Because of the differentiation between Belmont University and the School of Music, our paths never cross until our junior year when I attended a symphony held by her orchestra. The entire performance was impressive, but Carrie's solo earned a standing ovation from the captive audience. When I recognized her cloud of blonde hair on campus a few weeks later, I had to stop and compliment her, and our friendship grew almost overnight.

As the fall semester drew to a close, we decided to share a two-bedroom apartment. We renewed our rental midway through our senior year. At the end of the third lease term, when Micah and I were already married, Carrie found a lovely home for rent a few short miles away from ours. By then, she was part of a professional orchestra that kept her playing nine months of the year. The cancer diagnosis over the summer usurped her schedule, and I knew she missed the cello more than most other aspects of her life since her illness.

I texted Micah to ask him for Josh's contact information. Still Waters had a show that night, so I didn't expect a quick answer. In the meantime, I called the home health agencies on the hospital-provided list. Carrie listened in, answering the questions I was unsure of, and we found an option with flexibility in case her oncologist advised another round of chemo.

By the time I wrapped up the call and coaxed Carrie into swallowing a few sips of a chocolate Boost shake, visiting hours were coming to an end. Promising to forward Josh's number when I received it, I bent and pressed my lips against the top of Carrie's downy head. We had talked about shaving her hair before, but bringing out the clippers was too distressing. I hadn't brought it up again, and neither had she. Whispering that I loved her, I backed out of the room to head home for a date with my MacBook.

Constance's last day with Starship arrived, and the only good thing about it was the end of sharing a cubicle wall with Donovan. He and that squeaky chair had gotten on my very last nerve. And it wasn't just the chair. His judgmental huffs floated above my head with every phone call I answered. Some days, it seemed every keystroke I typed.

But worse was the way condescension coated each request. If I were heading to the coffeepot, which I often was, he'd say, "Bring me a cup, would ya, darlin'?" in that contrived twang he imagined was charming. I even overheard him referring to me as "the office girl" during a conversation with Shawn, like he had no idea of my name or that I'd almost had his job.

Or, maybe he did know.

I'd finally asked Henry what I could have done differently to earn the promotion. His answer left me feeling more insecure than ever.

"Elle, you absolutely could have handled this position. I wasn't worried you weren't right for the job—I just wasn't sure the job was right for you. I'd like to see you step out of your comfort zone. Push your limits. I think there's something that you might not see in yourself."

What could he possibly see in me that would make him think rubbing shoulders was my gift? I was a t-crossing, i-dotting, list-maker who pitched deals from the safety of a PowerPoint presentation. Off the cuff wooing as part of Artists and Repertoire certainly didn't play to my talents, hidden or otherwise, and I had every intention of staying comfortable behind the scenes.

That week, I spent my evenings torn between visiting Carrie, unpacking the remaining boxes from my mom's home, and trying to stay ahead of the constant flow of emails from Donovan. In a fit of frustration, I silenced his notifications, which were often causing my phone to buzz even after I'd closed up my MacBook for the night.

Micah called Thursday night, just as I was wriggling into bed. "Sorry it's so late. I booked my flight for this weekend. Just one layover—Edmonton to Denver. I'll land in Nashville just after three o'clock Sunday afternoon.

We'd have almost a full day together before he'd have to go back. Too bad he'd spend as much time traveling as he would home with me. "I can go in late on Monday. They'll understand it's our anniversary." I warmed, realizing what I'd implied, and changed the subject. "Speaking of relationships, guess why I asked for Josh's number?"

Micah chuckled when I told him about the flowers. "Josh is a good one. He may actually be worthy of Carrie. He certainly has a clean reputation." The contradiction to himself might have hit too close to home by the way he cleared his throat. "If you want to spend Sunday with Carrie, I understand. I can hang back. Do some laundry."

"I'm not expecting her to need me to stay, since a home health aide is coming. You don't have to worry about me leaving you home alone, though. And, hopefully, she'll be doing better by her release tomorrow."

On Friday, I left work mid-afternoon, slipping the project I hadn't been able to finish into my bag. I didn't want Carrie to have to wait on me after her discharge paperwork was complete. I was overly optimistic, though, as they didn't have her ready to go until after five that evening.

While we waited, Carrie filled me in on her conversations with Josh over the previous days. "He even came to have breakfast with me this morning. It was so sweet!"

As we gathered the last of her items from the room, including the beautiful floral arrangement that was retaining its blooms despite the dry hospital air, one of Carrie's doctors popped in. "Don't forget that you'll need a PET scan in a few weeks. Radiology will call to schedule it."

Carrie dipped her head. She knew this scan would determine if a fourth round of chemo was needed, or if she would be moving on to radiation.

Several minutes later, with the hospital wheelchair positioned near my car's passenger seat, Carrie deeply inhaled the cooling evening air. A young man swiftly transferred her into place before wishing us goodnight. As we exited the parking lot, she craned her neck to take in the twilight. She had a peace about her that calmed my own anxiety over being responsible for a life that a week ago had seemed so fragile.

I had an overnighter with what I'd need to get me through until Sunday morning when the first aide would arrive to take my place. Carrie would have day and nighttime helpers staying with her around the clock, except for weekends when I planned to spend from eight AM until eight PM with her myself.

When we arrived to Carrie's, I made a simple meal of sweet potatoes and shredded chicken. Then, taking advantage of her increased energy, I helped her bathe using a shower chair. As we watched, loops of her fair hair rinsed toward the drain. Carrie covered her face with her hands, pressing her elbows into her knees. After that, I made sure the sprayer stayed below her shoulders.

That night, Carrie lay quietly on the couch with her fingers laced over her chest. I was reading from one of my mother's journals, sharing portions aloud. This book covered my mother's pregnancy with me through my first months, farther back than most stories I'd been told. My father singing to me through my mother's belly, the anticipation of choosing a name and decorating the nursery, and the debacle of his diaper changing attempts.

When Carrie didn't laugh at a funny anecdote, I peered over the top of the book and discovered she'd fallen asleep. A tranquil smile parted her lips, and hopefulness replaced the current of loneliness that had carried me for so long.

Chapter Twelve

The disruption to her routine and the chemo meds caught up with Carrie on Saturday. She dozed on and off, nibbling crackers to settle her stomach, but vomited several times into the plastic bin we kept by her side. I alternated between finishing my work assignments and caring for her, heartbroken at the little I could do to ease her discomfort.

"This should be the worst of it," she assured me through tears. I could see how much it hurt every time her weak stomach muscles contracted to help purge the meager contents of her system. Eventually, she'd worn herself out so thoroughly all I could do was lightly rub her back and wipe her sallow face.

Josh sent Carrie a few texts that she weakly dictated responses to throughout the day. I could feel his agony through the phone at not being able to take away her misery. When she eventually fell asleep late in the afternoon, I scrubbed her shower and the spot on the rug where she'd missed the trash bin before I collapsed into the window seat within hearing distance of her sofa.

My heart begged a God who was out there somewhere not to be indifferent to this precious woman who held such trust in Him. Carrie had always reminded me somewhat of my mother; less gregarious but the same serenity, no matter her circumstances. I knew Carrie's home life before college held painful secrets she'd only insinuated. Her talent for the cello didn't impress either her parents or her siblings. However, her audition for the School of Music garnered a significant scholarship and seemed to free her from a family situation that had constricted the first eighteen years of her life. I'd taken Carrie home with me for Christmas the first year we were roommates and envied the way she and my mom related through their faith. Mom had similarly bonded with Micah. Both being extroverts, they didn't suffer trying to 'fit in' with each other when they first met. They just hit the ground running.

Now I gazed out of the window at the periwinkle sky, trying to reconcile a God who *could* do everything with the one who was choosing not to do anything for the person who surely deserved it most. Carrie attended church services on Belmont's campus, playing as part of a string quartet for holidays and special events. The few times I'd joined her on those occasions, I was inevitably overwhelmed watching her perform. It was as if she was infused with the instrument, or it with her, and I was transported.

But it wasn't only her playing. I gazed in wonder at the upturned faces surrounding me, marveling at the connection this congregation had to an invisible God and to each other. Of course, I believed in God. I had for as long as I could remember. My mother had raised me to pray before meals and bed, and she spoke as though He was as tangible to her as the pew I sat on. I'd always considered myself a believer. I knew He was the Creator and that He'd sent His son to die. As a child, I'd asked Jesus to be my savior, but was He also the Lord of my life? Had I ever *really* given control to Him?

The question, and the answer, were uncomfortable for me to consider. Type A personalities want to make the rules. I had my life mapped out, and I needed God to get on board.

Even if the past year was making me wonder if He had other plans.

I had arranged an altered schedule with the home health aide for this first Sunday. I planned to leave at noon, giving myself a couple of hours to buy groceries and wash and straighten my untamed hair before picking Micah up from the airport. It had been months since I'd put so much thought into what to wear to see my husband, and I wished I had something new for our anniversary dinner. Micah, always one for surprises, had only told me we had a seven o'clock reservation. When there was a soft knock on Carrie's door at eleven that morning, I looked at my watch, then double-checked the oven clock, unsure if the aide and I had gotten our wires crossed. I'd hoped she'd come early so I could show her around, but I wouldn't need a full hour.

Opening the door, I was surprised and then grateful to see Josh on the porch. Having read and typed responses to his texts the day before, I wondered if he and Carrie had been holding a covert conversation this morning. As I moved to the side for him to enter, he apologized for coming by unannounced.

"I, uh, wasn't too far from here, so I decided to stop by. I hope it's not an imposition. I thought maybe I could run to the grocery store or something for you guys before you leave for the day." He spoke in a low whisper, unable to tell if the motionless pile of blankets on the couch concealed a sleeping or awake Carrie.

I urged him to follow me to the living room, pulling the barstool I usually sat on at Carrie's side closer to the couch. "She's just dozing," I smiled at him. "I think seeing you is exactly what she needs this morning. And since I also need to pick up some things for my own house, what would you think of staying with her for a bit while I make a quick grocery run for us both?"

Carrie was less nauseated but severely dehydrated after the previous day. Still, I didn't want to leave Josh with more than he was comfortable managing. I showed him where I'd left a stack of washcloths to dampen for her forehead and promised to be back soon with ginger tea, low sodium crackers, and vegetable broth. As I headed out, their quiet murmurs made me pause. Josh was an answer to prayer.

Half an hour later with my arms laden with bags of fruit, fresh bread, and popsicles to soothe her scratchy throat, I returned to an empty living room. Almost immediately, Josh appeared at the end of the hallway, his brow drawn.

"She asked me to help her to the bathroom. She said she could handle things once she got there. I was hoping you'd come back before she needed any help."

I quickly handed off the shopping bags to him, calling over my shoulder, "There are popsicles that need to go in the freezer!" before tapping on the bathroom door and letting myself in.

Carrie stood at the sink, holding herself up with spindly arms on the countertop. Her toothbrush, topped with paste, protruded from her loosely gripped fist. She offered me a weak grimace, whining, "Why is brushing my teeth so much work these days?"

"Oh, Care-Bear," I laughed softly. "You're only doing this because you know Josh wants to kiss you!"

Rolling her eyes at me, Carrie sat on the closed toilet lid while I fashioned a makeshift method to brush her teeth using a cup of water and the tub. I darted to her room for a change of clothes, and she gratefully slipped into a soft pink sweater and silky pajama bottoms. I should have held off on teasing her about getting dressed up for Josh, but I couldn't resist asking, "Would you like earrings or a necklace to complete your look?"

By the time I guided her back to the living room, it was ten minutes before noon, and the aide was parking across the street, no doubt confused over the array of vehicles in front of Carrie's house. Josh had put the groceries away and made up the couch with clean sheets he'd found in the hall closet. I appreciated how he was making himself so useful.

"Maybe you can give the tour so I can get on my way," I joked.

As I showed the new Monday-through-Friday aide around the house, we could hear Josh and Carrie's muffled flirting in the living room. When I presented Elizabeth, I wasn't sure how to refer to Josh, so he introduced himself.

"I'm Josh Jenkins, a friend of Carrie's. I'll be here as much as she'll let me. And I'll leave you my number. You can always reach out if she needs anything."

I concentrated on hiding a smile over the hint of color he'd brought to Carrie's face.

While I gathered my empty coffee cup and purse, Carrie asked Josh to stay until she fell asleep, and I was happy to leave her in good company. With a kiss on her cheek and a wave to Josh and Elizabeth, I headed for my car. Micah would be landing in under four hours, and I was grateful I'd had the chance to pick up some necessities before leaving Carrie's.

I'd also found a lighthearted anniversary card at the grocery store. I wanted to give Micah *something,* but this past year had been a disaster in so many ways. We hadn't given each other Christmas gifts after I'd learned of his infidelity. He'd gotten me flowers for Valentine's Day, which I'd taken from his hand and pushed straight down into the trash. His birthday was in March, and remorse over my behavior on Valentine's Day prompted me to buy him pricey headphones he'd been eyeing. We were off-kilter again by June, and he was on the road, but he'd texted me that morning to look in the top drawer of his nightstand for my gift. The velvet box held pearl earrings, my birthstone, which I begrudgingly admitted were gorgeous and subsequently refused to wear.

This occasion was a chance to hopefully get it right. I planned to give him what I'd purchased for the previous Christmas. As angry as I'd been over his duplicity, I'd also been upset at wasting several hundred dollars on new basketball shoes and a sports watch. Micah loved to play and was perpetually on the hunt for a court to shoot hoops when he traveled. Now that he'd be coming home for a while, maybe he'd have an easier time getting in a weekly game.

After ensuring his arrival was on time, I left the house half an hour before he was due to land. Sunday traffic in Nashville was almost as heavy as weekday rush hour, but I wanted to avoid circling the airport. I'd done my hair and makeup, planning to only change from my jeans into a dress Micah hadn't seen me wear in a while before leaving for our reservation. After spritzing on my favorite scent and checking my teeth for lipstick, I cranked the music up for the drive.

My timing worked out perfectly. I glanced at his text, '*Leaving baggage claim now,*' right as I pulled up to the end of the terminal. Searching the crowd, I inched along the curb. When I caught sight of his wind-tousled hair, I raised my hand to wave, then realized his gaze was sliding over vehicles, not looking at drivers. It took him a minute to catch sight of my nondescript black Corolla. Even my mother had complained that I had the most boring vehicle of anyone she knew. Granted, this was in response to me calling her CR-V a 'clown car' due to its garish hue.

The ride home with Micah had a much different feel than this same journey a few weeks prior. Truthfully, our status was no different. I was still the scorned wife, and he, the adulterous husband. And he still spent the better part of the year traveling the world with the same floozy, theoretically doing who-knew-what.

But something was changing. I wondered if he felt it too.

At six o'clock, I emerged from the bedroom wearing a flowy emerald green dress, velvet navy pumps, and the pearl earrings that had been my birthday gift. The top of my hair was clipped back, and I'd lined my eyes with a striking deep blue. Micah had taken a shower while I dawdled in the bedroom, as nervous as I'd been on our early dates. He was dressed in slim-fitting charcoal trousers with a windowpane button-up. We both stopped and checked each other out in the narrow hallway leading to the bedroom. His low whistle made me blush, and I shyly accepted and returned the compliment.

"Let me grab my jacket from the closet and I'll be ready." A singular dimple appeared in his left cheek when he winked at me, and I nodded. Man, I'd missed my husband.

He followed me outside, where the sun was just beginning to recede from view. We headed toward his truck, parked to the right of my car. Both fit again with the CR-V at Carrie's. Soon, I'd have to put it up for sale, as we had no need for all three vehicles. My pondering was interrupted as Micah stopped abruptly. He had veered to the passenger side, intending to open my door for me, but suddenly he turned with a grim expression on his face.

"What happened to the yard?"

I peered around him to see what he was pointing at, although a sinking feeling told me exactly what it was. "Oh. Well, I had to park there a couple of times. I didn't want to block the sidewalk."

I looked behind me at the walkway at the end of our drive, wishing it would speak up and validate my struggle.

"Elle, why couldn't you have parked on the street? You know this is ruining the grass!"

Indignantly, I stalked to the truck and threw the door open myself. "You know what *you're* ruining? Our anniversary! But if the *grass* is more important to you, by all means, be mad at me. If you'd been here when my mom's car arrived, *you* could have figured out a better place to put it!"

Once again, my argument was irrational. I knew it even as I yelled at him. *Of course* I could have parked on the street. I could also have arranged for the CR-V to be dropped off at Carrie's house from the get-go. She had plenty of room, and she wasn't currently driving.

But I'd been frustrated about Micah leaving town, and I was overwhelmed making arrangements to empty my mom's house and upset he wasn't around to help with any of it. And most of all, I never expected to be taking care of my mother's final affairs when I was still learning how to be an adult. Who's prepared for that when they are only in their twenties?

He closed my door without a word and rounded the tailgate to the driver's side. Staring at some point between the top of the steering wheel and the windshield, he got in without speaking. The silence made me uncomfortable, and I wanted to shift in my seat but feared drawing his attention. Which was silly. Obviously, he was thinking about me already. Thinking what an idiot I was for ruining the grass. Or what a horrible wife I was for blowing up at him when he had only asked a question. My ears burned with shame, and I wished I hadn't added this stupid blue eyeliner that was about to end up in streaks.

Slowly, Micah turned toward me. His eyes were sad, and there was no hint of the dimple in his left cheek. I wished he would put me out of my misery. I prayed he wouldn't say he was tired of me. I waited, trying to stop my tear ducts and nose from leaking all over my painstakingly made-up face.

"I'm sorry." I glanced at him sharply, not sure why he was apologizing. "Elle, I know this has been a really difficult time for you, and it's only grass." He shrugged one shoulder, the same way he'd shrugged the same shoulder as he recited the wedding vows he'd written just for me. That incongruous thought had come out of nowhere, and the shoulder shrug solidified it:

I wanted *this* marriage with *this* man. I needed us to make it work.

With a catch in my throat, I reached for his hands. "Micah, I'm the one who's sorry. I don't know why I speak without thinking. I know I lash out, and I don't mean to. I promise I'm not always looking for a reason to ... to blow up." By the time I got to the end of my sentence, I was nearly wailing, and he pulled me to his chest, unthreatened by my tears or makeup or nose running on his shirt.

After a few minutes, I sat back. Embarrassed, I covered my face with my hands. It was almost 6:45 by this time, and there was no way to make a seven o'clock reservation, even though I still had no idea where he'd planned to take me. He appeared to have the same thought, but he didn't seem upset.

Instead, he reached for my hand and said softly, "You're beautiful, but why don't you also go get comfortable while I run and grab us some takeout?"

My husband still knew the way to my heart.

Chapter Thirteen

I woke the next morning in layers, gradually becoming aware of the sun through the window, the slightly twisted sheets, and the heat emanating from the body next to mine. I had grown used to sleeping alone, but it occurred to me now how I'd craved this. The night before had ended amorously with Chinese food enjoyed on the floor in front of our coffee table. We were wrapped in the same blanket, which made it difficult for him to use his chopsticks, but neither of us wanted to give up the intimacy. At midnight, we exchanged gifts, and he reacted like a little boy with a new toy when he opened his shoes and watch. He presented me with V.I.P. tickets to see an artist I loved, and while he had likely scored them through a connection, the gift of time with him was the most precious thing he could have offered after the many times I'd rejected it.

Anticipating a leisurely morning, I stayed in bed while Micah got up to start the coffee. But old habits die hard. When Micah hollered he was making bacon, I logged onto my work email and saw no less than half a dozen messages from Donovan that had come in over the weekend. I opened the most recent first:

> **I trust you're getting my messages and will be prepared with all the information I've asked for first thing Monday morning.**

I'd never received such an email from Constance or Erica, or even Henry. I'd completed my project on Saturday, but now I remembered muting email notifications from Donovan. No wonder I hadn't realized he'd been trying to reach me.

Sighing, I climbed out of bed to tell Micah I was on my way to the office after all.

I made it to my desk without running into Donovan. In fact, I didn't see anyone from my team, but I did notice Henry's door was shut. I booted up my MacBook with an unfamiliar clench in my stomach. Work was supposed to be my refuge. An escape from stress, not the source. At work, I knew what needed to be done. There were steps and procedures, unlike in my personal life. It seemed now that my relationship with Micah was recovering, I had a new wellspring of anxiety.

Donovan's first email had come in on Friday afternoon, sent minutes after I'd told him I was headed to the hospital for Carrie's release. He was reminding me to send status updates for the project I'd taken with me. The same project I'd informed him I was finishing up over the weekend.

The next three were all from Saturday. Requesting another update on the project. Reminding me of a report he needed before our Monday afternoon meeting—the same report I always ran before the meeting. And, finally, asking inane questions about an unsuccessful pitch I'd made before he even joined our team. In fact, the pitch I'd bombed the day he had come for his interview.

Two more emails came in on Sunday, including the one I'd already read. More of the same.

I started to respond to the most recent, which seemed to sum up all the rest, when I decided I needed a coffee refill first. As I stepped away from my cubicle, Henry's office opened and Erica backed out, closing the door behind her. Head down, she started toward her own desk, then glanced around before turning and intercepting me on my way to the Keurig.

"Morning, Elle. Do you have a minute?"

"Of course. What's up?" Erica didn't return my smile, and shook her head when I gestured to offer her first use of the single-serve coffee maker.

"Donovan called a meeting with Henry and me early this morning." Erica tugged the hem of her shirt but didn't continue.

"Okay." My insides twisted again. "What about?"

She reached for my elbow, as if hoping the gesture would soften what she was about to say. "He mentioned some...concerns. About your level of commitment."

"He *what*? Why would he say that?" I realized my voice had risen, and I continued in a whisper, "Not that it's his business, but I did just lose my mother."

Not to mention everything else I'd been dealing with.

"You don't need to worry. I just wanted to warn you, Donovan seems to be..." She paused, as though she didn't want to speculate. "Elle, from what I heard, maybe there's more going on with him than it seems."

Yeah, there's more going on with all of us. That's no excuse. Erica knew about Carrie's cancer, but no one here knew about Micah. That was my little secret.

I was just about to gripe over his deluge of emails from the weekend when her eyes flickered, causing me to glance over my shoulder to see Donovan heading back to his office.

"I'd better get back. He's waiting for some updates." Grabbing the lukewarm coffee I hadn't even gotten to refresh, I beelined for my desk.

For the next couple of hours, I focused on proving Donovan wrong. I dared him to find anything amiss in a single report or proposal. I followed up with Shawn on contract statuses and responded to each of Donovan's weekend emails with as much detail as I could squeeze in, preemptively answering whatever follow-up questions he'd possibly come up with. Maybe that's why he had nothing to reply and I never saw him step out of his office until it was time for our Monday lunch meeting.

At twelve-thirty, I printed a hard copy of my notes on the projects I'd been assigned and made my way to the conference room. I had facts and figures coming out of my ears. Donovan wouldn't be able to find anything to complain about. Still, I had no appetite for the burrito bowl I'd ordered, and Shawn's rehashing of his weekend went completely over my head.

Out of the corner of my eye, I watched Donovan scroll on his phone with his left hand while robotically crunching through nachos with his right. He hadn't spoken to me, other than a stiff *"Good afternoon"* when we approached the conference room's doorway from opposite directions. I didn't know if I should be relieved that Henry seemed to have set him straight or concerned about what was to come.

Henry arrived a few minutes later, gazing longingly at the communal chips and queso before uncovering his grilled shrimp salad. Sitting at the head of the table, he worried very little about the shredded lettuce dropping from his fork while he went over what we needed to concentrate on for the week. Donovan didn't interject even once, and left before Henry could finish thanking us for our good work.

Part of me wanted to just avoid my new supervisor. After all, he was making it easy today. But I'd lived most of the last year in fear of confrontation. Staying too busy for difficult conversations. And the more I thought about him going to Henry, the more peeved I became. So, later that afternoon, I found myself standing in front of Donovan's office door.

His closed office door.

I knocked.

He grunted. The genteel southern affect had apparently worn off. I took his second growl as an invitation and let myself in.

"I just wanted to make sure you didn't have any more concerns over the projects you'd emailed me about." I did my best to keep my tone cordial rather than caustic.

He looked up and it occurred to me that the shadows under his eyes were new. I hadn't paid him enough attention to notice them during the meeting.

"I have what I need." His response was to the point and not drawled out. "Thanks," he added as an afterthought.

I should have left. He wasn't encouraging me to stay.

But I sat. And we stared at each other.

"I didn't check my email this weekend." I didn't add that I'd silenced him. *At least he wasn't blocked.*

"I was under the impression you were a workaholic." He didn't say it like it was a dirty word, the way Micah used to.

"I've been accused of that, it's true," I tried to inject some levity. "But I had other commitments this weekend."

"Henry told me." Donovan didn't expound.

This conversation wasn't going anywhere. I stood to leave.

"You have a lot going on in your life."

I sat back down. It hadn't been a question, so I didn't answer. Was he going to use this as a reason to doubt my commitment to my job?

"Problems come when we let our personal lives interfere with our professional lives. I'd advise against it. If you want to make it into the big leagues, you can't let a challenge scare you off." The twang slid in somewhere between sentences, bringing him back—the Donovan Archer who got under my skin.

But, the truth was, he wasn't challenging me to be better. He was simply trying to make me look incompetent and give his misogyny a platform.

When I'd told Micah why I couldn't spend our anniversary morning at home with him after all, he hadn't reacted with the irritation I'd gotten used to. Instead, he'd asked when Henry was expecting my answer about the opportunity in A&R.

Maybe it was time to see what it was all about.

After closing Donovan's door behind me, I popped my head into Henry's office to tell him I was interested in visiting A&R. He didn't bring up the morning meeting I hadn't been invited to, but I left with the name of someone Henry wanted me to meet.

Raul Clemente, one of the top A&R executives, was easy to find. When I alighted from the elevator two floors up, the first person I asked simply pointed. "You can't miss him. Just follow the sound."

A voice boomed from around a corner. I headed toward it, continuing down the hall as the rumble, punctuated by laughter, grew louder. Just as I feared my eardrums would split, I came upon an open office. Peeking around the door jam, my eyes took in the source.

Raul leaned against the front of his desk, towering over his audience of two, who were seated in chairs facing him. He abruptly ended his story when he saw me and bounded to his feet.

"Henry just called up to let me know you were on your way." His guests took the hint and ushered themselves out, closing the door behind them.

I introduced myself. As I feared, Raul's voice echoed all the more when confined to four walls. But he had plenty of insight and his persuasiveness was tailor-made for A&R. Misconstruing my frozen smile for acquiescence, he took me around the floor to introduce several people whose names and job titles I barely absorbed. I decided once I processed what Raul had shared today, I'd come back and look for Sarah Sanderson, a bespectacled woman with a calm demeanor, to get my second round of questions answered.

That night, I was at the kitchen table sorting through cookware from my mother's house when Carrie called. "Sorry for the banging. I'm swapping out our old pots and pans for the good set from my mom's. How are you feeling?"

Carrie suppressed a yawn. "I'm getting there. Having home health has been such a help. And Josh has been great company."

"I bet he has." I chuckled before adding, "In all seriousness, it really is wonderful that he popped into the picture. To think how mad I was at Micah for leaving that week...yet, that's the reason you met Josh."

"Funny how things work out," Carrie murmured. "I really hope this chemo stuff is behind me. Three rounds were enough. But they haven't called yet to schedule the PET scan. Anyway, how was your visit with Micah?"

"It ended well, but it took a bit to get there." I told her about the incident on our way to dinner. "I think it was the only time in recent memory we've had an argument and actually talked it through. In the past, we would fight and storm away from each other and never bring it up again." I thought for a moment. "Or we just never admitted when we were upset about something, and it got added to the avalanche of things we resented."

"Even if you avoid talking, those emotions are going to come out somewhere. Whether in your relationships with others, or in how you view yourself."

Her comment made me think of Donovan, and I told her about him. "Carr, he's such a jerk. You know the kind—good looking and knows it. Superiority complex. Honestly, it's so hard to work for him, much less like him."

"Loving the lovable is easy, Elle. Everyone does that. It's finding a way to show the unlovable they are still worthy that means something."

I knew she was right, even if it seemed Donovan went out of his way to make himself insufferable.

Chapter Fourteen

I checked in with Carrie, or Josh if she was resting, every day throughout the week but didn't make it by her house again until the weekend. She had an overnight aide, usually a woman named Leslie. I hadn't met her, but Josh did, and he assured me she was an excellent caretaker. She stayed awake rather than only sleeping there, giving us extra security in having someone attentive to Carrie's nighttime needs.

It was 7:45 Saturday morning when I arrived at Carrie's. The front door was locked so, to alert Leslie, I knocked lightly before letting myself in. I could make out voices coming from down the hall and presumed they were in the bedroom or bathroom. I headed to the coffeemaker in Carrie's kitchen to refill the travel mug I'd drained before I was halfway to her home.

Hearing an unfamiliar accent encouraging Carrie to try sitting in the rocking recliner instead of going back to the couch, I called out to the pair in my rusty morning voice.

"Good morning!" The cheerful reply came from a beautiful Hispanic woman wearing colorful scrubs and a full face of makeup. Her wide frame obscured my view of Carrie, and I was halfway through thanking Leslie for her help during the week before she stepped sideways, and I gasped.

"Carrie!" I took a step back.

She reached up and stroked her smooth head, saying, "Yeah, well. It was time." I didn't know if I was more surprised about her shaving her hair without me or that she hadn't warned me during one of our calls. Then she threw another curveball, adding, "Josh did it. And he did his, too!"

After Leslie left, Carrie explained that while he was brushing her hair earlier in the week, the suggestion of shaving her head came so naturally that she wasn't sure which of them had brought it up. "Maybe that's one of those chemo brain things," she tried to joke, lifting her shoulders in surrender.

Bittersweetness tugged at my heart. Carrie's care had been my responsibility, and although I'd still be there for her, Josh was reaching for the baton, and it was time for me to pass it.

"Do you love him?" I sensed what they shared was deep but uncomplicated. Of course, this was a strange way to look at it. Their relationship was certainly unconventional, as she battled a life-endangering disease, and he'd appeared straight in the middle of it.

Carrie looked at me, her smile vulnerable. "Is that crazy? I've only known him for two weeks. I haven't said it, but I feel it. Maybe it's because of my cancer. I mean, I don't think it's only that. But it's hitting me how uncertain life is. I just never imagined finding someone like him." Her words faded, and the house was silent.

I reached out and ran my hand over her shiny crown. Words couldn't convey my joy.

The weekend with Carrie was peppered with fun as she sat up for increasingly longer periods. We played a game or two, watched a few of our favorite shows, and shared secrets like we had when we were roommates years before. As she napped on Sunday afternoon, I read from the forest-green journal I'd brought with me. This book covered the latter part of 2006, and I was aware of inching back toward the darkest period of my mother's life.

It wasn't long before I'd read through the entire summer of that year. Mom had sent me to sleepaway camp for the first time, and tucked between the pages of her ruminations were letters in juvenile handwriting I'd mailed her from camp. My mom was working full-time at a bookstore, one of the rare periods when she'd only held one job. Still, I recalled that come autumn, she had also worked in my school's front office a few days a week. She'd stayed on the hunt for more money and better hours yet always tried to squeeze in as much time with me as possible.

As I turned the page, the tone of her writing darkened. I realized this entry commemorated the second anniversary of my father's death.

Two years ago today was our last conversation. You called me early that morning because of the time difference on the East coast. You were afraid with the meetings you had scheduled and my plans for the day, we might miss each other if you tried any later. You wanted to check in to see how I was feeling. Midway through my second trimester and still dealing with morning sickness, and you were worried about leaving me alone. But this business trip couldn't be postponed.

You'd ordered room service, and they overcooked your eggs. I never understood how you liked runny yolks. That conversation was so typical of us. There was nothing to indicate it should be special or sacred in any way. Maybe that makes it better-the last time I heard your voice was like every other time you called, and you made me laugh over things I don't even remember now.

Elle was still asleep, and I went to get her ready for school right after we hung up. She didn't even get to speak to you one last time.

I could hardly read the words as my tears mingled with the dried smudges my mother had left on the page. I felt like broken pottery that had been glued back together so the cracks barely showed, now coming apart at fault lines jarred just right. For a moment, I was seven again. My father would pick me up as though I weighed nothing. He said I'd always be his baby, despite my insistence that I was going to be as tall as he was someday. He promised that after my little sister Brianne was born, he'd carry one of us in each arm. Brielle and Brianne. I didn't start going by Elle until after. I realized my mom began calling me that right around second grade. Like our matching bookend names were a reminder she couldn't bear of the daughter she'd lost within days of her husband dying.

I sat unmoving until the shadows grew long, stretching from the floor to the walls and ultimately absorbing the room entirely. My mom had been wrong. Just a little. She *had* come to get me ready for school after she'd hung up, but I wasn't still sleeping. In fact, I was sitting on the edge of my bed with my favorite doll, Poppy, in my lap. I had brought her with me to Mommy's room a few minutes earlier. Just in time to hear her say, "Don't forget, I told Brielle if she's really good, you'll bring her a present from New York City."

Why was I just now remembering? How certain I'd been that it was because I *hadn't* been good that Daddy hadn't brought me a present. In fact, I was so *not* good enough that he'd never come home at all.

I was in the same chair when the aide arrived. It was one of the nights Leslie didn't work, and I had difficulty conversing with the three-nights-per-week substitute. I never even caught her name. Carrie didn't wake before I left, but I murmured to the aide that I'd see her again sometime.

I drove home by rote, in silence with no radio. This journal entry hadn't provided me with any new information—I'd always known how and when my father died. Yet, memories I hadn't recalled until tonight flowed over me. I could picture him as though watching a movie. Kissing my mom every night when he got home from work; telling me stories as I squirmed across his lap in the rubbery, jointless way small children do; flipping pancakes from the skillet high into the air. I'd thought I barely remembered him, but images were washing over me in tidal waves, almost too colossal to process. Drowning me.

One of the large plastic tubs I'd retrieved from my mother's home was filled with framed collaged photos, albums, and loose snapshots filed in shoe boxes. I hadn't tackled this container yet, in part because of the sheer number of pictures and limited space in my own home to display or store them. That night, I popped the clips holding the lid and moved the collages to the side. I'd grown up with those framed photos adorning our walls until they blended into the landscape of my youth. I dug deeper until I at last uncovered the mottled red album with gold trim. The sticky pages holding a collection of 3x5 photos under Mylar plastic were yellowed after twenty years, and the chemicals used to secure the Polaroids in place were causing faint deterioration.

Sitting on the white rug that made me too afraid to use the dining room for meals, I scoured the album that revealed the story of my childhood before everything changed. Although my parents had a separate wedding album, some candid shots of their backyard ceremony and homemade cake filled the initial pages. My mother's high-necked lace dress was as lovely as the yellow roses she carried, but it was the adoration on her face as she looked up at her new husband that revealed her true beauty.

As I slowly turned the stiff paper, the photos came alive under my gaze. My parents, dancing in a kitchen wearing matching Christmas sweaters; an outdoor shot they'd tried to take of themselves with the tops of their heads cut out of the frame; my mom, looking tired and uncomfortable near the tail end of her pregnancy with me. Then, my first squawking cry with my face red and eyes covered in ointment, but my dad cradling me in his broad mahogany hands as though I were the most wondrous being he'd ever seen.

It was like watching myself grow through a flipbook. The ten years of marriage that had left my mother melancholy on the rare occasions they were discussed now provided in colorful detail I never thought I'd be privy to. My father wore Wrangler jeans and printed short-sleeved button-ups, or wide paisley ties with his suits for work. My mother radiated optimistic youth, then joy at new motherhood. Photos of any of us were scarce during my toddlerhood, and the few capturing her image exposed the despondency that correlated with two miscarriages within less than fifteen months.

My first day of kindergarten photos, taken with each of my parents standing next to me, showed me wearing my favorite Barbie dress with a pink headband holding my curls back. My first ever backpack was strapped over my narrow shoulders. I remembered that dress and how I'd continued to wear it long after it fit properly, fashioning it as a top to wear with leggings when it hit too high above my knees.

The final page was from my first day of second grade. So grown in my own mind, wearing jeans with plastic gem embellishments and my hair straightened and flipped instead of curly. Wide grin with two missing teeth, never guessing how my life would change in a matter of weeks. My father had lifted me up for this photo, keeping his promise that no matter how big I got, I'd always be his baby.

It was the last photo I'd ever have with him.

Chapter Fifteen

Work the next day was a struggle. Before bed, I'd read a few additional pages, trying to make sense of these new memories of my childhood, and how my mother's journey guided my own. The scripture she'd included in that journal entry was from Isaiah 55:8-13.

"For my thoughts are not your thoughts, neither are your ways my ways,' declares the Lord. 'As the heavens are higher than the earth, so are my ways higher than your ways and my thoughts than your thoughts. As the rain and the snow come down from heaven...It will not return to me empty, but will accomplish what I desire and achieve the purpose for which I sent it...Instead of the thornbush will grow the juniper, and instead of briers the myrtle will grow."

I've been harboring undeniable anger since we lost John. This thief took so much more than eighty dollars and a man's life. He stole a husband and a father and a friend. He ripped away my anchor...the one person on earth who knew my innermost hurts and fully understood them. The man who saw me grow from a teenager into a bashful bride and then a mother. This stranger didn't just take the future we deserved—he tarnished the innocence of the memories I had with John.

But I'm learning I'm not alone. God didn't leave me in a void. Every day, I get a little bit closer to believing in His consummate goodness. I may not understand why until I can sit at God's feet, but I can choose to believe that my trials and suffering are not divine mistakes but crucial parts of His plan. He allowed a terrible circumstance for ultimate good. God wants to draw me away from security in anything but Him. And He allows my frailty to remind me that I cannot trust what I feel more than I trust who He is.

God was beginning to show Himself, graciously allowing me to share in my mother's comfort. I couldn't always comprehend why He allows traumatic things to occur. I might not want to travail through 'the rain and the snow,' but God uses them for good. There's always a purpose, even for the hard things. *It will not return to me empty, but will accomplish what I desire and achieve the purpose for which I sent it.*

Trials reveal the <u>power</u> of Jesus in me. His utmost desire isn't my comfort on earth but shaping me for everlasting joy with Him.

Josh's words on the day he helped me with the pod now made sense. "God doesn't allow anything He can't redeem." Mom had eventually reached acceptance, but I wondered if she'd ever begun to understand how He could *redeem* the losses our family suffered.

I admit, I'd experienced flashes of resentment toward my mother since her death. She'd kept so many secrets. But now I was confronted with how she'd purposely locked my father's memory away. In boxes in the attic. In photobooks we never looked through. And as a secret between her heart and her beloved journals. She thought she was protecting me, but she was teaching me to hide. My mother was a grief counselor and a survivor herself, but she didn't recognize how much her own daughter never healed.

My fear of rejection. My fear of abandonment. My incessant need for a glaze of fondant-smooth perfection and control. Could it all stem from my unaddressed childhood loss? Was this the root of my refusal to tell Mom about Micah's affair?

Catherine had been a beacon of inspiration. A tragedy had taken half her family, yet she'd heroically given me a wonderful life. A husband she loved so much she never replaced him, yet, she'd harbored feelings for Paul. An unwavering faith in God's goodness, but only after battling an earthquake of instability and peril.

All these years and I had never understood the complexities of my mother's life.

There were no easy answers as to why she'd not unburdened herself to me about the other miscarriages. Or why she'd never crossed the particular barrier in her grief that would have allowed her to share memories of my father with me. Maybe that would have been part of the reparation of our relationship. Perhaps losing her this year robbed me of more than just a future with her.

"For my thoughts are not your thoughts, neither are your ways my ways."

It wasn't meant as a rebuke, but it struck like a persistent reminder popping into my head throughout the day. My marriage, Carrie's health, my career, and lately, even my emotions felt as uncontrolled as a vortex. But like a prodding, that line of scripture wouldn't leave me alone.

What if I took this new job opportunity? Losing the promotion disappointed like rain on a parade, but maybe this rain would lead to a juniper instead of a thornbush.

I shook my head at my attempt to create a simile for the current situation as I rode the elevator upstairs to track down Sarah from A&R. Donovan's managerial directives see-sawed between patronizing and tangled. Either way, they made me feel dense. No wonder he considered me incapable of making decisions weightier than what to order for Monday lunch.

Henry continued to drop hints that my go-getting attitude would serve me well in A&R, but I still dreaded the starry-eyed gazes of hopeful artists willing to put their careers in my shaky hands. Donovan had chewed up my confidence and spit it back out, but Henry may well have been oblivious.

Sarah was easy to find when I got off the elevator, as she was waiting to take the same car down. She had her bag and jacket thrown over her arm, and I was dismayed to realize she was heading out of the building. I hesitated, then reintroduced myself, intending to ask if we could speak on a later day. Instead, she graciously assured me she wasn't on a tight schedule and would be happy to give me a few minutes right then.

I followed her to her office, which was small but private. She pointed out that with the layout on this floor, there were no cubicles. However, the requirements of the job meant they were rarely *in* the office. That said, she'd decorated her space with accolades on the walls mixed in with autographed photos of famous musicians, and several more I assumed were of her teenage children. This was confirmed when I noticed a whimsical family portrait of Sarah with a balding man and the same boy and girl at younger ages.

"Thank you so much for seeing me right now. I only have a few questions, but I didn't want to badger Raul with them."

With a knowing look, Sarah replied, "He is a little difficult to have a quick conversation with, isn't he? He can be overwhelming!"

Taking a chance, I leaned in conspiratorially and added, "And *loud!* Is it because he's spent so much time in clubs, he's used to yelling? Or do I need to worry about losing my hearing if I take this job?"

With the ice broken as we settled into the two guest chairs at her desk, I started by clarifying some points Raul had covered. As the conversation unfolded, I expressed to Sarah my biggest worry.

"The thing is, I'm not very good with crowds. Especially meeting new people in a crowd." I felt silly admitting it. "It's something I'm working on."

Sarah's glasses slid down when she smiled. "A similar fear first led me to *this* side of the business. I'm also a singer myself, and I always wanted to 'make it,' but I couldn't bring myself to sing in front of anyone other than my family. I was drawn to this profession because I wanted to encourage others who have the talent but need guidance on breaking into the industry. 'Those who can't do, teach,' I guess." She pushed her tortoise-shell frames above the bridge of her nose.

She continued, "I'm not generally intimidated by strangers, so I can only somewhat relate to where you're coming from, but I do use a trick now when I perform. Which I do, believe it or not! I've learned to filter out everyone except one or two people. Then, I move on to one or two others. Directing your focus when you're in a group will not only let everyone else evanesce into a kind of 'white noise,' but will also let the person you *are* focusing on know they have your undivided attention. And I'm sure you realize, ego-stroking is a major part of this industry." She rolled her eyes.

We spoke for several minutes more and discussed her typical schedule. She made sure I understood I'd be working a lot of nights and weekends. In fact, she was on her way to an open mic night at The Bluebird Café when I stopped her.

I glanced at her family photo. "Do you feel you have a good work-life balance?" With Micah home for a while, I didn't want him to think I was avoiding being dedicated and present to tend to our relationship.

Sarah assured me she had plenty of time for her husband and kids, but she'd also spent years developing a routine that worked. "Of course, with teenagers, things are always changing. They stay crazy busy, but they are also more independent. The great thing is, I make my own schedule, so if they need me, I improvise, and hope I'm not missing out on a gem."

I thanked her as we walked back to the elevator. She'd answered the questions I'd come prepared with and addressed my most urgent fear, which I was now glad I'd brought up.

Now, if only I could stop Donovan from gloating over belief he was scaring me off.

Chapter Sixteen

Micah's quick visit for our anniversary never presented the opportunity to discuss his plans to continue, or not, with Still Waters. At least that's what I'd maintained as we'd cuddled on the couch that night for a movie. In truth, the incident with the damage I'd done to the grass kept me from wanting to introduce the delicate topic, and I had no regrets about just enjoying the night with him. But now he'd be back on Monday, and I wasn't sure what he'd decided—or if he'd decided anything.

His flight landed in the middle of my workday, but the agency sent transportation to the airport for them. They were also holding a wrap party for the end of the tour on Tuesday night, and I had agreed to attend. At Micah's skepticism, I'd cupped his face in my hands and promised I wouldn't be late and would stay as long as he wanted. Biting my tongue, I didn't bring up Martine or what it would take for me to be in the same room with her.

I couldn't tell if Micah was home yet when I pulled into the drive on Monday evening. I knew he had some work to do at his office, and he planned to use a ride app when he finished. Finding the house empty gave me the chance to take a shower and start dinner while I waited for him. I'd picked up ingredients for his favorite meal of steak fajitas after I left Carrie's on

Saturday night. I wanted to start on the right foot—especially since I was determined to bring up his future career plans.

Micah finally texted at seven that he was on his way. By then, I'd prepped everything for dinner and moved most of my mom's belongings so we could eat in the rarely used dining room. I had emptied the boxes of dishes, stored her jewelry and clothing, and purged most of her files when I called to cancel credit cards and other accounts. There were a few remaining copies of her death certificate, which I'd need to sell her house. Endless considerations and so much to learn along the way. I thought again that I was too young for all of this. I hoped my mom would have been okay with the decisions I was making on her behalf.

The four boxes containing my father's items had gone upstairs into my own attic. It wasn't easy to move them up there myself, and I'd wished I had accepted Josh's offer when he asked if he could do anything else to help until Micah's return. He was already doing so much for Carrie, though, and I didn't want to impose.

I'd gotten to see him again on Saturday when he brought lunch for Carrie and me. His head was still bare, and I could tell he'd continued to shave it rather than letting it grow back, in solidarity with Carrie. Their affection was evident, but I didn't feel like a third wheel as they talked. We each stood at Carrie's side to support her on a stroll around her block after she complained about being trapped inside for two solid weeks. The scheduler from radiation had called to inform her of the next PET scan, and it was slated for October 31st, Thursday of this week. Josh and I both insisted on going with her, even though we weren't expecting the results right away. However, we'd prayed together for good news before Josh left on Saturday. It was my first time praying aloud with anyone other than my mother since back in youth group days and my timid words came out jumbled, but Josh and Carrie agreed wholeheartedly with the prayer anyway.

Seeing the flash of headlights beam through the window, I slid the flour tortillas into the oven to warm. Micah called out to me as his luggage clattered on the hardwood floor. Our kiss confirmed that the closeness we'd reached during his previous trip home was intact, and I wasn't in a hurry to pull from his arms.

"I'm so glad you're home! But let's not end up with burned tortillas." I disentangled myself to grab the oven mitt. I didn't want to bring up anything divisive with the band, but I asked, "How was the trip home? Are you exhausted now that it's over?"

After a short leg of three months, followed by a stretch of almost nine months, with segments across the US, parts of Western Europe, and Canada, the band's success hadn't diminished. With the debut they'd released the previous year still hovering on the charts, they just needed to keep the momentum as they headed into the studio to finish recording their sophomore album. It would be an ideal time for Micah to look for a different artist or band, but first, he needed a stint off the road, and we needed to spend time together.

Over dinner, Micah shared stories from the tour, but I could tell he was censoring himself. Otherwise, how did Martine's name never come up when I was sure she was front and center for many of the tales? Occasionally, his gaze slid to the corner of the room as he considered how to word a particular anecdote, or his story would drop out partway through with a hedging "anyway…" followed by a subject change. I tried to believe he was just being sensitive so we could enjoy a happy reunion, but I wondered if I'd ever completely trust my husband again.

I decided to change the subject before I said anything regrettable. "I went to meet with A&R again this week. I'm actually considering making the change."

Micah scooped a wayward bell pepper from the edge of his plate before it could drop. "I really do think it could be good. How's the pay?"

"That's the other thing. It's mainly commission-based. To be honest, that scares me. Especially now." I didn't add that if Micah left Still Waters, we wouldn't know where his next paychecks were coming from either. It wasn't only Martine I was asking Micah to give up. I made a mental note to check in with Vicky regarding the sale of my mom's house. That would help, if only a little.

Before bed, Micah reminded me of the wrap party the next night. He wanted to meet at the venue, the Union Station Hotel, by seven-thirty. Driving together would have been preferable, but I needed extra time to change clothes and touch-up my makeup. There was no way I was going to show up at this party to face Martine looking like I'd just put in a full workday.

The next morning, Micah was leaving as I emerged from the shower, and he kissed my cheek while reminding me that he'd look for me in the hotel lobby. "Let me know if you're running late or anything." He smiled as he said it, but I knew we were both tallying up all the times I'd bailed on him.

With my best intentions to be waiting when and where he expected, I promised to see him after work and went to get ready for my day.

Shortly after six, I pulled into our driveway. Micah had taken a fresh shirt and sport coat with him, and he planned to change at his office and drive straight to the hotel. I hurried inside, thankful I'd used a lunch break the previous week to go shopping. The dress was more daring than anything I typically wore, but I wasn't messing around tonight. I intended to make it clear to Martine she hadn't won.

After I visited her home last February, she'd vindictively made another bid for Micah's attention. And she'd tried to make me believe she succeeded. One chilly March night, my heat had gone out. Micah had been gone for two weeks, and nothing I tried to restore it was working. It was after midnight, and I didn't want to contact an emergency service if there was any way to avoid it, so I'd begrudgingly called Micah to ask for advice.

On the third ring, a voice purred, "Hey there, Micah's phone."

With my hand over my eyes, I tried to remember what time zone he was in. Was it the middle of the night there, too? "Where is my husband?" I seethed.

Martine's taunt poured thick and saccharine sweet. "Micah stepped away, but I'm expecting him *right back.*"

I was freezing and exhausted, and the suggestive way she responded when I questioned why she'd picked up did nothing but rankle me. I wished for the olden days when I could have slammed the phone back into the cradle, but instead, I furiously disconnected and waited for him to call back. And waited. And waited.

I don't know why I believed Martine would give him my message, but I refused to try him again. Instead, I fumed beneath every blanket I could find, then surrendered and headed to work before seven the next morning. No one was at the office yet, and I didn't have a key to the building. I ended up sitting in my car with the motor running, blasting myself with heat and banishing away tears until people began trickling in almost half an hour later. I was still livid when I called Micah again after several hours.

Of course, he hadn't known I'd tried to reach him previously. Martine had gone so far as to erase our conversation from his call log. They had been in London, and it was six hours later there. He'd left his phone with the rest of his belongings while he walked away to check out of the hotel. They were taking the

Chunnel to Paris on a rare day off, and Martine didn't have permission to do anything with his phone. She'd alluded to having spent the night with him—audaciously suggesting I was calling *awfully early* in the morning. She'd punctuated the rebuke with a yawn, which I envisioned was being delivered while stretching in tangled hotel sheets. I burned with humiliation, but all I could do was accept his promise to deal with her. Micah tried to appease me by arranging for a repairman to be waiting when I got home, but Martine's antics warned me a broken heater was the least of my worries.

That was the way this entire year had gone. Suspicions and accusations, attempts to placate and appease, apologies and forgiveness, around and around, until we were both worn down to nubs. I put all my energy into work, telling myself I could be just fine without Micah. Now, almost a year had passed since the start of this mess last Halloween, and we were at last wading our way out of the fog.

As I fastened sparkly drop earrings to my lobes and loosened the tendrils framing my face, I was ready to remind both Micah and Martine it was me he loved.

Chapter Seventeen

When I pulled under the overhang at the Union Station Hotel to valet my car, it was actually a few minutes earlier than we had arranged to meet. Entering the grand lobby, I was transported to the glamourous 1900s as my gaze was drawn toward the barrel-vaulted ceiling with its deep colors and rich history. Chandeliers dripped like crystal raindrops, and soulful jazz from the grand piano filled the space along with the heady scent of lilies, which adorned marble tabletops throughout. The landmark hotel, transformed from a train terminal that had been in use until 1979, was where my mom and I had stayed during our first trip to Nashville.

I strayed to the edge of the spacious room, drawn back in time and daydreams, nearly forgetting I should be looking for Micah. When I regained my focus, I saw him standing under the ornate clock, watching me with amusement as I meandered. I hurried to join him, balancing on the slim heels of my shoes. Glancing above his head and seeing the time, I bubbled an apology, "I was here early, I promise! I got distracted and forgot to look for you!"

He laughed as he bent to kiss my cheek. "I just came in, right as you saw me. I'd only brought a clean shirt, and then I ended up spilling coffee in my lap." He surreptitiously lifted his jacket to show me a dark spot on his left pants pocket. I assured him it was inconspicuous, and we made our way toward the Front Porch, the space reserved for the evening's celebration.

As we squeezed through the developing crowd, I gripped Micah's arm, suddenly unsure of myself. I remembered Sarah's advice to focus on one or two people at a time as Micah led me between groups gathered around the bar, the firepit, and out on the lawn. I did my best to recall those I'd met before and to retain the names of new faces. I was complimenting a young woman named Lacey on her necklace while Micah went to refresh our beverages when I heard a familiar throaty laugh directly behind me, as though she'd leaned down to my ear to make sure I caught it.

"Micah, how sweet of you to remember my favorite drink! You're joining me for one, right?"

I turned, watching Martine swoop in to pluck my wine-glass from Micah's hand. It wasn't difficult to make the rest of the crowd disappear as Lacey's prattling dimmed to a buzz, and Martine and Micah were all that existed. Her coquettishness was fake and overdone, and Micah's narrowed eyes indicated he wasn't buying her act. For a brief instant, I wanted to scream in exasperation. Micah and I hadn't discussed how we would handle interactions with Martine tonight, but I knew he wanted to avoid her, as did I. Yet, her obnoxious behavior was being thrown in our faces, and remaining dignified was difficult.

Micah wasn't one to cause a scene, and as much as I wished he would tell her off, he instead extended the remaining glass to me. "Elle, there's someone I want you to meet. Care to walk with me?"

Taking the stemware from him, I made sure Martine heard my reply, "Of course! And why don't we share this wine?"

My heels perforated the grass as I stalked away, making my exit ungainly, but Martine was the one left alone, clutching her pettiness and trophy of stolen chianti.

I was surprised at the number of well-known people who cared that Still Waters had returned from headlining their first major tour, and I said as much to Micah. As we worked our way around a circle of famous names and faces, a nasally twang caught my ear.

"... women are usually just not worth the aggravation, know what I mean? I sent her packin', alright ... "

"Donovan?" I hadn't known he'd be here.

"Well, well, if it isn't ... "

Don't you dare call me the office girl, I mentally telegraphed, then decided an interruption would be more effective. "Micah, this is Donovan Archer. He took Constance's place when she moved on," I explained without giving him the satisfaction of calling him my boss. "Donovan, Micah Reed."

The two of them sized each other up in the rivalrous way that men often do.

Donovan spoke first while thrusting his hand toward Micah's midsection. "The husband, I take it." His accent was more Matthew McConaughey than Andy Griffith tonight. He must have been working on it while he waited for his Just for Men to set.

Micah knew enough about Donovan to not concede by moving a step back, and he waited for some of the smugness to leach from the aggressively offered handshake before gripping it. "Appreciate you coming."

It was a subtle nod to Micah's position with the band, and the fact that Donovan was only here to rub elbows. But not so subtle that Donovan's jaw didn't clench. Micah had asked around after I'd let my indignation at Donovan's demeaning behavior get to me one day. He found out a Donovan Archer had been with Warner Music Group, working out of Los Angeles. Being the son-in-law of one of their executives had surely helped put him on the fast track, but that had also been the beginning of the end for his marriage. When Micah shared this, he'd prudently avoided the parallel he could have made. Donovan had begun making mistakes at work and gotten a reputation as someone who would throw anyone under the bus to stay on top. He'd left his family—and his previous position—in disgrace.

"It was all really hush-hush but he's finished in L.A. He came here to start over."

Well, that might explain why he was always trying to make himself look important. He didn't understand that wasn't how we do things in Nashville.

I looped my hand through the crook of Micah's arm, effectively ending the interaction with Donovan by saying, "See you tomorrow," before letting Micah lead me away.

So, now I was evading both Martine and Donovan. No wonder I didn't like attending these parties.

A few minutes later, Micah was waylaid by several crew members laughing over inside jokes, and their rehashing of road tales couldn't hold my attention. My gaze wandered and landed on Donovan and Martine, both getting their drinks refilled. Apparently, all I had to do was avoid the bar.

I turned to check out the view from the bridge beside the hotel, my imagination conjuring up the ghosts of old trains lining the yard. The daydream ended when my senses picked up on someone watching me. Glancing over my shoulder, I saw Donovan outlined near the corner of the building. Our eyes met, and he gestured.

Did I have to go? He wasn't my boss tonight. Not here. But an interaction with someone I knew and didn't much like couldn't be worse than getting pulled into conversation with people I didn't know at all, so I followed.

"I just wanted to ask you before I forgot, where do we stand with the proposal from last week?" Donovan turned, shielding me from the crowd on the lawn.

I scrambled for a minute, my mind aligning details into the mental grid where I stored my checklists. "Shawn is waiting for a couple more things to finish the contract. I've got a tentative schedule put together. I think we should be good before the end of the month to start..."

Donovan moved closer, the crocodile that had been sacrificed for his leather shoes invading my personal space.

"...to start..." I couldn't remember where I'd been going with this sentence. He leaned in, and I didn't have time to figure it out.

I smelled whiskey. Definitely not the scent that lingered from *my* last drink. It must be him.

I stepped back—at least, as far as the slit in my dress let me step.

He kept leaning.

"What are you doing?" I wasn't panicking. After all, it was just Donovan.

I realized that his unfocused eyes were still managing to fixate along the edge of the slightly daring dress I'd worn.

"Donovan!" I raised my voice, but not enough to attract attention. Not much, at least. In fact, only one person's.

Martine.

Martine disappeared so fast, I wasn't sure I'd even seen her. Or that she'd seen me. Night was falling. The building, in shadows. And Donovan had stood so close, we might have appeared to be only one body. Wearing a cocktail dress covered by a blazer.

I hadn't done anything wrong, and I would tell Micah what happened. But that conversation would be had in the privacy of our home. Not here. Not risking a scene.

Still, I needed to find him.

Most of the crowd was clustered near the firepit in the cooling air. The glow enticed more people than there were chairs, and several guests huddled together on a blanket on the lawn. In true Nashville style, the group burst into song, their voices melding and harmonizing, filling the air.

Weaving my way through, in the crackling firelight, I saw Martine perch on the arm of Micah's seat, bending down to whisper something in his ear while running her fingernail up his left thigh. Micah jumped to his feet, and Martine barely caught herself when the chair tipped. Her squeal of surprise wouldn't have drawn much concern, but her follow-up hiss caused the singing voices to dwindle in confusion.

"You're gonna regret treating me like this, Micah. You can act all high and mighty, but I know what you're really like." She swiveled, a snake seeking out her victim. "Besides, your wife has a secret of her own. I just caught her in a very *un*businesslike meeting. Why don't you ask her about it?"

The provocation hung in the air as Micah turned to find me on the other side of the firepit.

I *really* had no interest in having this conversation here. A hundred pairs of eyes watched and waited. Everyone except for Donovan, who had mumbled an apology and staggered back toward the bar, hopefully in search of copious amounts of water.

"Micah, let's go." I tried not to plead, no matter my desperation. This entire night had been a disaster.

Long strides brought him to my side, and he draped his arm protectively over my shoulder. Micah nodded goodnights and I held my head high as we worked our way through the gathering and headed back toward the lobby.

Neither of us spoke until the valets left to get our vehicles. The cloud hanging over us was heavy with the realization that our attempts to restore our marriage while co-existing with Martine weren't working.

The journal my mother wrote in January flashed in my memory. *"I wish she could see that mere human love won't be enough to build the kind of marriage God intends for her. A cord of three strands is not easily broken."* I flexed my aching fingers, suddenly aware my nails were denting crescents in my palms. I had done my best to ignore those words, to forget them, after seeing the entry. But they had lingered, reappearing now to convict me.

Micah broke the silence. "She noticed the stain from the spilled coffee. That's why she touched me."

I looked into his eyes—saw the frustration mixed with shame. Donovan was still too close for me to tell Micah what he'd done. I didn't need my husband defending my honor, even though he wasn't typically one to make a scene. My car arrived, and as Micah tipped the valet, I mumbled, "Let's talk when we get home."

Donovan wasn't really the problem, no matter what spin Martine tried to put on what she thought she saw. The man was obviously inebriated and allowing his inhibitions to run amuck. But Martine was clearly not finished with her games. I needed to know if Micah had been putting up with these invitations from her the entire time they were on the road. Had she felt brazen enough to come onto him tonight because he'd given in before, or was her adolescent behavior solely to provoke me?

The road blurred and I let the tears fall. I couldn't let Martine keep getting to me. I knew her performance was for my benefit. It wasn't as though there was a chance Micah could have slipped away with her tonight. My logic clarified and returned as we neared the last series of turns into our neighborhood.

Parked side-by-side in the driveway, we each waited for the other to disembark. What might be going through his mind? After a moment, his truck lights extinguished and I followed him wordlessly to the porch and into the small entryway where I stopped to remove my shoes.

He jumped right in. "What was Martine talking about? Who did she see you with?"

I pulled Micah to our couch, angling my knees to touch his. "Donovan had too much to drink." I realized that the excuse I was making for him was the same one Micah had made for Martine. "But nothing happened. I don't even know what he was doing. Or trying to do."

Micah's gaze leveled. I remembered when constant uncertainty had left me jealous and mistrustful. We'd rehashed the same argument more times than I could count, until ultimately, Micah stopped coming home for breaks. Now, even though I didn't doubt Micah's version of what happened with Martine tonight, she continued to create suspicion between us, and Donovan's boorish come-on didn't help.

I hadn't believed in Micah for so long. Would he believe me now?

Chapter Eighteen

Exhausted and admittedly cranky the next morning at work, I was distracted when I answered a call from an unknown number. "Elle Reed!" I snapped into the phone. I swiveled and was jerked to a stop, forgetting my cell phone was plugged into the wall because I'd neglected to charge it the night before. The '608' area code should have tipped me off, but I was several beats behind when it occurred whom I was speaking to. "Oh, Vicky! I meant to call you today. Please tell me you've got good news."

The realtor was calling to tell me that two couples from the open house the previous weekend intended to put in offers. The house had only been on the market for a week, so I was relieved to hear there were interested parties so quickly. She promised to email me with updates after they each went through the pre-approval process. I sincerely appreciated Vicky arranging for the appraisal and necessary minor repairs, and I was thankful for her expertise and willingness to take the lead. She'd run things by me via email, but this was the first time she'd called from her office phone instead of her mobile.

As soon as we disconnected, I added the number to her contact information. A modicum of relief wafted over me. I hadn't realized until then how much the sale had been weighing on my subconscious. It was no wonder: between Micah and Martine,

Carrie's health, my career, and remorse over the friction with my mom, I kept shuffling my stressors between the front and back burners, unsure where to focus my anxiety on any given day.

And now, the discomfort of Donovan figuratively breathing down my neck at work was nothing compared to the memory of his literal looming last night as he was about to cross all sorts of lines.

He'd shown up late this morning, squinting under the fluorescent lights like a mole coming to the surface. I'd pretended not to see him. The hours since our interaction had confused my recollection. Maybe he'd just stumbled, pitching toward me in the dark. Perhaps I'd made assumptions. Or what if *now* I was overthinking, and it had happened just as I remembered—and he'd been trying to kiss me?

It was a conversation I wasn't ready to have. I wouldn't know where to begin. Besides, all that mattered was Micah had believed me when I told him there was nothing going on between Donovan and me.

The afternoon dragged on. I was watching for three o'clock when Henry would be back from an offsite commitment. I had decided to let him know I accepted the transfer to A&R. The question was, would I tell Henry that Donovan was a bigger factor than Henry's encouragement to spread my wings? Not just what happened the night before, which, if true, would make it impossible for me to work under Donovan, but just as problematic, his overall demeanor toward me since day one.

Once Henry finally returned to his office, I gave him time to regroup, then knocked on the doorframe. His brow furrowed, attentiveness creasing his face. "Elle, what can I do for you?"

I closed the frosted glass door behind me. "I wanted to talk to you about the position in A&R. I've decided to try it. To take it, I mean. I know it's a permanent move." I drew my shoulders

BEAUTY IN THE BITTERSWEET

back, hoping to appear decisive to counter the bags under my eyes and the third-day hair that were diminishing my poise.

Henry looked like he would have stood, but his ample form was comfortably wedged into the wide office chair he surely missed during his external meetings. Instead, he hunched forward, digging his elbows into the desk calendar and steepling his fingertips.

"You're making a good decision. And the timing seems right. I think you'll discover a side of your personality you didn't realize was there. You have an authenticity that draws people in. Don't be afraid of that gift. Not everyone has it."

I blanched. Apparently, I hadn't even been able to hide my avoidance of crowds from Henry.

"You held up well under Donovan's way of doing things but it's alright to cut yourself some slack, especially for your last couple of weeks in my department. Believe it or not, I was once your age, all bright-eyed and bushy-tailed. But I bet you didn't know I worked myself into a heart condition." He rapped the knuckle of his right index finger on his chest. "I've got a pacemaker now, and it's a constant reminder for me to slow down. Of course, it's also a reminder to lose some of this padding. But that's a story for another day."

Now was my chance to tell him about Donovan. After all, Henry's grimace when he mentioned my new supervisor's *way of doing things* implied he didn't necessarily agree with them. But I remembered Erica's comment that there might be more going on with Donovan than we knew, and there *had* been some hints over the last few weeks that he wasn't holding himself together as well as he wanted people to believe.

As much as I dreaded it, I was going to have to talk to Donovan myself. About last night, and about the notice I'd just put in to change departments.

But first, I shot a quick text to Micah. *It's done*, I typed. *I told Henry I'm taking the new job.*

His response was immediate: *I'm so proud. Dinner out tonight to celebrate?*

I waffled, thinking of the work I'd planned to take home with me since I hadn't been able to do so the evening before. But Henry's words buzzed in my ear, and I glanced over my shoulder as though he'd been reading my thoughts. He'd want me to take tonight off.

Sounds good, I texted back.

Then I went to find Donovan.

Micah and I chose a low-key Turkish restaurant near our neighborhood, and after meeting at home to change into jeans and sweaters, we were seated by 7:30.

Over crispy Sigara Borek, I explained everything Sarah and Raul had told me about my new position. Then I told Micah how surprised but excited Erica and Shawn had been when I told them the news. And the entire time, deep down, I knew I was the one now censoring myself by dancing around my conversation with Donovan.

After ordering our dinners—he opting for Turkish gyros and I, getting my favorite, Hunkar Begendi—the conversation flowed to his plans now that he'd almost finished the paperwork from the Still Waters tour.

"Tonight is about you, and I don't want to ruin it, but you should find out now." An opening like that was ominous, and I gripped my napkin. "Martine went to the management head. She said I coerced her into having an affair and harassed her for most of the tour."

My eyes widened, and the tzatziki I'd unabashedly coated the cheese-filled cigarette rolls with soured in my gut. *How could she?* Especially after what I'd learned from Donovan today.

My hands flew to my burning cheeks. I had to tell him.

"Micah, that's not all she's done."

When I'd gone to Donovan's office to tell him I'd be leaving the department, I'd tapped on his door with my fingernails. At his mumble, I let myself in and found him in the semi-dark, with only his desk lamp switched on.

It was hard to feel bad for him. A grown man should know how to handle himself around an open bar. But, clearly, he hadn't, and was now paying the price.

"We need to talk." Perhaps a cliché, but for someone who hates confrontation, those words were a big step for me.

He looked up, and I could see signs of physical and mental unease, making me want nothing more than to say what I'd come to say and move on. I wasn't even going to sit.

"I hoped my memory of last night was just a nightmare but it's been coming back to me all day." Donovan's words were all but suppressed behind the hand over his mouth. I watched the flush start at his collar and flood to his hairline.

"I don't know what made me agree. She told me you'd wanted it all along. Elle, I promise I hadn't been thinking of you like that, but something about the way your husband acted when we met brought out my competitive side."

Now, I needed to sit. "Donovan, what are you talking about? Who told you I'd wanted it all along?"

"Martine Vaughn. Isn't she one of your best friends? She said you'd told her you had a crush … " His voice dwindled in confusion when I gasped.

The flush had worked it's way from his hairline, across his desk, and now overtook every inch of *my* body. I was mortified and couldn't even explain why Martine would have tried to use Donovan against me without also admitting to my husband's affair with her. I stumbled out of the office without giving Donovan a heads up about my move to A&R.

What would Micah do when I told him?

Well, I was about to find out.

The other restaurant patrons may as well have been on a different planet as Micah and I stared at each other across the flickering battery-operated candle in the center of our table, each trying to digest what we had just learned from the other. Martine's villainy had reached an incomprehensible low.

The truth had been bad enough: Micah had fallen into bed with the headliner of his first major tour. That was wrong even if he weren't also married. Now, Martine was accusing him of harassment, while masterminding an assault on me—by my boss.

The scandal itself was compounded by the timing as I moved to work with a new team where nobody really knew who I was. This would be the first thing they found out about me. Secrets spread like wildfire in this business, and we all knew it. Martine was willing to sacrifice the man who had facilitated one of the most successful tours ever of any new band because of her pride.

Micah didn't have the opportunity to reply before the waiter appeared with our dinners. My favorite dish, always mouthwatering and fragrant, steamed in front of me, turning my stomach. I furtively glanced at the surrounding tables, all seated with carefree couples. *This couldn't be happening.* The waiter hovered, refilling our water glasses, then our wine. My heartbeat thrummed in my own ears, drowning out whatever he was offering me now. Micah's gaze never left my face, and the waiter finally realized he'd interrupted *a moment.*

"Elle, I was planning to quit anyway, but now it will be under a shadow of suspicion until all of this is ironed out, I'm afraid." The corners of his mouth were down-turned, and I realized the permanent smile lines could just as well have been from frowns of disappointment.

"And I won't be working with Donovan much longer, but maybe I should talk to Henry about it. Or even Lorna. Even if he believed I liked him—nuts, right?—Donovan should have known better than to try anything with his assistant, no matter how much he'd had to drink."

Micah had scheduled a meeting for the end of the week with the president of his company. He had two days to round up statements from anyone who knew what had actually gone on while they were on tour. The next day was Halloween, and it was like we'd come full circle back to when this had all begun one year before. Sorting out who had witnessed what and if the impression they'd gotten would shed a negative light on Micah would be daunting since we had tried so hard to keep the brief affair under wraps.

But the situation needed to be cleared up quickly. Micah was leaving Still Waters, and now perhaps the management company altogether if the president wasn't satisfied with his version of events. His success as a tour manager wouldn't mean much if this ruined his reputation.

What if an opportunity for another tour didn't come up because of the mess Martine was instigating?

Chapter Nineteen

If I'd known a year ago what I knew now, I would have called my mom, most likely from the bathtub, and justifiably in tears. She would have listened, given sage advice, and I would have gone to bed with a plan for how to handle the next day, and the day after that, and the day after that. No matter how I always wanted to be in charge, I'd valued her advice. Despite our personalities and experiences being so different, I knew I could count on her. So, why was I too stubborn to let her know when my marriage hit a bump? The kiss, while indelicate, could have been a forgivable offense. My mother would have reminded me to look at the bigger picture, and perhaps the future betrayal wouldn't have occurred.

Dreams featuring all my regrets being batted around like badminton birdies plagued me for hours that night. I woke at almost three AM, my hair a knotted mess from tossing and turning. Leery of more nightmares, I slipped from the bed and used my phone's flashlight to reveal the row of journals on my closet shelf. I chose one at random, sneaking to the living room to avoid waking Micah.

Wrapped in the blanket from the back of the couch, I drew my knees to my chin in the flowered chair. The glow cast from the lamp on the small table allowed me to see the scripted dates of December 2013 to August 2014. Before I began reading, I did the math. I would have been in my junior year while Mom worked toward her bachelor's degree. By then, my focus was on doing well in school and what I wanted to do afterward. I'd taken my first trip to Nashville with my mom, thrilled that I loved it as much as I hoped.

The journal illuminated my mother's perspective during that year. I mostly skimmed, using the familiar handwriting to alleviate the longing for her presence in my life. I was starting to feel drowsy again when a February entry roused me.

Paul called tonight after avoiding me for the last six months. The woman he dated after me, Alison—I guess it's gotten serious. He wanted to tell me he's going to propose. I don't know what he expected me to say. It was almost as though he wanted me to object. But what good would that have done? He was the first—the only—man I've had feelings for since John. I was ready to take a chance. If my rein on Elle hadn't been so tenuous back then, I believe Paul and I would still be together. But I made the choice, and he said he understood it. I sometimes wish that he'd tried harder. If he had made it clear he was willing to work through the difficult teenage stuff with Elle, I would have been all in. I'm grateful we've been able to stay friends, but I don't know why he thinks I should have a say in his love life. He met someone else, and they are suited to each other. What good do regrets do me now?

Being reminded I was the reason my mother had broken up with Paul was disconcerting after the myriad of bad dreams.

I closed the book for several minutes, thinking back to what I could remember about my mom's relationship with Paul. Nothing stood out, and I realized she'd strived to keep from revealing more than friendship between them. My eyes grew heavy, and as I fought to stay awake, I had a flash of murky recall. My mom, bent over the kitchen counter with a wedding invitation in front of her. I scampered into the room, heading for the refrigerator. Mom startled, balling a tissue in her hand, then reached for a pen from the jar. "Elle, I'm sending back our acceptance for the wedding. Do you want the chicken or the steak?"

Paul and Alison had been married in the rose garden of a museum, and Mom and I had taken the opportunity to wear big, over-the-top "church" hats. At the time, I'd thought she was indulging in her exuberance for her friend and his new bride. Now, I recognized the underlying ache she had been trying to shield from view. My mother was heartbroken over losing a great love before it had begun. She'd become friends with Alison over the years, though. Together for dinners and birthday parties, reconnecting in Monona, and being in the same women's Bible study. I wondered if Alison ever asked how her husband and my mom had met.

Renewed just enough, even though it was going on four AM, I continued to scan the next couple of months after the wedding as I flipped toward the end of the journal. I found a scripture reference and my mother's thoughts about it.

"You, God, are my God, earnestly I seek you; I thirst for you, my whole being longs for you, in a dry and parched land where there is no water. I have seen you in the sanctuary and beheld your power and your glory."

This passage has been my reminder that You are all I need. My life isn't lacking. Even when I feel alone and like I'm missing out, You provide. Nothing in this world could satisfy me as You do. There are hard days, but I am trying to remember that although the heart is fickle, Your love and provision are steadfast.

Although my mom didn't mention Paul by name, it was evident by this entry she was still struggling with 'what might have been.' I wondered if, at the end of her life, she'd wished she could have gone back and changed things. I contemplated how thirteen-year-old me would have taken her introducing Paul as the new man in her life. By then, it felt as though it has always been just Mom and me. My father existed in remnants, memories of him indistinct and impersonal, like a secondary character in a book I'd once read.

I wanted to believe I would have been happy for her, but chances were, I would have been more focused on how a new relationship for her would have impacted *me*.

It would have been pointless to go back to bed, so I moved to the sofa sometime between four-thirty and five in the morning. I woke to Micah nudging me, mild alarm in his voice. "Elle, are you alright? It's almost seven."

Blinking my eyes into focus, I swung my legs to the floor, trying to get a handle on what day it was and what I should be doing. It wasn't coming. Micah sat on the edge of the coffee table, picking up the journal to make room.

"I'm sorry. I was having a hard time sleeping, so I came out to read. And I didn't want to wake you when I got tired again. I'm sorry," I repeated myself, although Micah was shaking his head, trying to halt my words.

"It's fine. I know you had a rough night. It was difficult for both of us to fall asleep. You don't need to apologize." He didn't ask about the journal as he tapped it against his palm. "I have to get ready for work." He stood, setting the book back on the table and leaving me to shake the remainder of the cobwebs away. Before he showered, he sympathetically made me a mug of coffee and left it on my dresser.

As we danced around each other while completing our morning routines, I reminded him I was spending the morning with Carrie at the hospital for her PET scan but expected to make it to work by early afternoon. I was not looking forward to finishing yesterday's conversation with Donovan, but I'd have to face it sooner or later.

Neither of us mentioned Martine's false accusations, yet I knew she was at the forefront of our minds. The only thing Micah said about it as he pocketed his wallet and phone was, "I'll try to get as many statements as I can from the roadcrew today to back myself up. Wish me luck."

I spent an extra thirty seconds watching him trudge to his truck, his posture dejected as the brisk air blew his hair into disarray. It was Halloween, and red, orange, and gold maple leaves covered the lawn. We had no plans for tonight, neither of us interested in attending the annual costume party thrown by his company and bound to be attended by the one person we had no interest in seeing.

I needed to be at the clinic before nine, when Josh and Carrie would meet me in radiology. Making a blonde roast for the road, I sent a text to let her know I would be leaving by 8:15. I hoped the caffeine jolt would get me through so I wouldn't have to settle for a boost of hospital coffee. I'd joined Carrie for enough scans in the past months to know exactly where to park, and I effortlessly arrived at the reception desk on the second floor where Josh and Carrie were already waiting. He was busy figuring out the electronic tablet the department used for completing forms.

The nippy fall air called for Carrie's head to be double wrapped in a peach scarf and the hood from her wool coat. As she glanced up at my entrance, the hood slipped from her head, and I saw the scarf tied in a fashionable knot at the nape of her neck. Her smile was wide as she unnecessarily thanked me for coming.

All three of us tried to curtail our apprehension over this test. A mass might still be present, but the PET scan would show any chemical activity within the tissue indicating active lymphoma. We were praying for a negative scan, meaning remission. She'd be able to avoid more chemo and move on to radiation. The five-day-a-week schedule would be grueling, but the treatment itself would be much easier on her body.

As we waited, it occurred to me to ask Josh, "So, what are you doing for work that gives you all this free time?" I knew he had been spending at least a few hours with Carrie almost every day since they had started dating, if that's what you'd call it. I also knew he'd had the flexibility to help Micah, of course. I was curious how he kept up his livelihood, but there wasn't a delicate way to find out. I wished I'd asked Carrie when we were alone, but now the question hung in the air, and Josh didn't act put off by my frank curiosity.

"Well, I've been working some freelance stuff. I went to school for sound and video editing, so I've picked up jobs like that in the last year. Sunny is about to start touring again, and she wanted me back, but I told her I wasn't available."

Sunny Parker was the prominent artist whose tours Josh had been coordinating for the last several years before she took a break for a starring movie role. I wasn't surprised she was going back on tour, as I'd heard a new song of hers on the radio over the summer. I *was* surprised Josh wasn't working with her, and I wondered if Carrie was the reason he was holding back.

Before I could contemplate further, a redheaded young man, hardly old enough to be out of school, called Carrie's name from the doorway. I had the ludicrous thought that he had dressed as a doctor in honor of the holiday. He allowed us to accompany her, and we followed his swishing, oversized lab coat to the exam room.

The scan required a tracer delivered by IV, and we sat with Carrie while it worked its way through her system. Josh prayed aloud, but mostly we kept to our own thoughts, waiting for someone to take her to the imaging room. By the end, the process had taken its toll on Carrie's energy, but she mustered a weary smile for the lab technician, who assured us the images had come out clearly and would be sent to Dr. Greer.

It was 11:30 when we pushed the button for the elevator. Two floors below, with Josh supporting Carrie's tiring body, we stepped into the main lobby. We were walking toward a group of chairs so she could rest while Josh pulled his car around when Carrie gasped and staggered. Afraid she had tripped, I reached for her as Josh tightened his grip. Carrie wasn't aware of either of us. Her gaze was on the graying gentleman standing in our way.

"Dad! What are you doing here?"

Chapter Twenty

I looked from Carrie to the gaunt man I'd never even seen a photograph of. Neither of them had the expression I would expect after not seeing each other in ... how long? At least four years. Carrie's features were strained. No, more than that. Distraught. Her father kneaded a knit cap in his hands as he shifted his weight. Josh and I glanced at each other over the top of Carrie's scarf-covered head. His face, cast in confusion, mirrored my own bewildered thoughts. But Carrie's legs were closer to giving out than they'd been moments before, and she was our priority. I whispered, "Carr, why don't you sit," then, resolutely, "Mr. Stephenson, Carrie's tired. We need to let her rest."

The shock on Carrie's face had not dissipated by the time we guided her to a small grouping of deep chairs away from other visitors. I urged her to relax back into the cushion, but she sat stiffly, the flakey skin of her slender fingers pale as she gripped her kneecaps.

Her father sat down warily in the seat across from her, his rheumy eyes flickering between Josh and me as though waiting for Carrie to introduce us, or, perhaps, for us to leave him alone with her. I'd never seen my friend look this uptight and I had no intention of walking away. Josh must have felt the same, because he kept his hand on her shoulder.

The four of us waited in an interminable silence until Carrie spoke.

"What do you want, Dad? Why are you here?" Her voice was low and flat. I cringed at her bluntness.

Her father licked his thin lips, once again glancing up at Josh and me as though we should be taking his silent hint. After a protracted sigh, he wheedled, "Carrie, your mother called and told me you had a three-month check today. I thought you should have family here." He shrugged, and although I didn't understand what was going on, a twinge of pity for him scraped away at my disapproval. I caught Josh's eye, wondering if he knew more about Mr. Stephenson than I did, but he met my gaze with his own skeptically knit brow.

Carrie's tone didn't change. "As you can see, I was just leaving. You missed the appointment, and I won't have an update until tomorrow. I'll let Mom know what they say." Carrie strained to rise, so determined to leave the man with no further consideration that she forgot she didn't have enough strength to pull herself to her feet. Josh, recognizing her frustration, bent to help. The entire encounter was over almost before it began. Carrie moved as though she couldn't get away fast enough, and I could see bright spots of color high on her cheeks.

I glanced behind me as we left her father sagging in his seat. He gave one last shot, undoubtedly knowing it was futile, as he didn't bother to stand. "Carrie, we really should talk...."

Carrie acted like she didn't hear him, her tight expression unaltered. Josh and I were almost entirely supporting her frame as we led her away, yet somehow, she was still dictating the rapid pace. When we were out of earshot, approaching the revolving glass door, Josh broke through to her.

"Carrie, please, stop for a second. You'll never make it all the way to the car, and it's too cold for you to wait outside. Stay here with Elle for a minute. You need to take a breath—take a minute. Calm down."

With a tormented cry, Carrie started to collapse, as though the lack of forward motion forced her knees to give in. Josh accepted her full weight in his arms, against his chest, as Carrie whispered, "I can't! You don't understand. I can't be here. He can't be here!"

Josh ended up staying with Carrie while I brought my car around to shuttle them to his truck. I searched my memory for an explanation as I pulled up to the revolving door and waited for them to notice me. Carrie looked depleted as Josh helped her into the backseat and followed, pulling her close. He directed me to where his pickup was parked but didn't comment on the scene we'd left behind. I didn't know what, if anything, Carrie had explained after I'd hurried away, but the tension in her face and body had diminished. She silently wilted into Josh, closing her eyes.

When I stopped in the empty space next to his truck, she finally reached forward to acknowledge me, whispering, "I'm so sorry. I'll explain, but not right now. Thank you for coming to the appointment with me." She was back to her gentle self, and it was like I'd dreamt, or at least exaggerated, the incident in the lobby. Josh buckled her in while assuring me he'd stay home with her, and I reminded them both I was only a phone call away. I hated to abandon her, but figuring out what to say to Donovan after yesterday's revelation, waiting to hear from Micah, and expecting an update from the realtor were also crowding my mind.

Poor sleep and the anticlimactic wait while Carrie's test was completed had lulled me into a sluggish state, and despite the ensuing drama that jolted my mind awake, my body wasn't catching up. I jiggled my coffee cup, hoping to hear a remaining slosh, and grudgingly pulled into a drive-through Starbucks. As I idled in the dwindling line, my phone disrupted the radio as it connected to the car's speaker. The screen displayed Vicky Miller's name, and I answered, now praying the two cars ahead of me would take their time.

"Elle, I hope I'm not interrupting!"

"It's always good to hear from you. I may have to put you on hold, though. I'm about to order coffee. What's going on?"

Vicky concisely explained the reason for her call: both couples had been pre-approved and were putting in offers. "I know you want to close as soon as possible. I thought the forewarning might help you make travel plans, especially with the holidays coming." Vicky promised to forward the offer letters when she received them, and we disconnected as I pulled up to the speaker. I ordered an amped-up version of my favorite hot coffee along with a sandwich to allay the jitters from four shots of espresso. Waiting for my drink to be made, a line I'd seen several times in the various journals ran through my head.

"When I am overwhelmed, lead me to the rock that is higher than I."

While driving to the office, my mind swirled in a dizzying array of 'what ifs.' The management company might side with Martine simply because she was one of their biggest successes. I could be terrible at this new job and end up back working for Donovan. Or what if Carrie's test results weren't what we hoped? And even with two interested buyers for the house, it was plausible neither would work out.

For most of my life, I called my mom to talk me through—if not my emotions, then practical next steps. Now she was gone, Micah himself was a part of my problems, and I couldn't burden

Carrie, especially after today. The weight of unknown outcomes was heavy, and I wished I could just lay them down. Leave these burdens for someone else to carry for a while.

Instead, I put my bag and coat down in my cubicle and shuffled through my agenda. The holidays were coming, as Vicky had pointed out. We had planned for a closing date forty-five days from acceptance of an offer, but I didn't want to make the trip too close to Christmas. I wondered if either party might agree to close in thirty days. When I'd left the house in September, I'd dreaded the idea of flying back up after the first snow, but it might not be avoidable. Even after living for almost twenty years in those often-sub-zero winter temperatures, my blood had thinned after moving to Tennessee. I didn't suffer nostalgia for the cold.

I'd have to let Raul know I'd be taking a few days off even though I'd just accepted the job. Donovan would have had plenty to say about priorities, but fortunately, this trip wouldn't be any of his business. Still, before Henry scheduled any interviews for my position, I should give Donovan the courtesy of telling him about my decision. And I was determined not to let anything he said get to me. I decided to get it over with.

As I neared his office, I saw the door was cracked. But I doubted he meant for it to be, as the one-sided conversation I heard as I approached was surely not meant for public consumption.

"Caitlin, please. It's been four months. Knox is going to forget who I am... yes, of course... but you know I was still a good father... Caitlin, wait...." He ended with an expletive, and I jumped when I heard what sounded like his phone slam to the desk.

Silence. I waited, each breath thin as I tried to figure out if there was any way to turn around without my heels tapping. Suddenly, the door was yanked open, and Donovan stood in front of me.

JESSICA STONE

"Why are you eavesdropping?"

His Ferragamos must have more cushioning than my shoes.

"I wasn't! I mean, I'm not. I was just..." I stopped. There was no graceful way out of this. Why did my interactions with this man always end up so uncomfortable? I took a breath and started over. "I didn't mean to eavesdrop. I was coming to talk to you, but it can wait." I started to turn, then realized that, really, it couldn't wait. I was leaving the department and Donovan didn't need to hear it from someone else.

"Actually..."

"Actually..."

We'd spoken simultaneously. I gestured for him to go first.

"Actually, I'm taking the rest of the day off, and I won't be here tomorrow, so you'd better say whatever it is now."

I noticed a cowlick in his normally coiffed hair when I followed him into his office, carefully pushing the door closed behind me until I heard the click.

He was distracted. I could tell him I was moving on and it might not even register. Now was my chance.

Instead, "Is there anything I can do for you?" tumbled from my lips before I could stop it.

I expected indignation. Perhaps he feared I'd heard more than I did.

He had a son named Knox. He hadn't seen him in four months. And, apparently, his ex-wife was the reason.

I guess I had heard enough.

But Donovan simply looked resigned. And, for the first time, I heard his true timbre. Low and broken. "My wife was the love of my life. But she left. And when I turn it off, when I shut my feelings down, I'm done." He stopped, and for a moment, it seemed he'd said all he intended to. Then he continued, his voice tightening like his vocal cords didn't want the next words

158

to escape. "When she left, she took the only good thing I've ever done: she took our son. Without him, I don't know who I am anymore."

Long seconds passed before his gaze met mine. What I found there made my heart ache. I could have been staring into the recesses of the deepest, darkest ocean. An ocean of misery. No longer was he Donovan, cocky and ruthless supervisor. His pain was so stark, so jagged, it was untouchable. And not meant to be shared—not with me, certainly.

But here I was, and I realized I hadn't had any control over what led me to *this* chair in front of *this* man during what seemed to be one of the hardest situations of his life. If I'd had my choice—any of my choices as of late—this wouldn't be the case. So, what purpose did God have for me in this moment?

"I can't begin to imagine how much you must miss Knox," I spoke timorously, knowing it was useless to pretend I hadn't heard his son's name. "And I can understand trying to keep yourself distracted with work, even on weekends." I wasn't ready to confess I'd fallen into the same trap to avoid the pain in my personal life.

The way Donovan raked his fingers through his hair explained the cowlick. "If I don't work, I drink." He swallowed. "No matter which trap I fall into, it seems you've had to suffer from my abuse."

It might be the only apology I'd get, so I nodded an acknowledgment. "That leads me to what I came to tell you. I've accepted a position in A&R. I'll be starting there in a few weeks."

Donovan tipped his head, his chin nearly touching his chest, then he nodded. "I hate to lose you. You leave some big shoes to fill."

Would wonders never cease?

As I walked from my office to my car, I tried to call Carrie, but neither she nor Josh answered. As tired as she'd been after her test, I assumed she was napping, and I hoped my call hadn't disturbed her. Micah was home when I pulled into the drive, and I parked strategically, giving him room to back out first in the morning.

The fragrance of rosemary and anise seed greeted me at the door. Micah peeked his head out of the kitchen, wiping his hands on a dishtowel. His grim smile broadcasted the kind of day he'd had. My afternoon had been so busy that I hadn't taken time to text him after getting to the office. I wanted to tell him about Carrie's father, but I was more interested in hearing if there'd been any developments with Martine. I hated that she had taken over so many of my thoughts and our conversations for the last year. It was as though she could sniff out every moment we started to put her behind us, and she'd instigate something else to bring the situation to the forefront.

Micah had potatoes roasting in the oven and was waiting for me before searing Ahi tuna. It was nice to be welcomed home with dinner, and while setting the kitchen table, I updated him on the news from Vicky. It wasn't until I was putting the finishing touches on our salads that Micah brought up his conversations with the other members of the road crew he'd been able to reach during the day.

"Most of them are already on other tours, so I'm waiting for some to call me back, but I got a few statements." His ears turned red, and I could tell he was holding something back. "I don't want to keep anything from you, so you should know all the details of this predicament. Martine, she…ah…there were quite a few times that she tried to start stuff up. I never entertained it again. I didn't even consider it. But I plan to be upfront with management. I don't want you to hear anything through the grapevine."

I focused my attention on dressing our salads while Micah plated the tuna steaks and potatoes. He'd put out a large bucket of candy for Treat-or-Treaters to help themselves, and we heard laughter as a group stomped up to our porch.

He resumed, "Sometimes, she'd show up at my hotel room door. Once, she even convinced the front desk to give her a key. And after I turned her down, *which I did, every time,* she'd always have an attitude the next day. She'd complain about everything, trying to say I'd not taken care of making arrangements that I should have at the venue or in her hotel suite. She'd pout and rant to anyone who would listen. I'm sure, on one of those occasions, she admitted something she shouldn't have."

"What time is your meeting tomorrow?"

"I asked if we could meet at the end of the day. I wanted to give the crew enough time to send any written statements they were willing to make."

Josh's comment about Martine being *more trouble than she was worth* popped into my head. I wondered what he'd specifically noticed or heard, or if she'd directly made any remarks regarding Micah to him.

I tucked that in the back of my mind while Micah finished his thought. "I wanted to wait until tomorrow to ask the other members of the band. Maybe I won't even need to involve them. They probably had a bird's eye view and could be a lot of help, but if Martine found out they spoke against her, it could cause repercussions. That's if they would even be willing to stand up for me. As talented as they are, they aren't Still Waters without her."

I brought up Josh and the possibility that he could provide some insight regarding both Martine's general attitude when he was around and how to approach the other three band members, should that become necessary. "It might be worth a phone call to him, you think?"

As we cleared our plates and I started to rinse them, Micah rested his hands on my waist. The reflection of his worried eyes met mine in the kitchen window as he stood behind me. "Elle, I can't say I'm sorry enough."

"I know you are. It just doesn't erase the consequences."

While I finished cleaning up the kitchen, Micah turned down the television in the other room, and I heard him say Josh's name. He must have decided to take my advice and call tonight. His tone sobered and what I overheard led me to believe Josh had a lot to unload. Micah exclaimed several times, and they were still talking when I bypassed him to refill the bowl of candy. I sat on the porch for a few minutes to enjoy the costumes and give Micah privacy. He was sunk into the couch when I came back inside, his hair mussed from scrunching his fingers in it. He always does that when he's upset, and I wished I could comfort him. What could I say, though? He'd brought this on himself. I'd forgiven him, but I couldn't fix the aftermath.

I waited to see if he'd tell me what Josh said. He'd promised he didn't want to keep secrets, but a new kind of resentment would develop if I pried into his every thought. I wanted to be his safe space, not elicit guilt if he wasn't ready to talk.

It was time to regain some trust in him.

"Josh just left Carrie's. He wanted me to tell you she slept all afternoon and only woke up long enough to eat dinner." I nodded without commenting. I didn't know how to explain the encounter at the hospital when I didn't understand it myself. Micah had enough on his mind for tonight, regardless.

He continued, "Yeah, so Josh definitely had a few interactions with Martine when he covered shows."

"Oh?" I waited, hoping he'd elaborate without my having to pry. I took the cushion next to him.

Micah scrubbed his hands down his cheeks. "I can't believe it."

"What? Did she trash you that bad even to him?"

"No, she didn't trash-talk me." He shook his head with a humorless chuckle. "She tried to get him to sleep with her, too."

Chapter Twenty-one

I kept my ringer turned up the next morning, not wanting to miss Carrie's call when she got her scan results. The first bit of news that came in, however, wasn't via phone call but rather a chime indicating an email from Vicky. Her introduction was brief, stating the first offer letter and purchase agreement were attached, and we could expect the second by the end of the day. There were several pages, and I quickly scanned through them to determine the most crucial information.

Eventually, I came to the dollar amount on the first offer, which was just below our asking price, and their requested closing date of mid-December. After getting the second offer, I would need to accept or counter within a day. My hope wasn't for a bidding war but to receive our asking price as well as a reasonable closing date. Bonus if they would buy the piano. The house had a small mortgage, thanks to my mother's handling of the money she'd received from my father's life insurance, but I still wanted to avoid paying much more of it.

I had run out to grab a salad from the deli across the street when Carrie's assigned ringtone—"Oath" by Cher Lloyd—played from my phone. I stepped out of line and moved toward the quietest corner to answer. "Care-Bear! Did you hear from the doctor?"

Her voice was grave. "I'm sorry I didn't call you back last night," she began. "I just needed sleep, and I was kind of out of it. But the news is good. No more chemo and I get another week to rest before six weeks of radiation start."

"Why do you sound like something's wrong? This is the best news we could have hoped for!" I was more excited than she seemed to be, and I wondered if she'd heard from her father again. "Is it … your family? Have you called them? Do you want to talk about it?"

"Actually, yeah, I do want to talk. Are you still coming over tomorrow? Can you come in the morning? If not, I think I'll be okay without an aide here. I'm feeling better."

"Don't be silly. I'll be there bright and early. With bells on!" Another one of our inside jokes, as she knew good and well how I felt about mornings, but she didn't laugh. After making sure she wouldn't need anything before the next day, I disconnected. Carrie had been eagerly awaiting this exact outcome from the PET scan, and to hear her tepid relay of the positive results was disheartening. Her reaction to seeing her father came to mind. There was definitely more to that story.

Paying for my salad and a molasses cookie—*it's all about balance*—I stepped out into the chilly air and hurried back to my office. I had a lot to accomplish before the end of the workday, and I wanted to be home when Micah arrived.

He texted me later that afternoon. He'd gotten four statements, plus Josh's account, of Martine's behavior that had been witnessed by others. Two of the roadies had observed Martine, on separate occasions, knocking on Micah's hotel room door late at night. One of them overheard Micah ask her firmly and persistently to leave. According to the statement, Martine had been loud and belligerent. A different crewmember saw Micah guide her to her room. He added the caveat that it was clear Micah was returning—not joining—her, despite Martine begging him to stay. Another document included Martine's scheme to sabotage

Micah's arrangements with a venue by showing up hours late for a soundcheck. She insisted to everyone that Micah told her it was scheduled for one PM instead of eleven AM, despite the rest of the band being on time.

He could fill in the gaps later, but it all sounded promising. The management head would surely understand Martine had initiated all of this. Of course, Micah would still have to tell him the drama was retaliation for his refusal to continue their original affair.

Unfortunately, that was a big problem to counter. Martine and her crocodile tears could play the scorned lover to a T, and Micah could still be disciplined or even let go before he'd found a new tour. And after whatever twisted versions of the story started going around town, he'd have to explain his personal business to the next artist or band and possibly a new management company.

He texted me again at 4:45. *Going up to talk to Joe. Say a prayer.* I was struck by the fact he'd asked for prayer instead of 'luck.' Micah had always said he believed in God, but I knew he didn't share my faith. Since before we'd met, my own beliefs hadn't much affected my day-to-day life. But that was changing, and I did stop and say a silent prayer after glancing around to make sure I wasn't being observed.

God, I'm so grateful that You're healing my marriage. Please show me how to be supportive of Micah, no matter the outcome of this meeting. Please help Joe to see what kind of person . . . Micah is. I wanted to pray for Joe to see what kind of person Martine was, but a strange conviction pressed on my spirit. I could hear God reminding me of the grace He lavishes on me.

The feeling left me uneasy, and I pushed it away. I'd already excused Micah. There was no way I was going to forgive Martine. It wasn't like she'd even asked, and in fact, she was continuing to make trouble.

I left my office at 5:30, and after stopping at the grocery store, I pulled into the empty driveway an hour later. Not up for cooking, I'd grabbed a rotisserie chicken from the deli for dinner. It would keep if Micah was in the mood to go out instead.

The second offer letter for the house had come, and I printed both emails and their attachments to peruse. The most recent was for our asking price, but they needed to push the closing until after Christmas. I was just starting to respond to Vicky when I heard Micah's door slam shut. That wasn't a good sign, considering how he babied his truck.

He entered and shrugged out of his leather jacket. Deciding my news could wait, I discreetly slid the printed pages underneath my MacBook. I handed the glass of wine I'd poured to him as he bent down to kiss the top of my head before dropping next to me on the couch.

"So, here's a mystery. Joe got an anonymous email about Martine trying to use Donovan to keep you out of the way during the wrap party. Who do you suppose knew about that?"

"Wait, you're saying Martine wasn't just trying to start a fight between us?"

"Not according to what Joe said. He implied it claimed explicitly that Martine suggested Donovan keep you occupied for as long as he could, however he could. Do you think Donovan would have ratted himself out? It could be disastrous to his career if the right people find out."

I never told Micah about my latest conversation with Donovan. It would have been a breach of confidence. But not telling Micah also meant he didn't know we had ended on good, or at least semi-good, terms.

"Honestly, Donovan might have sent that email. Or maybe someone else overheard the two of them talking that night. Or maybe Martine bragged to the wrong person. I really don't know."

"Well, I guess your prayers along with that email gave Joe what he needed to make a decision. I still don't have a tour to manage, but he's got some ideas for the meantime. Unfortunately, even with that level of manipulation from Martine, Still Waters is worth too much for him to cut ties, but at least he understood that although I made a mistake, it wasn't at all what Martine claimed."

If I'd ever wished I could go back and unmeet someone, it was now. How different our lives—our marriage—might have been without the detour she'd sent us on.

Micah tipped his head against the back of the couch for a moment, then pulled himself upright. "Josh detailed quite a bit in his statement. Now I feel bad for asking him to fill in so often. I'm surprised he didn't turn me down. Last year, at the end of December, I guess Martine had a pretty bad attitude when he first stepped in. Then she *really* started showing her colors when I didn't come back in January." He picked up the glass of merlot, swirled it, and set it down again without sipping.

Josh's first time covering for Micah had encompassed a month of shows, starting when I found out that he'd gone to bed with Martine. I'd put the kibosh on all travel plans for the foreseeable future. His tour schedule, including the clandestine overnight to NOLA, of course, was canceled, along with my mom's holiday visit. I started to kick him out but retracted out of fear I'd be handing him to Martine.

Screaming, yelling, and sobbing had echoed off the walls of the cramped house that no longer welcomed either of us. I moved into the guest room. He'd try to apologize or explain, and I'd stonewall. The weeks in the wake of his confession had been the

BEAUTY IN THE BITTERSWEET

most agonizing of my life. In the midst, I'd avoided my mother's phone calls, finally telling her both Micah and I had the flu and didn't want to expose her. She hadn't been able to get a refund for her plane fare, and I apologized more than was reasonable for wasting the price of a discount ticket. I couldn't own up to my true guilt, though. She patiently waited for me to confide to her what was going on, but I dodged. My case of the "flu" lasted far longer than was believable, and by late January, my despondency over Micah and the lies I was telling my mother became too much.

On a cold Saturday afternoon, after a painful counseling session with him, my mother called. I'd barely mumbled *hello* when she implored, "Elle, honey, please tell me you're doing something to make up for the holidays. Working yourself to the bone is the reason you've been so sick!"

I yearned to confess, but admitting I'd been made a fool of by my husband with the woman I'd introduced him to wasn't something I could face. I told her I was simply trying to get caught up, and she nagged I was pushing myself too hard when I should be taking advantage of Micah being home. In my head, she was inferring I should be trying to get pregnant, and it lit me up. I wish I could forget the rest. Unfortunately, I recalled the conversation almost verbatim.

"You have NO idea what I want for my life! I love my job, and I'm not ready to give it up because of some outdated itinerary that says by now I should be sitting at home changing diapers! The last thing Micah and I need is a baby! I'm not like you, Mom!"

I took a long pull of my wine, hoping the flush it brought would mask my humiliation. That last part was true. I wasn't like her.

Outside of my self-reflective brooding, Micah and I talked for hours that night. The stories Josh shared with him about Martine made us both livid. My clenched hands longed to retaliate somehow against the woman who sought out ways to hurt me. To hurt those I cared about. Didn't she remember her career started with my help?

Micah had flown home to be with me on the day of my mother's death, and Josh made it up to Canada that same night. The band was performing in Quebec City, and Micah did as much as he could over the phone until his plane took off. Josh arrived at the venue halfway through the show to find Martine incensed about the six hours there wasn't a tour manager on site, despite the urgency of our situation.

Josh had graciously flown up for two days so Micah could console me in Tennessee, but of course, she blatantly ignored him once he arrived. It was unfortunate Josh couldn't cover long enough to allow my husband to attend the funeral, but he had other obligations. And the way Martine treated him while he was there was inhospitable, to say the least.

Although it could have been helpful to have Micah in Wisconsin to help pack up Mom's home, part of me hadn't wanted him to come. I was grateful he dropped everything to be with me when she died, but in a way, I still blamed him for the months I'd lost with her beforehand. If it weren't for his affair, I wouldn't have lied to her, and our relationship wouldn't have been fragmented for the last year of her life.

Letting go of those hidden resentments felt like coming home after a long trip where everything had gone wrong. We had vacillated so frequently between talking and not, loving and not, that neither of us grasped how many layers of hurt we were covering up. He also hadn't known the depth of injury I'd inflicted on my mother in January. I hadn't fully realized it myself—not until I'd come to read many of her journal entries.

I retrieved the book I'd left in a drawer of the side table earlier and shared some of the pages I'd skimmed through during my night of insomnia. With a heavy heart, I told Micah about the lost siblings I'd never known existed and how my spiteful words must have impacted my mom during our argument. I admitted I hadn't yet found the peace I would need to read journals she'd written since last Christmas when my lies first began.

He didn't push me. Maybe he knew I wasn't ready to forgive myself. I was lying with my head in his lap, the wine mellowing my racing thoughts. I blinked heavily as my muscles relaxed. Our conversation veered back to Josh's troubles with Martine. He'd first met her the week after Christmas when he managed the series of gigs in Vegas and Colorado. Still Waters was scheduled to play a private party at the home of a movie star on New Year's Eve in Brentwood, one of Nashville's affluent suburbs. I would have attended with Micah, but instead, we both stayed home—each in our own bedrooms. Josh handled that show also, thankfully, and continued with the East coast segment for most of January. While Micah and I were seeking couples' therapy, now we knew that Martine was planting her sights on Josh. She might have thought pursuing him would make Micah jealous. At the very least, he'd be a good rebound.

Josh put the sordid details into his written statement, which had been provided to Joe along with the others. I didn't need to read it myself. Micah shared enough to leave me embarrassed on Martine's behalf. She had blatantly thrown herself at Josh. When Josh covered for Micah in Canada, maybe it wasn't malice but humiliation that had driven her insolence toward him. He had denied her so thoroughly in January that she may have hoped their paths would never cross again.

Pulling back the sheet on our bed, I reminded Micah, "Don't forget, I'm heading to Carrie's early in the morning." I was eager to hear what she had to say. "While I'm there, I'll respond to the potential offers on Mom's house. They're due by noon."

"I'll have your coffee waiting," Micah offered.

I half joked, "I'm already looking forward to a nap tomorrow afternoon."

But it didn't stop me from reaching for Micah as soon as he slid under the covers.

Chapter Twenty-two

$\mathcal{J}$ had to run back inside twice—first after forgetting my laptop and then again for the printed offers—as I was trying to leave the following morning. My grogginess was worse than usual, but the lost sleep the previous night had far and away been worth it. I'd loved drifting off and waking with Micah's arms secured around me.

The aide who covered a couple of the overnight shifts each week was sitting with Carrie at her kitchen table when I arrived. Her name was Tina, I'd learned, and she was wearing her coat already. "I'm sorry, I don't mean to rush out on you, but my babysitter can't stay past 8:30."

It was only our second meeting, the first being the night I was too emotional for conversation. Yet this would be the last I saw of her, as we wouldn't need the aides after today. I exchanged pleasantries briefly before closing the door behind her and heading back to the kitchen, where Carrie waited.

"Your color looks good." It was true, but also the only compliment I could tender. Her expression was solemn, and she smiled grimly in reply, wrapping her hands loosely around a mug of herbal tea.

"Are you hungry, Ellie? Tina left some oatmeal in a pot on the stove." Carrie's use of my nickname felt like she was trying to lighten a moment heavy with foreboding. Goosebumps rippled along my arms.

"Maybe in a bit. I'll wait until it's nice and congealed." My attempt at humor didn't go over well. Pushing my laptop to the side, I glanced at the microwave clock. In an hour, I would need to contact the realtor so we could send responses to the offers in time.

I sat across from Carrie, taking in the puffiness around her wide-set eyes. "Have you been sleeping? Did Josh come over yesterday?" My powerlessness when we first found out about her cancer didn't compare to this. At least then, the enemy had a name. The desolation Carrie was combatting right now was an enigma to me.

"I asked him to give me a little space." Her detached voice belied the glisten on her lashes that threatened to fall with her next blink. "I just...it was too much to put on him along with the cancer. He has his own life and doesn't need to give up everything for me."

I'd never heard this defeatist attitude coming from Carrie before. I moved from my seat and slid into the chair beside hers. "Carr, tell me about your dad."

Tears dripped from her chin, but her voice remained impassive. I listened in revulsion as her story started when she was seven years old. Her father had taken her out on "daddy-daughter dates." My eyes had begun to be opened to the horrors of child trafficking in our country by recent news stories, and I dreaded what Carrie would say next.

"For five years, I was shared by my own father."

My blood careened between fire and ice.

"He would say there was a friend he wanted me to meet. The *friend* always happened to be staying at a certain motel." Carrie's nose pinked and she wiped its tip with her sleeve. "I knew my father was supposed to protect me. Instead, I endured heinous harm and betrayal."

"Didn't you tell anyone? Your mother didn't step in?" The sharp questions sliced my vocal cords. I rested my hand on her baggy sleeve, attempting to soften my reaction.

Carrie swallowed hard before answering. "It was years before my mom claimed to have finally realized what I was going through. During that time, I was forced to participate in at least two dozen encounters with more than ten different men."

She sketched the scenes for me in more detail than I wanted to accept, and undoubtedly less detail than she remembered. My stomach roiled as her memories putrefied the atmosphere. The occasional shaking of her hands rattled her mug against the tabletop, but her eyes never left the rippling surface of the tea.

"By the time I realized that this wasn't normal, I was afraid to speak out. What if people didn't believe me? My father was a Little League coach for all my brothers' teams. Everyone liked him. Even my mother didn't recognize the signs, or so she said. She'd left me to fend for myself for so many years that, at first, I was grateful for the attention he was giving me." Carrie chewed the inside of her cheek. "I wasn't planned, you know. My youngest brother, Scott, was six years old when I was born. And Mic and Chris were in high school when the abuse first started." Squint lines appeared at the corners of her eyes as she gazed into a past only she could see. "People always assume big brothers take care of their little sister, but mine had their own activities, and I wasn't interested in tagging along. So, I was just alone. A lot. And when he'd bring me back after a 'daddy-daughter date,' the fact that I'd go to my room to be alone didn't trigger any questions from my mom."

Tears poured down both of our faces. A million questions I didn't want to hear the answers to swirled in my head like crows searching for a place to land. She finally raised her hazel eyes to meet mine, and even though I had been her best friend for four years, it was like I saw her for the first time.

Sending responses to the offers on the house was the furthest thing from my mind, but by now, it was almost ten o'clock, and my deadline was approaching. Carrie wanted a bath and insisted she was stable enough to relax in the tub unsupervised. I left the door cracked, so I'd be able to hear if she called to me and sat on her bed with my laptop and the printed pages. How was I supposed to concentrate on something like this with the echoes of Carrie's story reverberating in my head? Gradually, my heart slowed to a dull thud, and I decided to call Vicky instead of attempting a coherent email and awaiting the response.

I was grateful for the way she cut to the chase, hardly acknowledging my lackluster response to her obligatory *hope you're well.* We decided to counter the first offer. If they would close in thirty days and come closer to our asking price, I could save a month of mortgage and avoid possible flight delays with January snow. Neither party was interested in the piano, so I'd need to be more proactive about finding a buyer. Deciding to get Micah's advice, I assured Vicky I'd have it moved before the closing.

Less than fifteen minutes later, I received her emailed CCs to both buyer's agents. I carried my MacBook to the living room where I'd left my charger, stopping to peek in on Carrie as I passed the bathroom. She was staring unblinkingly at the wall, only rousing herself the second time I said her name.

"Yeah, hey. I'm ready to get out. I'm starting to prune here." She squinted at her fingertips, which were indeed wrinkling. I asked her to hang on for a minute while I plugged in my laptop, then joined her at the side of the tub. She was still seated, watching the water gurgle down the drain when I handed her the fluffiest towel I could find. She seemed resolute after unburdening herself, and I wondered what she'd decided in the time she'd been floating. This wasn't the type of trouble you could soak away in a bubble bath.

Carrie and I were side-by-side on the couch soon after with the television on but the sound low. To bring some levity, I'd found a channel playing old episodes of *Gilmore Girls*, and Lorelai and Rory were speed talking in sotto voce with the volume on two. I was updating Micah with an audio message so I could simultaneously fill them both in on the sale of the house.

"If the offer is accepted, I'll be going to Wisconsin the first week of December for the closing," I finished before turning to Carrie. "Micah's playing basketball with some guys this morning, so I don't really expect to hear back from him, but at least he'll get my text later."

Carrie swiveled her head from the television to me. Her eyes were glassy. "He's with Josh. Micah asked if he wanted to get together to shoot hoops today." Before I could comment, she continued. "I always figured you and your mom were like them." She gestured toward the television. "I wondered what that would be like, to have a mom that you could tell everything to."

"Oh, Carr! For starters, let's not watch this," I blackened the TV screen with a quick mash of a button. "Secondly, can we talk about Josh? How did he take your ... news?" I wasn't sure what to call it. Even 'nightmare' was too trite for what she'd been through.

"He cried for me. Then he was angry. Furious. Disgusted. He wanted to go find my dad and ... I don't know. Perhaps kill him." Her lips twisted in a lopsided smile. "You know men—they always just want to fix things. It was difficult for him to accept that the past can't be fixed."

I reached for her hand and moved it to my lap. My next question was delicate, and I needed her to feel my support, no matter what the answer was. "Carrie, why is your father still walking free? Why isn't he locked up?"

She didn't answer for so long that I thought she was ignoring the question. I squeezed her hand, trying to convey that it was alright, she didn't need to talk about it, but her words blurted out as soon as I released my grip.

"My mom didn't want to pursue it. She filed for divorce and wanted to just leave it at that. I was young and traumatized. She got me into therapy. Individual for a long time, and then a support group. That's where I met Dean, my high school boyfriend. He'd been through some trauma also, so he was the only guy I was ever comfortable around. My *dad*," she snarled the reference to him, "ran away to Florida, and it just seemed easier, somehow, to put it all behind me once he was gone." Her voice softened as she concluded, "He tried to call a few times. I answered once or twice. He begged for forgiveness. Said he'd changed and knew how wrong he'd been. He's remarried. I don't even know her, but I know she doesn't have kids. I never thought I'd have to see him again. I didn't even tell him about my cancer, but I guess my mom did. Or one of my brothers."

"Your brothers still talk to him? Don't they know what he did?"

"They know. And no, I don't think anyone still talks to him regularly. My mom probably only told him about my cancer in case, you know, I didn't live through it. But my brothers, I think they must all suffer from a form of survivor's guilt. They don't know how to approach me or deal with me. I feel like I'm the black stain on the family, and they just want to wish me away."

"You know that's not true. The 'black stain' is him, all of them! Not you. They didn't stop him, and they chickened out of reporting him. You were just a child! Whatever blame there is, none of it is on you." I gently rested my head on her bony shoulder. "And Carr, don't push Josh away. He's been such a blessing in your life. Let him love you. You know he does."

We sat in the same spot for far too long, until the growl of her tummy reminded me it was getting late and neither of us had eaten. The oatmeal was, indeed, congealed, and I scraped it into the trash and left the pot to soak while I made grilled cheese sandwiches. Carrie's appetite was gradually improving since her chemo had ended, and her hair was patchily growing back around her hairline. Radiation would end the week before Christmas—another blessing. While she'd be weak and feel as though she had a severe cold, according to the doctor, we could start the new year with her cancer almost entirely a thing of the past.

If only the rest of her awful past could be wiped out the same way.

Chapter Twenty-three

Couple number one accepted the counteroffer that evening. I hadn't wanted to leave Carrie, so she and I were folding laundry when I got the call from Vicky. Relief coupled with root-lessness washed over me. The last ties to my home state were being broken. I checked flight options, then decided to wait a few days and look again on Tuesday, when prices tended to drop.

Later that night, Micah and I were talking about the piano when he suddenly snapped his fingers. "You know, last Thanksgiving, Paul's wife, what was her name? Alison, right?" I nodded. "She played for us before dinner. Do you think they might be interested? I heard Paul say they don't own a piano, but Alison definitely had skills."

Contemplating for a moment, it occurred to me my mother's address book was still in a box in the corner of the dining room. Nine o'clock at night might be too late to phone them, so I asked Micah to remind me to reach out to them in the next couple of days.

But it wasn't too late to check on Carrie before bed. I still felt uneasy leaving her alone for the first time since her fainting episode. She answered my call like she'd read my mind. "Elle, I'm fine. It's been three weeks since I finished chemo."

She was stronger, but now I was concerned about her mental state. "Did you at least text Josh?"

"No. That's what taking some time apart means."

"Okay, okay. I'll let it go. But from what I see, it may be you who is struggling with Josh's newfound knowledge more than he is."

Lying next to Micah that night, I asked him how Josh had behaved during their basketball game. "Carrie asked Josh to give her some space because something major about her past came to light the other day. Was he okay when you saw him?"

"He wasn't himself, but whatever is going on, he didn't want to talk about it. His game was off, but it was our first time playing. He got angry a few times when he missed shots, and that seemed out of character. Do you think we should get involved or just let them work it out?"

"It's hard to say. But Carrie really needs him right now. Even if she won't admit it."

Carrie had given permission for me to tell Micah what was going on, and it would have been odd if he was the only one not to know. Her story started to flow out of me, and I couldn't stop until I'd revealed all I knew. Seeing my own horror echoed in Micah's expression brought tears to my eyes.

He laid back, stunned, when I told him about meeting Mr. Stephenson on Thursday and how he'd approached Carrie with such a charade of caring about her well-being.

"How could any father do that to his daughter? It's inhuman. I can't even fathom how scarred she must be. If we had a daughter, she'd never know anything but love from us. What kind of man would intentionally destroy his own child like that?"

My head lay on his chest and I felt his heart racing as he processed the thoughts filling his mind. It was an abhorrent situation, and I could only guess how Josh was dealing with it. So many of Carrie's comments, reactions, and introverted ways were making sense to me now. The way she'd kept her distance from college boys, her reluctance to go home for school breaks, her vagueness when we talked about our growing up years. I desperately wished I could go back and insist that she join me for every trip I'd made to Wisconsin.

Our soft murmurs faded, and eventually the lack of sleep from the previous night, as well as the emotional turbulence of the day, caught up with me. I fell asleep pressed against Micah with our fingers loosely laced, dreaming of a daughter he'd talked about loving.

I called Carrie at eight the next morning when I would have been arriving at her house. She'd made me promise to grant her some independence and managed to convince me of her improved spirits. I agreed to give her some time to relax before coming by and rolled over to go back to sleep.

Unfortunately, my brain was awake. After tossing and turning, I decided to see what Micah was up to. The house was silent as I emerged from the bathroom. Where he could be so early on a Sunday? I glanced out of the living room window and noticed his truck still in the driveway.

Mystery unsolved, I padded to the kitchen to make coffee. Movement caught my attention when I shuffled past the back door that led to the patio. Bypassing the coffeemaker, I peered through the blinds, glimpsing Micah on the glider. His eyes were closed, and his lips moved in a silent monologue. I was curious but decided to give him a minute before joining him. The brisk morning required a hot beverage just as much as I craved the caffeine. Before the cup finished brewing, I heard the latch quietly disengage, and Micah slipped in behind me.

"You're up! I hope I didn't wake you."

"I was going to join you if you were staying out there. How did you sleep?"

"Honestly, not great. You were right—hearing about Carrie made it difficult. I know I said we should let Josh and Carrie work things out themselves, but I don't think I can sit by and watch them break up. Josh said something when we talked about the Martine thing that makes me believe he's in love with Carrie. It's a tricky situation, but they're good for each other."

I noticed that even speaking Martine's name caused his eyes to dart away, but she was being reduced to just a brick we tripped over rather than a wall between us.

Although not as amusing as playing matchmaker, we devised that I would get Carrie to agree to see Josh, and Micah would try to meet up with him today. If it worked out, the four of us could be having dinner by tonight.

After a quick shower, I donned jeans and a turtleneck and told Micah I was heading to Carrie's. He had already texted Josh to see if he wanted to meet for coffee but hadn't heard back yet. Micah seemed more relaxed now than earlier when he first came back inside, so I gently inquired before I left, "When you were on the patio, what were you doing?"

He blushed and rubbed the back of his neck. "I don't really know. Praying, I guess. I just need help figuring some things out." He shoved his hands into the pockets of his athletic shorts. "Helping Josh is only a temporary reprieve from thinking about work. Of course, I realize that my issues are rather insignificant compared..."

To Carrie.

"Comparison is a road we shouldn't go down. But I do think what any of us go through is meant to grow our faith. Maybe God uses both the good and the bad to bring us closer to each other, and ultimately, to Him." I paused, unsure where the words had even come from. I hadn't looked at any of our issues that way before now. I was starting to sound like my mother.

For a moment, I considered suggesting we look for a church together. Sunday mornings always made me feel that way—like I was missing the routine from my growing up years.

But I kept the thought to myself. Instead, I brushed Micah's cheek with a quick kiss. My thoughts about church reminded me I would probably not be able to catch Paul and Alison until later in the day after their service let out.

At Carrie's, I wasn't sure how to bring Josh into the conversation without annoying her. I bided my time, searching through her pantry for ingredients to make a cake to celebrate the end of her chemo.

"It's such good news, and we didn't get to revel in it as we should have. So, today we bake, and I'll help you with any big chores you might have difficulty with since..." I hesitated. I'd started the sentence intending to point out that she wouldn't have Elizabeth, Leslie, or Tina from the home health agency here anymore. But the blanching of her lips, the only feature that held much color, jerked me back. Unless she agreed to see Josh, he was who she'd really be missing.

"Cake sounds good." Carrie seemed determined to clam up when it came to Josh, and she helped me gather the rest of the ingredients in silence. After raiding her pantry and fridge, we decided on a Sock-It-To-Me cake, one that I'd grown up making with my mother.

As she grabbed the sour cream and eggs and preheated the oven, I measured the oil and sugar in with the cake mix. Instructing her on the cinnamon and nut mixture for the middle was our only conversation until she slid the Bundt pan into the oven. Setting the timer to go off in an hour, I finally decided that I'd have to be less passive to get Carrie talking to Josh by this evening.

"I'm ready to text Josh."

Carrie's words stopped me just in time. "Thank goodness, because I was about to give you a pretty stern lecture." I laughed, then caught myself. "Unless you're texting to break up with him. Carrie, tell me you're not gonna do that!"

She laughed ruefully. "No, I'm not breaking up with him. I just think he's had a few days to process everything, and it is probably time for us to talk about if he wants to keep seeing me. C'mon, Elle. You have to admit, this was a jaw-dropper. I've known you for four years and didn't even tell you."

I searched her eyes. "I've been thinking about that. I suppose that it wasn't something you wanted to bring up, but, Carr, if your father hadn't shown up at the hospital, would you have ever told me? I'm your best friend. You can trust me with anything. I've been unloading *my* ridiculous drama on you since we met, and certainly for the last year. I don't want you to think I'm not here for you."

She gave me a side hug, her fuzzy head barely reaching my shoulder as she sat on a barstool pulled up to the island. "I would have told you. Eventually. Probably." She pointed. "Can you pass me my phone? Gah. I don't even know what to say to him right now."

I grabbed both our phones from the far side of the counter. Micah had texted me, *Waiting for Josh to get here. We are grabbing coffee.* The message had come in just a few minutes before. Intending to be sly about Micah's plans with Josh, I responded with a 'thumbs up' emoji in return as I slid Carrie's phone to her. Chances were, Josh would receive her text while he was with Micah and would hopefully not leave Carrie hanging.

She started to type, then backspaced several times, rewording the message more than once. I didn't ask what she'd decided to say, but she turned her phone toward me with a questioning look.

"Is this ok? Do you think it sounds contrite enough?"

I read her screen: *I'm sorry if I didn't give you the chance to say what you wanted to since Thursday. I needed a little time myself to process. Seeing him, and telling you the truth, took a lot out of me, so thank you for letting me have the space we both needed. If you're willing, I'd like to see you. I have a birthday gift for you, if nothing else.*

"Birthday gift? And I think it's perfect. Send it. Is it his birthday?"

"It's coming up. Tuesday of this week. I ordered him something small online a couple of weeks ago. He plays guitar, and I personalized this super cool pick box on Etsy. I'll show it to you later."

"Well, here we are with cake. Maybe he'll want to come over!" I couldn't have planned it better if I'd tried. I was hopeful Josh would agree to see Carrie. I wondered if I could slide a text to Micah to see if he had any insight.

The cake still had a while to bake. We used the time to clean out the refrigerator and wash the resulting stack of dishes. Carrie thanked me more than once for my help. It was more of a distraction for both of us as she waited for Josh to text back, and I waited for Micah.

As I pulled the cake out of the oven, both of our phones vibrated within moments of each other.

Micah's message read: *The smile on his face when he got that text from Carrie blinded me. I don't think I'll be able to see to drive.*

I peered over the top of my phone at Carrie. She had the same smile that Micah had described on Josh as her thumbs flew across her keys in reply.

Chapter Twenty-four

When the guys showed up at Carrie's, we were painting our fingernails as a deterrent from busting into the heavenly-smelling cake we'd glazed and left under a dome on the dining room table. I hollered to them that the door was unlocked as Carrie and I furiously waved our hands to dry the polish.

Micah hadn't seen Carrie since the day my mother passed away, and I recognized his effort to recover when he saw how much she had changed in the previous month and a half. She registered his surprise before he'd wiped it away and reached up to adjust the scarf tied around her head. Leslie had always had a way of getting it to look fashionable, and the way I'd tucked and arranged it when Micah said they were on their way wasn't nearly as chic.

"We heard there was cake!" Micah bellowed to cover his momentary fluster.

Josh followed him, raising two pizza boxes stacked on top of each other. "So, we figured we'd better bring some dinner to go with it."

"Then the cake is for before, or after—or both! You and Carrie choose. We are celebrating the end of her chemo and, apparently, your birthday!" It was the first time we had all been together, and chatter gushed out of us for the next several hours.

Only when I caught Carrie stifling a yawn did I check my watch and discover it was after eight o'clock.

"We should probably be getting home, don't you think?" I suggested to Micah. I assumed Carrie and Josh still had some talking to do, although the way they were bantering and flirting didn't suggest there had been any sort of break in their relationship. He was attuned to her needs, keeping one eye on her during the meal and subsequent dessert.

As I hugged her goodbye and Micah and Josh did their manly fist-bump, we figured out a schedule for checking on Carrie. Between the two of us, someone could come by every day to provide her company. Carrie shooed me out, promising she'd be fine when we weren't there. The widening of her eyes was a signal to me alone that she'd update me on her talk with Josh the next time we spoke.

Making our way toward our vehicles, I informed Micah that Carrie had promised my mom's CR-V was fine to stay in her drive for as long as we needed. "I just want to get through the sale of the house before I deal with it. I'm spread a bit thin," I admitted.

"There's only so much I can do, but I'll help in any way I can," Micah assured me. "By the way, did you ever call the Spencers about the piano?"

"I didn't. I intended to try this afternoon, but now shouldn't be too late. I can call while I'm driving. See you at home!"

After finding the number in my mom's address book, I dialed while giving my engine a minute to heat up. Micah's headlights flashed behind me as he backed out of the driveway and U-turned, avoiding Josh's humble pickup parked on the street. I switched into reverse once Alison's questioning "Hello?" chirped on the other end.

"Mrs. Spencer, hi. This is Elle, Catherine Miles' daughter."

"Elle, dear. What a nice surprise! How have you been? I was so sorry to hear about your mother." Her animated voice was full of compassion, and I thought back on Paul being alone at the funeral. It seemed accusatory to ask why, as a friend of mom's, she hadn't been there, and I wondered if she'd offer the reason without me having to ask.

"Yes, thank you so much. I've been alright. In fact, her house has a buyer, which is sort of why I'm calling you."

When I explained Micah's idea that she might be interested in the piano, she parroted my question to Paul in the background.

After a brief discussion, Alison returned her full attention to me. "We would love to buy it from you, for whatever price you would like. We can make space, and I do love to play." She continued without taking a breath. "When are you coming up? And, Elle, would you like to stay with us when you do? It would be silly to pay for a hotel when we live so close. You know we would love to see you again."

The offer caught me by surprise, but I promised to call her back when I had my flight arrangements. We hung up as I pulled into my driveway, and I considered what a kind gesture it was for Paul and Alison to invite me to stay. A night or two with them could be nice.

I updated Micah on Alison's offer when I walked inside, but was turning on Sunday Night Football and only half answered me. "Micah! I didn't tell you. I found out my mom and Paul used to date."

That drew his attention briefly from the television. "Huh. Does his wife know?"

"I have no clue. I mean, she hasn't alluded to it, but we've never had a heart-to-heart. Maybe I'll find out while I'm there."

With the closing on Tuesday, I'd need the piano moved beforehand. "I'll find a flight for Monday morning. Depending on the timing, I can come back on Tuesday night, or Wednesday, if necessary." I'd ask Vicky about the lawyer's schedule before I booked it.

While Micah watched the game, I searched for piano movers in Madison and requested quotes. Micah's yelling at the television was an ironically comforting sound, and I was sure he appreciated the diversion of cheering for whoever was playing against the Patriots. Even I knew they were everyone's least favorite team.

It was nice to know Micah was home for the foreseeable future. Joe had set him up helping another band develop their tour budget, but odd jobs like that were a step back in his career.

We had no idea what the next few months might hold, but at least our relationship was on steadier ground.

I cringed as I confirmed my selected flight back to Madison for the day before the closing. I would need to be at the airport by six AM, but with the piano movers scheduled for noon, a later flight simply wouldn't work.

Paul and Alison offered to pick me up from the airport and loan me one of their vehicles during my stay, but the use of their guest room was more than generous. Besides, my return flight on Wednesday morning also left insanely early, and I couldn't have asked them to drive me.

With the details hammered out for the trip and the paper-work I would need for the closing sealed in a manila envelope, I was as prepared as I could be for now. Additional documents would come from the escrow office, and our appointment was scheduled for mid-afternoon.

On Thursday, Hank hired my replacement—a young woman straight out of college. After one conversation with Amanda, I was sure she could hold her own. I was working out my schedule for the next two weeks when my desk phone rang two successive chirps, indicating a call from within the building. I answered distractedly, my pen and my mind still hovering over the tasks I was listing.

"Brielle, hello. It's Lorna."

I dropped the pen, then quickly grabbed it back, in case she said anything I needed to make a note of.

"Hi! Hello. What can I help you with?"

"If you have a few minutes, I'd like to chat with you. And I'd love to get out of this office for a bit. How about it? Can we run to the deli for coffee?"

The pressure of everything I needed to finish doubled at being called into a meeting with Ms. Mackenzie. Her suggestion to grab coffee instead of meeting in her third-floor office was probably a positive sign, though. After agreeing to join her in the lobby in fifteen minutes, I ran to the restroom to make sure I didn't look as wrinkled as I felt. Smoothing my hair and touching up my lipstick, I figured things were as good as they were going to get. I dropped by my cubicle for my coat and handbag before taking the elevator to the main floor.

Ms. Mackenzie, *Lorna,* I reminded myself, looked as flawless as always. Her pantsuit today was charcoal, and she'd paired it with a deep teal silk blouse with a bow tied fashionably at the neckline. I'm 5'7", but she still had several inches on me in off-white heels, which perfectly complemented her ensemble. Slipping her arms into a black and white trench coat, she graciously held the door open for me an instant before I reached out, intending to beat her to it. Blushing, I tried to make friendly chatter as we darted across the street in the chilly air.

"It's almost fireplace season—this year went so fast."

She chuckled at my comment. "It seems they all do the older we get, doesn't it?"

The deli was almost empty this time of day, and the staff brewed us a fresh pot of coffee when we ordered. Lorna slipped the young man a ten-dollar bill, well over the amount they charged for coffee, and waved away the change.

"We'll bring them right over, ma'am." He couldn't have been older than twenty, but he gazed at Lorna in awe, and I wasn't sure if he was entranced by her stateliness or an aspiring musician working up the courage to introduce himself.

We chose a corner table that appeared recently cleaned by the streaks of water still marring its surface, and we each doffed our outerwear. Lorna's gaze was direct as she immediately steered us to the purpose of our meeting. "Brielle, you've been with us for a while now. Firstly, I want to tell you your hard work and dedication have not gone unnoticed by Henry or me. I appreciate how you learn quickly and are willing to take on so much."

"Th-thank you," I stammered. I sensed there was a 'but' coming even though her eyes were soft with kindness, and her smile appeared authentic. The young man from the cash register appeared at my elbow, dropping off our drinks along with two of the molasses cookies he'd seen me order innumerable times. With a smile, he disappeared back to his station.

"Ooh, these always did look delicious! I never treat myself, though." Lorna laughed and didn't hesitate to pop open the plastic wrapper encasing the chewy treat. She indulged in the first bite for a moment, leaving me to awkwardly blow at my steaming cup of joe. "Yes, just as scrumptious as I'd imagined."

Her girlish delight at a cookie I splurged on regularly made me hide a grin. I enjoyed them immensely, but she was taking it to a new level with her closed eyes and indifference to the crumbs adhering to her coral lipstick.

She abruptly switched topics, and my grin faded. "I started in this business when I was sixteen, you know. I worked from the time I was in high school until I got my MBA. I took my first industry job only because the hours fit with my school schedule, but once I fell into the music biz, I was hooked. I started Starship because I wanted to pave my own way. I worked hard, experienced failure, and learned as I went. I let my career goals dictate everything else in my world. If it was a choice of A or B, I chose what would lead to greater success professionally. Every time. Do you see where I'm going?"

I nodded slowly, then sighed and shook my head. "I'm not sure I do. Have I done anything wrong?"

"Heavens, no. In fact, you have always done pretty much what I would have done in your shoes. Which is why I wanted to have this talk. You work hard. You're dedicated," she reiterated. "And I don't want you to look back when you're my age and wish you'd applied the same energy to the rest of your life."

I heard my mom's words, Micah's words, even Henry's words echoing with Lorna's. I set my cookie on the napkin already discolored with oils from the confection. Before I could respond, she reached to touch the back of my hand.

"I can't tell you what to do—or what not to do. But I can tell you that working all day and then going home to curl up with more work isn't where I realized I was headed when I made my choices over the last twenty-five years. And I'm still learning to stop and savor the little things." She held up the last morsel of her cookie, then winked as she popped it into her mouth.

I looked down, heart stinging, though her intentions were good. It seemed trifling to point out I was already making small changes in my life, because they were being made out of necessity. Carrie needed help, I needed to wrap up Mom's final affairs, and Micah, well...I was figuring out on my own that marriages require attention to survive.

But with Josh's help, Carrie needed me less. Mom's house was about to be sold, along with her piano, and soon after, her vehicle. My new job would be the sort of thing to draw me into the sixteen-hour days I allowed for myself until recently.

All of this ran through my mind as I now saw Ms. Mackenzie in a new light. She appeared so impeccably put together, with the kind of life I aspired toward. Her hair wouldn't dare frizz, or her slacks dare wrinkle. Her pointy-toed heels wouldn't consider giving her blisters. Her company might not have been the biggest or most coveted, but it was run solely by her, and nothing had been handed to her—she'd built it from the ground up.

Yet, if I understood her correctly, her accomplishments, impressive as they were, hadn't been enough to fulfill her. The coffee turned bitter on my tongue.

I would have never guessed she didn't have everything she ever wanted.

Chapter Twenty-five

Micah and I decided to eat out that night, and spontaneously invited Josh and Carrie to join us. She had more energy these days as she readied herself for radiation. I'd seen sheet music on the table when I visited, and she'd pulled out her cello for the first time since August. She finally had confidence in her life resuming. Despite her optimism throughout the last five months, she'd lost almost half a year of normalcy. We talked by phone every day, but I'd only seen her on Wednesday. Josh was also spending time with her, and they had professed they loved each other. They'd been together nearly a month at this point, and we agreed it had both passed quickly and seemed much longer to us.

I'd gotten so used to seeing Carrie wrapped in a blanket that my eyes initially slid past my stylish friend. She wore a long, richly-toned dress topped with a thick cardigan and cute blocky sneakers. She'd opted to forgo buying wigs and had a beanie slouched on her head with baby hairs peeking out. Now with chemo a month behind her, the side effects were abating, and her soft new fuzz was lighter than the drab tone she'd had before shaving the lifeless strands. Her complexion improved every time I saw her, and the puffiness was being replaced with a healthy roundness to her cheeks. Above all, she was glowing with a serenity I had never witnessed in her, even before the diagnosis.

We'd let Carrie choose the restaurant, and she was eager to go back to her favorite Italian spot. After selecting appetizers, Micah raised his wine glass. "May I propose a toast? To friends and health and new opportunities!"

A moment later, Josh suggested we pray before our stuffed mushrooms and fried zucchini arrived. His prayer of gratitude for those same blessings felt more appropriate than the clinking of glasses had.

Over our hearty meal, which Carrie exuberantly dug into, Josh suddenly cleared his throat. "So, no pressure, but Carrie's coming to my church on Sunday if you two would like to join us."

Carrie's eyes lit up, and she clapped her hands without letting go of her fork, flinging a dab of tomato sauce into space. "Yes! That would be so fun! Please come!"

"So much for no pressure!" I giggled at her enthusiasm and pretended to wipe the stray sauce from my cheek. "I don't see why not. Micah?" I thought it was serendipitous how I so recently wanted to bring up finding a church, and Josh's offer fell right into place.

"Sounds good. Just give us the when and where." Micah's reply wasn't quite as spirited, but at least he was amenable. I was interested to see how he'd react to the service.

I had some time to myself on Saturday while Micah hooked up with Josh and a few other friends to play basketball. Although I'd brought a little work home, my conversation with Lorna kept coming back to me. While putting laundry away, my attention was drawn to my mother's journals on the closet shelf. After thumbing through them, I chose a book from two summers earlier.

Clippings from bridal magazines were tucked between pages, including our cake design. Micah and I had gotten engaged that summer and Mom and Carrie were helping plan the big day. Mom tried to talk me into polka-dot bridesmaid's dresses with matching bowties for the groomsmen, and various color choices were paperclipped together. I'd rolled my eyes and decided on a simple moss green and tangerine palette, ideal for autumn.

Tucking the clippings into the back of the book, I began to read the journal entry dated August 24th:

When John and I were wed, the pastor read from Ephesians 5. The scripture commands wives to submit to their husbands, as he should lead her in the same way Christ leads His church. Likewise, a husband is to cherish and sacrifice himself for his wife. This is God's command for marriage and the covenant we take when we commit to spend our life with someone.

I was so afraid to make the wrong choices when raising Elle that now I worry I let her down by not providing an example of godly marriage after we lost John. I adore Micah, and I believe they are in love with each other. But he isn't yet saved. I constantly lift them both up in prayer, even more fervently since he proposed. I know that You have a beautiful plan for their lives and their marriage. Please help Elle to see they need to invite You into their relationship. I know that Elle has to find her own way to You, just like I did—and continue to do. It's not about religion or rules, but a relationship. Falling in love with You leads us to crave time with You and grows the desire to know You intimately. I don't think she has come to that point yet, and no matter how much she wants to marry Micah, I pray they both come to understand that the greatest love story of all is Your love for us.

I had spared my mom the details of my college adventures as I found myself swayed by the people surrounding me, eventually drawn away from church by my shame. Meeting Carrie seemed coincidental at the time, but now I realized how she'd reminded me in her subtle way that I was worth more than cheap dates with frat boys.

When my mom realized how serious Micah and I were becoming, she asked, "What about his beliefs, Elle? Will he lead you, or will he draw you away from God?"

I hadn't known how to tell her I'd left God in Wisconsin and had hardly spoken to Him since.

On Sunday morning, Carrie and Josh were waiting outside the sanctuary doors when Micah and I rushed in a few minutes after the service had begun. We were able to slip in without causing a commotion, as the worship band had begun with an upbeat number that had the congregation on their feet. Josh's church was smaller than Carrie's, but it still required some shuffling to get four seats together.

I looked around, comforted by the voices lifted in praise. There was a holy presence, and I stood on the precipice. Micah stood stiffly beside me, but I observed Carrie and Josh with their eyes closed and hands raised. Several of the songs were updated hymns, and I softly sang along with the next one I recognized.

When the pastor walked to the pulpit, we sat, and the couple in the row behind us gripped Josh's shoulders in greeting. His receding hairline and a slight crepiness to her skin put them a couple of decades ahead of us, I guessed. She smiled at me before turning to whisper in her husband's ear.

The sermon was based on a quote by theologian John Piper. "Love is the overflow of joy in God that meets the needs of others." The pastor's words reflected my mother's spirit, and many of her journal entries echoed in the points he made.

"...And not just meets, but gladly, eagerly, and cheerfully does so. In 2 Corinthians 8:1-4, Paul speaks about the overflowing joy and generosity the Macedonian churches display, despite their extreme poverty. How they gave, even beyond what they were able, and considered it a *privilege* to do so."

I thought about the needs Micah had in our relationship. The needs I had begun to treat as an inconvenience to my schedule and preferences.

"Abundant and overflowing joy in God allows us to relate to others through *His* love rather than our own. Human love is flawed and full of manipulation. It is self-serving rather than sacrificial. We look for what it can do *for* us rather than what we can offer. But the 'sacrifice' isn't negative when it is this kind of love. Instead, it's an honor and a privilege."

Being there for kids in community programs had been that kind of privilege for my mom. And she gave more than just time: meals during vacations, tutoring, school supplies—but not just buying off a list. I remembered the purple backpack with a matching notebook, pen, and binder my mom had dug through the racks and bins for. They were for Anya, a sixteen-year-old whose mom was killed during one of her father's episodes of

PTSD. Mom always searched for a way to show every person she assisted they had a purpose. No one encountered my mother, no matter how briefly, without feeling *seen*. This was overflowing joy in Him happily meeting the needs of others.

Once again, I glanced at Micah. Each time I looked his way, he was focused on his clasped hands. I wondered if he was thinking of all the ways I'd let him down that led him to search outside of our marriage, if not for love, at least to have his more primitive needs fulfilled. Attention, understanding, commonality. All of that leading to the *most* primitive need being satisfied.

He hadn't loved me sacrificially. But neither had I. We had both been serving ourselves.

So, how could I find this joy?

As the sermon wrapped up, the pastor seemed to be speaking directly to me as he walked toward the corner of the stage nearest our seats. "The abundance of generosity the Macedonians were known for wasn't because they had it all! They didn't have it easy. Remember, they were in extreme poverty. Have you ever experienced being broke? I have. Let me tell you, it wasn't fun. In our early days, Millie and I were always worried about the electricity being shut off. Starting a church is not a lucrative endeavor, and it shouldn't be."

He paused to let the chuckles die off. "Joy in God is a result of being free from *focusing on* the worries this world tries to shackle you down with. The joy comes from living with a hope that never dries up and never runs out." He let that sink in as he returned to the pulpit.

"Maybe you're not worried so much about money. Hey! It could happen," he shrugged at the murmurs. "Money isn't the only affliction here on earth. Maybe your lack of happiness with your life is due to a job you don't like. Regret over past choices.

A broken heart. Maybe it's a health circumstance." Josh's knuckle brushed my shoulder when he slid his arm around Carrie.

"This world is not short on troubles, is it? There is almost always something going on that keeps us from being carefree. But our ability to share the love of God by gladly meeting the needs of others isn't based on our own lives going swimmingly. It is based on our pursuit of joy in God—notice I said *pursuit*—that overflows into the kind of uncontainable love we can't help but share. I stress pursuit because you may feel a long way from joyous right now. It may feel out of reach. But going after it—that's the *only* step. All we have to do is hold on to hope, which is where joy in Him is found."

As the pastor closed in prayer, my heart welled up. I was meant to hear this message.

After the service, Josh introduced us to the couple sitting behind us. Will and Celia Hart were, in his words, his honorary uncle and aunt. The couple was excited to meet Carrie, and I got the distinct impression they knew how she fit into the picture by the way Celia reached over the pew to squeeze her and Josh into a combined hug.

When they turned to Micah and me, their eyes lit up and they smiled warmly. They left us on a clear-cut assumption they'd be seeing us again the following Sunday, and Micah surprised me when he responded, "Great! See you then."

After agreeing on a nearby restaurant so we could join Josh and Carrie for lunch, Micah and I walked back to our vehicle. I asked Micah what he'd thought of the sermon.

He chewed his lip thoughtfully before replying. "I've never experienced joy like he was talking about. I think maybe joy comes from purpose. I've never wondered if God had any sort of plan for me personally."

By then, we had reached Micah's truck. I waited, curious where his thoughts were leading. He started the engine and I turned down the radio as a prod for him to continue.

"Maybe I complained about you working so much, but I always admired your focus. I've always made my choices by what was available and easily within reach." He rubbed a finger across the bridge of his nose with the admission. "Being able to charm people has always come easily for me, so that's what I rely on to feel confident."

Micah's cleared his throat. "Anyway, that's not so much about the sermon. But maybe I haven't been able to love you the way you need because I was so focused on what I wanted from you instead of what you needed from me. And when I didn't feel like I was getting what I wanted... "

My chin jerked. Did his affair really come down to my not feeding his ego? But the sight of him wiping his eyes with the back of his hand made the flash of anger subside. I reached over and rested my palm on his leg, willing him to finish his sentence.

" ... I'm so sorry. I just ... I'm really sorry."

I hadn't anticipated my question leading to this. Rubbing his knee, I reassured him we were going to come through this stronger. We decided we should talk more later, and our discussion continued that evening, as well as over the next few weeks.

During one of our conversations, Micah finally brought up how his night with Martine had come to be. I'd always suffered a morbid curiosity about the details, so I waited, perched on my floral-patterned chair in the corner of the living room with my arms squeezing a throw pillow.

"Not long after our Thanksgiving trip, the band had the show in Brooklyn. Several of us went to explore the city during a break. Walking through the snow with Martine, seeing how energized she was by the crowds—it put me in a different frame of mind about her. The venue that night was packed, and she put on one of the best performances I'd ever seen from her. It was like we were drunk on a perfect day, and when the night was ending, neither of us was ready for it to be over."

My stomach twisted in anticipation of where this was going. I didn't want to see it through his eyes. Hated having to relive it. But like a car wreck, I couldn't turn away.

"When she showed up at my hotel room door, someone else took over my thoughts. Took over my body entirely." Micah pressed a white-knuckled fist against his chest as he sucked in a breath, quelling tears.

Part of me wanted to go to him—to close the distance between us, but I couldn't bring myself to make that move. He still owed a penance. The idea of my husband entwined with another woman flooded my senses, and my grace for him was too shallow.

"The next morning, I had nothing but regret, but she was so chill. It was like she didn't see it as a big deal or that it changed anything between us. So much that after a few days, it almost seemed like it *wasn't* a big deal. Then she suggested wrapping up that leg of the tour before the year ended with a quick two days in NOLA. I forgot I already gave you my schedule and thought I could get away with it."

The confusion, fear, and remorse that had cycled across his face the day I'd found out had been as glaring as neon signs. Less obvious was my self-reproach over letting appreciation for the sporadic time we had together flutter away like dandelion fuzz.

"Martine and I . . . there were never feelings involved. I know that might not make it any easier, but it's true. Then she started dating that drummer. At first, I thought she was trying to make me jealous, but she doesn't care enough to do that. She just doesn't like to lose. We were only speaking when we had to, and you've seen how she goes out of her way to cause trouble."

"Elle." His voice broke. "I never stopped loving you, or, at least, what passed for love then. I was getting so frustrated with you using your job as an excuse. We weren't connecting. When I tried to get you to engage in the things I wanted to do, it seemed like you just guilt-tripped me about how busy you were. It felt like an excuse not to spend time with me."

Rising from the couch, Micah came and knelt at my feet. "I see now how selfish I was. I never considered I was only seeing the faults in our marriage from my viewpoint. I didn't even think about how I could meet *your* needs."

I pushed the pillow to the side and fumbled for his hand. I wanted to believe things would be different now, but how could I know? Should I trust his love for me was enough?

He'd confessed to more than just his affair. Sharing the resentment that led to it had been difficult for me to hear, and I could tell it had been hard for him to admit. But there was no healing without pain. No fresh start without scraping out the gunk.

We both needed this clean slate. I was grateful for the chance to show him that I'd always make time for another hug. Another kiss.

From now on, I vowed to myself, *I'll start making time.*

Chapter Twenty-six

We continued to attend church with Josh and Carrie in the following weeks, both of us drawn to the down-to-earth sermons as much as the friendly atmosphere. Thanksgiving was right around the corner, and my new job would start on Monday. I spent the afternoon of my final Friday moving personal items from the second-floor cubicle to my new four-walls-and-a-door office on the fourth floor.

I'd always found it surprising Ms. Mackenzie had chosen the third floor for herself rather than the top of the building. During our coffee meeting, she explained that not only did she prefer being in the literal middle of things, but at one point, the third floor was the "top" of Starship. Back then, the majority of her staff occupied the area Henry now oversaw. Even as her company grew, she didn't see the need for a larger space herself.

The office allocated to me shared a wall with Sarah on one side and the kitchen on the other. I basked in the autumn sunshine coming through the window and considered bringing the peace lily given to me by my former co-workers to fill the empty top of the credenza.

I stepped onto the elevator carrying a box of office supplies. Raul was already inside, his presence making the car feel small.

"Getting settled? Need anything?" he boomed.

I needed to scratch my nose and my hands were full, but he couldn't help with that, so I answered, "I'm good." The elevator slowly rose. I wriggled my face, trying to alleviate the itch. Raul raised an eyebrow.

"Oh! Don't forget, I'll be gone few a few days after Thanksgiving. I have the closing on my mother's house."

He gestured for me to go ahead as the doors slid open. "That's not a problem. We'll hit the ground running when you return." With a nod, he went left while I went right.

I'd left my phone in my cubicle and came back to a missed call from Micah, and moments later, the indication of a voicemail. "Hey, hope you're having a good afternoon. I got called into Joe's office about twenty minutes ago. Jonathan, the bass player, talked to him. I didn't ask him to, but he said he couldn't stay quiet. Apparently, Martine had been spreading lies even before all this went down and has continued to do so. He said she told everyone in the band she was going to ruin me. Anyway, if you can, call me when you get this."

I glanced around. Although it was a quarter after five, I wasn't alone. My team had thrown a going-away lunch for me that afternoon, and it had taken up more time than we'd planned. No one was quite ready to wrap things up for the day. It would be better to call Micah back during my drive home rather than sneaking it in now.

Making one last check of all my drawers, I wrote a quick "Welcome" note on a generic card and poked it into the corner of the over-used bulletin board. Amanda's work email wasn't active yet, but I had a draft saved with notes of everything I had been working on to send her on Monday. Laying my coat and bags in the office chair I'd occupied for the last two and a half years, I made the familiar trek to Henry's office. His side of a jovial phone exchange sounded as though it was concluding.

I hovered in the doorway, not quite sure how to thank him for all he'd done for me. Henry didn't remain seated but pushed himself up and pulled me affectionately into a hug. "So, this is it, kid."

"This is it." I swallowed around a lump forming in my throat. "You know, I worked under Donovan and Erica, but I look up to you, and I want to thank you for giving me this opportunity. I learned so much from everyone, and I never could have made it through this last year…." I paused, then started over. "A lot happened this year, and this job gave me a reason to keep going. Henry, I have to tell you, I always imagined my dad was like you. I always wanted to make you proud."

"You did, and you always know where to find me." I noticed a glassy sheen in his eyes. "You're like the daughter every dad wishes he had." He cleared his throat, determined to cover with the slightly grumpy veneer he tried to hide behind. "You'll do great, kid. Raul is lucky to have you."

With a last embrace, I promised to check in with him before the Thanksgiving break. After gathering my belongings from the cubicle, I made one more pass to say goodbyes to Shawn, Erica, and even Donovan.

Donovan was also putting his coat on and rode the elevator down with me. As the doors slid closed, we both began to speak.

"Well…"

"Well…"

He grinned and gestured for me to continue.

"I just wanted to thank you," I started.

"That's funny. I was going to say the same."

I fiddled with the PopSocket on my phone. "Are things any better?" I hadn't brought up anything about his personal life in the last few weeks. In exchange, he hadn't brought up anything about mine. It turned out, we worked pretty well together when we kept things purely professional.

Donovan shot me a glance out of the corner of his eye. "Actually, I'll be spending Thanksgiving with Knox." He paused, then finished, wonder in his voice, "And Caitlin."

Genuine happiness for him flooded over me. "Oh, Donovan, that's amazing!"

We stepped off the elevator and I experienced a tug of the old awkwardness as I tried to figure out how to recap the time I'd worked for him.

He beat me to it. "I can't wait to see all the great things you'll do." Donovan's Bruno Magli sneakers carried him away before I could reply.

I dove into the protective confines of my car. Fall was turning into winter early this year, and if it was this cold here, I could only imagine what Wisconsin would be like by December.

Micah didn't pick up when I called him back, and I was almost home when the Christmas music I was singing along to was interrupted by his ringtone—"Livin' the Dream" by Drake White. I navigated with my thumb to answer the call through the car speaker and started by letting him know I was a few minutes away.

"I'm not home yet. Not sure when I'll be back. There's this new band looking for a manager—a little country duo—and they're here at the office. They're fairly low-budget. I think Joe was going to push me to take them on to keep me around, but then this meeting he had with Jonathan might have changed things. He's been trying to reach Martine by phone ever since, but she's not answering. Which, of course, is not helping her any."

Shaking my head, I agreed with him that Martine was biting the hand that fed her. She could leave and find a new management company, but the mature thing to do would be to 'fess up to her deceit and try to work things out. She had a contract, and running would only cost the band money. And time. They were working on their second album, but they had to stay relevant and not lose momentum. She should know better than to do anything to delay the release, not to mention their next tour.

After hanging up with Micah, I stopped to see Carrie. She was doing well with her radiation and had begun driving herself. She played her cello a little every day, intending to resume practices with her orchestra by spring. Radiation was fatiguing, at best. Although she'd finish before Christmas, she would continue to feel run-down, likely for a few months into the new year. But she'd begun talking about *when* she'd rejoin her orchestra's performance schedule, rather than *if*.

Carrie was in the kitchen putting away groceries when I stopped in her entry to unzip my boots. I pitched in, as familiar with her home as I was my own. Rescuing one of the small round pumpkins that had started to roll off the countertop, I joked, "I guess we should talk about the holidays since you're buying props."

"Those aren't for show! I want to make pies, and if I'm going to do it, I may as well go for the real deal instead of canned filling."

"I can't help you there. Pies are not my specialty. But, since we're hosting our first holiday, let's plan the rest of our menu. I can't believe Thanksgiving is next week. We haven't even ordered a turkey!"

Micah and I had tried alternating trips between his family and mine. We'd both preferred holidays with my mom over going to North Carolina. I guessed we would spend some future Christmases there, but we had acknowledged after our first visit that the day and a half with his parents dragged on. He said he never knew how staid they were until he compared them to Catherine. Micah complained that while the three of us at Mom's was a party, five—including his younger brother, Sam— at his parents' was tedious by comparison.

His parents liked me, at least. Maybe they appreciated my career-mindedness, which the conversation kept coming back to, no matter how I tried to avoid being the center of attention. The dynamic between his mother and father was polite, but it was like they'd run out of things to say to each other after thirty years together. I'd like to think my parents wouldn't have been that way. And I'd really like to think Micah and I won't.

Regardless, Carrie wasn't leaving Nashville, and I'd over-heard Josh tell Will and Celia, the couple from church, he wouldn't be joining them for Thanksgiving this year.

After chatting with Carrie for almost an hour, I let her get on with her preparations. She was making a romantic dinner for Josh, and I didn't want to be hanging around when he arrived. We arranged to get together for grocery shopping the next day and agreed to cook and eat at my house on Thursday.

Micah still wasn't home when I pulled into the driveway, and I checked my phone to make sure I hadn't missed a text from him. My screen showed nothing but the wallpaper photo, which I'd recently updated to a shot of my mom and me from my wedding day. She wore navy blue with an over-the-shoulder corsage of hellebores, lisianthus, and strawflowers. I had the same flowers interspersed in my intricately woven braid. We were facing each other, laughing through tears, in the shot captured by Carrie before the ceremony.

It seemed a lifetime had passed since that moment.

Once inside, I changed into yoga pants and a hooded sweat-shirt of Micah's. It still smelled faintly of him, my favorite unnam-able scent—a blend of soap, pine, and leather. With time to kill and, for once, no work peeking out of my satchel, I reached for the red journal, which encompassed September of 2004.

Uneasiness wrinkled my brow when I looked closely at the cover. It was splattered with stains, and I could vividly imagine my mother clutching this book to her chest, rocking back and forth in the throes of the deepest grief. I almost put it back on the shelf, but I'd been battling the urge to confront it ever since the first church service we had attended with Josh. My mother had discovered a joy in God that transcended the suffering of that time in her life.

I craved a taste of that, and this was the way I hoped to find it.

When Micah arrived home hours later, he found me lying on our bed surrounded by used tissues. He halted in the doorway, his brows rising in concern. It occurred to me his long day at work didn't need to be made worse by my current state, and I grabbed a fresh Kleenex from the box to use as a bookmark. With a shuddering breath, I swung my legs to the side of the bed, gathering the tear-soaked tissues into a wad while trying to convince him I was alright.

Warily, he came toward me and tucked a loose strand of hair behind my ear. "I'm sorry for getting home so late. Do you want to talk about...whatever this is?" His eyes swept over the rumpled bed and splotchy pillowcase before landing on the stack of books, which now included all three of the journals from July 2004 until February 2006.

I shook my head, not yet trusting myself to speak without dissolving into more tears. He followed me to the hall bath, where I splashed my face with water. I was mortified at my appearance in the mirror. "I was trying to find my mom's joy, believe it or not." I sniffled again. "I'll explain later. Tell me what happened at work."

I had no idea it was after nine o'clock. I remembered a hunger pang not long after I opened the first journal, but soon I was caught up in that book, and then the next, and food was the last thing on my mind.

Micah grabbed a selection of cheeses, smoked and cured meats, and olives from the fridge. I sliced a day-old baguette, drizzling it with olive oil before sliding it into the oven for a few minutes to mask the slight staleness.

Despite the hours he'd spent with Joe and the country duo, Micah's news regarding them was brief. He'd confirmed managing a two-month tour, with the first show early in January. They were planning on two or three gigs a week, weekends only, and it would pay less than half of what he'd been making. So, low pay, and his duties would include production management, accounting, promotions, and any other hat he could wear. The upside was, per Joe, he'd come back to take on an even bigger tour than Still Waters' previous run had been.

"And, speaking of Still Waters, Martine showed up in Joe's office while I was with the new guys. I didn't see her until she was storming out. Unfortunately, she saw me too." Micah didn't seem to know what to do with his hands, tugging an earlobe, then loosening his watchband.

"What happened?" I didn't like how fidgety he got when her name came up.

"Oh, you know. Veiled threats and general nonsense. Joe let me know afterward that he's canceling Still Waters' contract. They had been planning to start their next tour in March. I already started bookings, some of which required down payments." He threw up his hands. "No longer my problem, I guess."

I swiveled the hors d'oeuvres platter to bring my favorite BellaVitano cheese closer. Tucking my toes under Micah's thigh, I contemplated the news. "I guess she got what she had coming to her. I just feel bad for the rest of the band." I brushed bread-crumbs onto the floor while vowing to vacuum first thing the next day. "So, you ready to hear why I was such a mess when you got home?"

Sharing what I'd read in my mom's journals that evening was heart wrenching. On the night of September 28th, she'd finally opened her journal. It had been one week. Seven days without her husband, and forever to go. Chaotic words tumbled out of her—all the things she wanted to say to my dad: How she'd never stop loving him. That she'd hidden his favorite white button-up after mistakenly washing it with new blue jeans. That some of her favorite things about him were when he danced her around the kitchen and how he paid attention when she rambled. That what she'd miss the most was him playing with her hair while they were falling asleep because she knew he was thinking about her.

Her writing was ripe with longing and heartbreak, and I realized they had a faith and love that bound the fibers of their spirits. In their fourteen years together, they had experienced the greatest bliss and deepest tragedy. I recounted her words, numbing the emotions that had already dragged me under tonight. Her tears over losing him had lasted days, and then longer, with Mom shut into her room and family and friends coming to take care of me and sit with her.

I only vaguely recalled the flurry of new activity the following week and strangers in blue uniforms rushing into the house, then carrying my mother out. It was the end of October before she wrote about losing Brianne that Thursday. She described the unequivocal horror of enduring labor and delivery for a stillbirth. Of holding my sister's lifeless body, begging her to take just one breath. The death of her husband blended with the loss of the tiny newborn, yet more than doubled the anguish. I still couldn't wrap my head around the agonizing image.

My mom grew to steadily depend on scripture passages with daily, and sometimes pages-long, journal entries. I paraphrased some of the Bible verses she'd relied on, all the while carefully searching Micah's face. Was he receptive to the Word? Was he listening? "I think the one verse that indicated a turning point for her was the beginning of Psalm 40. It said, 'I waited patiently for the Lord; He turned to me and heard my cry. He lifted me out of the slimy pit, out of the mud and mire; He set my feet on a rock and gave me a firm place to stand.'" I still had Micah's attention, so I continued.

"She took that to mean God didn't leave her to pull herself together and dig herself out of the pit. Instead, He showed mercy and picked her up to place her on higher ground. The verse promised God would give her a new song, a song of praise. I think that passage led her to see He doesn't expect us to be strong enough on our own. She always said the quote people use—that God never gives us more than we can handle—isn't true. If we could manage everything, we wouldn't need Him. Now I see what she meant. She didn't have to figure out how to be okay. She just had to cry out to Him, and He would lift her out of the infinitely dark place she was in."

Micah reached for my hand. I had never imagined one day I'd be sharing scripture and thoughts like this with my husband. In another entry I'd read tonight, my mother had thanked God for blessing her with a Christ-centered marriage. She wrote that she could praise Him because John was a citizen of heaven, and she'd see him again.

And, although I didn't tell Micah, in so many of her journal entries, this was what my mother had prayed for us to find: a relationship that would transcend this earthly plane.

Chapter Twenty-seven

The first two weeks of my new job were skewed due to the holiday and my scheduled trip. Raul provided me with a list of showcases to attend when I returned, and Sarah showed me the contracts various labels required. By Wednesday, I was looking forward to the days away. This side of he business was quite different from the one I'd left.

Our Thanksgiving was a success. The turkey was perfectly roasted, and Carrie's pies were delectable. I made my mother's cornbread dressing, which had been her mother's recipe, and her mother's before that. My first taste when it came out of the oven left me sliding to the kitchen floor in sobs. The nostalgia of the familiar smell and the blend of flavors hit me hard, as did the realization I'd never experience another holiday with my mom.

My aunt Jan wasn't distant, but her career, husband, and teenage son kept her schedule full. We traditionally only exchanged phone calls and gift cards for birthdays and Christmas. My dad's parents had lived in Mississippi, but neither lived long enough to see their son become a father himself. However, looking around our dining room table, I was thankful for the new family surrounding me and the memories we were making.

Before I knew it, it was Sunday afternoon, and I was choosing my heaviest sweaters and lined wool pants for the trip to

Wisconsin. I called Alison Spencer to make sure they had cleared space for the piano and slid the sheaf of legal paperwork into the inside pocket of my luggage. In a nod to my mother, more so than because my own case had the broken wheel, I packed my attire for the trip into her colorful, smiley-faced carry-on.

As I landed on Monday, the pilot announced, "Welcome to Madison, where the high for today is a pleasant thirty-five degrees." A trace of snow lingered, wind blowing it in skids across the asphalt.

I hurried to the rental booth to pick up the keys to my reserved vehicle. Following the signs to parking lot A, row 6, I bypassed black, blue, and silver cars to stop short at my assigned space. The Kia Soul in front of me was the color of mustard, and I had to snicker. "Thanks, Mom. I don't know how, but I'm sure you had a hand in this!"

When I pulled into the driveway that had been my mom's, I had thirty minutes until the piano movers were scheduled to arrive. I slung my purse over my shoulder and alighted in the driveway. I was so focused on making sure I had traction on the film of ice, I didn't immediately notice my mother's neighbor, Mae, in her front yard. When she called out to me, I yanked the plaid scarf away from my mouth to answer, picking my way carefully across the frozen ground.

"Elle, I thought maybe you were your mom in that yellow car!" Mae was tickled, but there was a hint of sadness behind her smile. "Is today the day? I saw the 'sold' sign go up."

"No, it's tomorrow, but I'm having her piano picked up shortly." I bent down to hug the fragile woman and could barely feel her through all the layers she wore. "How have you been? How's Tom?"

"He's fine—we both are. Gearing up for another long winter. These old bones don't like them as much as they used to."

Encouraging her to go back inside her toasty home, I assisted in filling the two birdfeeders, which immediately attracted an array of cardinals and finches. She made her way down the side of her house to store the birdseed in her enclosed patio. I watched her round the corner and made a mental note to pick up a dessert of some sort and drop it off while I was in town. She'd been a wonderful friend to my mother in the years they'd been neighbors, and it devastated Mae to find Catherine on the day she died.

I let myself into the house, noticing the scent of lemon no longer lingered. The piano stood alone in the front room, a witness to two decades of our lives, and I was grateful it was staying within my mom's circle of friends. Still, disappointed to be letting it go, I lifted the fallboard, resting my thumb on middle C.

Unexpectedly, a complex melody came to mind, and from my mind to my fingers, without me being aware I knew it by heart. I let the keys tell me where to go next, reaching the end before ever recalling the name of the song. As the last note faded away, footsteps shuffled behind me, and I glimpsed the piano movers standing on the other side of the screen beyond the door I'd left cracked open.

It took the professionals less than half an hour to load the instrument into the back of their truck. I verified Paul and Alison's address for them and let them know I wouldn't be too far behind as they left to deliver the piano to its new owners.

Once they backed out of the drive, I walked through the rooms one last time. I expected a rush of maudlin sentimentality, but this hadn't really been my home. I had memories, but the empty walls and floors no longer reflected Mom's hospitality. My rumination amounted to making sure the cleaners had done a thorough job and that the pipes weren't frozen.

Piano movers are efficient. They left before I arrived at the taupe stucco residence with the house number in extra-large script on the post of the arched entry. Unsure of my hosts' morning routine, I parked at the curb and carried my bags the length of the drive and up the front steps. Paul answered the door before I finished knocking. I spotted Alison bent over, already perusing the music books stored in the piano bench.

Their home was large and comfortably decorated, with collectibles displayed in glass hutches and layers of texture formed from blankets and throw pillows. It gave a more cluttered impression than my mother's house but fit Alison's bustling personality. Even now, she fluttered toward me, one hand still holding sheet music, and halfway through her greeting as she embraced me.

"You must be freezing walking all the way up from the street. Why didn't you park closer? Well, never mind. You're here now. How are you, dear? How was the trip?"

"Hi, Mrs. Spencer. Thank you so much for having me. The trip was good. Uneventful, which is always important when flying."

"Please now, it's Paul and Alison, right, honey?" She reached for her husband to draw him into the conversation. "We are more than glad you could stay with us. The timing is perfect—we just got back yesterday from spending Thanksgiving with my sister's family."

"Oh, where does she live?"

I noted that Paul hadn't uttered a word other than 'hello' as he stepped back to usher me past the foyer. Still, his eyes hardly left my face. I was flustered, having learned what I did about his relationship with my mother. I tried not to imagine him calling for her input on marrying Alison. However much it couldn't be helped, he'd broken my mom's heart.

As Alison told me about their Thanksgiving, I followed her through the house and up the staircase. Paul waited in the living room as she showed me to their guest room, which was decorated with a collection of antiques, including a vintage Singer sewing machine table. I set my overnight bag on the large chest pushed up against the foot of the bed and agreed to join them downstairs after freshening up.

I sank onto the edge of the soft mattress, craning my neck to inspect my lackluster reflection in the ornate mirror above the dresser. I could lie back and fall asleep if given the opportunity. Reluctantly I rallied, shaking out the travel creases from my outfit for the next day as I unpacked, and took my small toiletry bag to the bathroom Alison had spruced up for my stay.

Somewhat refreshed, I headed back downstairs. I found the couple in the kitchen, Alison's prattle guiding me to the cheerful room. Her hands were wrapped around a mug covered in a crocheted cozy. A box of various hot teas sat open on the counter in front of her.

"Oh wonderful, you found us!" She was so enthusiastic I suppressed a laugh. "Paul is having coffee, but I only drink tea. We also have hot chocolate or juice, if you prefer. What can I get you?"

I scanned the flavors of teas in her metal tin and selected spearmint. "As much as coffee would recharge me, this sounds yummy. I've been up since five, and I will probably try to go to bed early tonight to make up for it."

"Tea, it is! The water is still hot." She busied herself preparing it, waving away my insistence I could do it on my own. It was kind of nice to be fussed over. That thought reminded me again of my mother, which led me back to her relationship with Paul. There was no way to bring it up delicately, so for now, I sat and made idle chitchat. Paul was opening up, more comfortable with having me as a guest in his home. It wasn't long before the topic of my mother's funeral came up, and the couple exchanged a glance before Alison reached for my hand.

"I need to tell you why I wasn't at her service, Elle. I'm sure you felt it was impolite of me not to attend."

"No, of course not, Alison. That day was such a blur for me. I didn't even think about it until my husband asked about you."

Alison had pulled a stool up next to mine at the breakfast bar, and Paul had his back to me as he refilled his mug. The smell of the fresh coffee he was pouring tempted me again, but I sipped carefully at the steaming cup of mint tea as it chased away the last of the chill from my stiff fingers.

Paul was taking an inordinate amount of time to make his coffee, and when he finally turned, his face was resolved. He nodded at Alison, and they had a silent exchange, the way married couples do.

"Elle," he began, "I think it's time for me to tell you how I got to know your mother."

I considered sharing what I'd read, but I wanted to hear things from his side, so I didn't interrupt.

"Quite a while back, well before Alison, I knew Catherine." His eyes took on a faraway look, and even if he hadn't thought of those days in a long time, he was now seeing all those years ago clearly in his mind. "You were about thirteen when I met her, and she was working at the hotel, if you remember. I admit I was smitten with your mother from the first moment."

I glanced at Alison, wondering if she'd heard this version before. She surprised me with the soft smile playing around her lips.

"We dated for a couple of months, but your mom was always worried about how you'd feel about her bringing me into the picture. When she started to pull away, I gave her space, and we tried to just be friends for a time. Well, we were both in love, I think, even if we weren't ready to admit it then. We stayed close, only going out together in groups. She finally introduced me to you during one or two of those church get-togethers. You were such an ornery thing back in those days, never wanting to hang around us old fogies." His guffaw came close to snapping the tension I felt listening to him talk about how much he'd loved my mom right in front of his wife.

He continued, "Over the next year or two, Catherine and I tried again. You were getting older, more mature. She thought maybe you'd be alright if we started to see each other openly. But, although the attraction wasn't broken between us, she always had other things going on. Raising you, of course. And she started college. We both decided maybe it wasn't meant to be."

I watched his dark eyes as he spoke. He didn't sound concerned about hurting Alison, and while she hadn't interrupted, the same gentle smile hadn't left her face.

"Then, Alison came along."

Her grin widened, and she took over the tale for the moment. "He was so handsome I had to introduce myself. I'm sure you won't be surprised, but I asked him out first. He told me almost immediately he was not quite over someone else." Her eyes left his and rested on mine. She must have seen something there because her brows knit together, and she turned to give me her full attention. "Elle, we don't want to hurt you by telling you this. Please don't think I stole him from your mother, or he was unfaithful to her. That honestly wasn't the case, believe you me!"

For the first time, I spoke. "No, I don't think that. I have to say, though, I only recently found out about some of this. Some, not all of it." *And also, the other side of the story that included my mom's not-so-happy-ending.* I addressed Alison. "Were you ever jealous? Or resentful? Is that why you didn't come to her funeral?"

"Oh, heavens, no!" Her sparkling eyes widened. "I loved your mother. I honestly did. And it was easy for me to see why

Paul had, too. What they had didn't upset me. The time he spent with your mother had a hand in shaping him into the perfect husband for me."

Once again, she smiled sweetly, first at him, then back at me. "Your mother and I had an understanding. She may have had some secrets about her feelings for Paul, but as time went on and I got to know her, I accepted they'd had a connection, and their friendship was important to them. I trusted her, and, of course, I trust my husband. As far as why I didn't attend the service, his relationship with her ran deeper than my own, and I wanted him to have the time and space to grieve her loss in private. Or, at least, without me hovering."

I sat quietly for a minute. Despite the fact Paul and Alison had no compunctions about speaking candidly about the situation, I still had questions. In the journal entry my mom had written when Paul was going to propose to Alison, palpable emotion leaped off the page. She'd wanted him to fight for her. So, why hadn't he been willing? I couldn't ask him this in front of Alison. I shouldn't ask at all. It wouldn't change the past. But deep down, I wanted to know.

Had my mom not been worth it to him, or had he viewed me as the deal-breaker?

Chapter Twenty-eight

*W*e had a quiet evening with a home-cooked meal Alison wouldn't allow me to help her prepare. Afterward, we relaxed around the comfortable family room chatting, with mindless sit-coms and canned laughter providing background noise. At one point, Alison plinked out Christmas carols on the piano, which was slightly out of tune after its relocation. "Oh, this is going to be fun!" she gushed, flipping through the music book for a song she hadn't played yet.

I tried to stifle my yawns, but around nine o'clock, one escaped, then another a minute later. Paul, observing quietly from the leather recliner where he'd ensconced with a thick book, suggested to Alison that perhaps the music hour should wrap up. With a dramatic sigh, she lowered the lid over the keyboard and arranged the music books inside the bench.

"What time is your closing tomorrow? Do I need to make sure you're up by any particular time?" Alison was in full hostess mode.

"Ali, dear, I'm sure Elle has an alarm," Paul tried to tone down his wife's enthusiasm.

To lessen his chastisement, I convinced Alison the smell of coffee brewing would surely wake me. Since the appointment wasn't until two o'clock, I was planning on a laid-back morning.

"I don't want to disrupt your routine, though, so if you need me to be up or out of the house, it's no problem."

"We will be fine! You do your thing and let us know what we can do to help. Sleep well, and if you need anything during the night, we have night lights on both levels."

I gave her a quick hug, murmuring, "You truly are the best hostess." Waving to Paul, I mounted the stairs, my feet dragging as I wished I were already crawling under the thick quilt.

After I washed up, I called Micah as I piled the throw pillows from the bed into the emptiest corner. In a quiet voice, I apologized for not texting more during the day and shared the greetings the Spencers had asked me to pass along. He said his day had been productive but not newsworthy, and I promised to check in again when I woke up. I immediately fell asleep without setting an alarm.

I slept soundly and late into the morning on the plush mattress. When I checked my phone, it was indeed after nine, and I'd been out for twelve hours. I hoped my hosts didn't think I was a complete slug, and, without sending Micah the text I'd planned, I jumped up and ran to the shower. Piling my hair on top of my head, I washed quickly. Without stopping to apply makeup, I dressed in the wool slacks and blouse I'd left hanging and crept down the stairs.

Alison was washing dishes and didn't hear me coming. She was humming as I stepped hesitantly behind her. After a moment, I cleared my throat, hoping not to startle her. Unfortunately, I did, and the bowl she was washing plopped into the dishwater, splashing a froth of bubbles into the air.

She turned with an eruption of laughter. "Good morning, sleepyhead! I'm so glad you were able to sleep in. Silly Paul started the vacuum first thing this morning, and I was worried he woke you. Let me brew some fresh coffee."

As usual, Alison's sentences tripped over each other coming out, and I smiled. "I can make the coffee." My protests were ignored as she filled the carafe with cold water and hit the start button.

"It won't be but a jiff! And now, what can I get you for breakfast?" She was already pulling eggs, sausage, and a can of biscuits out of the refrigerator. "We also have oatmeal and fruit, or I can whip up some hotcakes..." Her voice was muffled as she rifled around in the back of the fridge, turning back to me with her arms laden.

"Please, you're too kind. I usually just have coffee." I pleaded, but she produced juice, milk, coffee creamer, and two tubs of berries to add to the assortment.

"You can't only have coffee! Besides, if you'd stayed at a hotel, they'd have offered you all this for breakfast also, so pick what you want."

I relented and popped two slices of bread into the toaster before she could do it for me. "I'll have some eggs and berries with toast, then. Thank you so much." I thought that would be the end of it, but when I expected her to return her other offerings to where they came from, instead, she turned to me with three different flavors of jam for my toast.

"Strawberry, cherry, apri-" she interrupted herself, "Oh! Or apple butter, or cinnamon and sugar?"

I gratefully poured a steaming mug of coffee, praying it would help my brain catch up with all she was hurling at me. After I convinced her my needs were simple, I sat with a small plate of toast topped with a fried egg, and a handful of blueberries. She fluttered around the kitchen, wiping and tidying and keeping up a chatter I found surprisingly pleasant.

"Paul went to the store for me. Today's not as chilly as yesterday, but geez-a-loo, I don't want to go outside until it's at least forty degrees! Speaking of, my book club meets this afternoon. We usually do it at seven, but it gets dark so early these days. I'll be home to cook supper, though, and then we'll send you off to bed since you need to be up at the crack of dawn." My ears could barely keep up, but I caught the gist.

I waited until her back was turned before carrying my dishes to the sink to wash them myself. By now, it was going on eleven o'clock, and I needed to finish getting ready. My hair had gotten damp in the shower, and it was going to take some work to tame the waves into an intentional style. I thanked her for talking me into breakfast, considering the long afternoon stretching before me.

Climbing the staircase, I sent Micah a brief text: *Overslept and then got caught up with Alison. Hope your day is going well. Also, can you water the lily in the living room window today? Thank you!*

My phone chimed a short while later, but it was Vicky checking in to say she'd be at the escrow agent's office by 1:30. She sent me the address again, then ended the message with a final note: *The Dales completed their walk-through this morning and found no issues whatsoever. They are going to take excellent care of Catherine's house. Let me know if you need anything. Otherwise, I'll see you before two o'clock for the closing!*

I had a little time to kill once I was fully dressed and made-up. After making sure I had all the necessary documents, I went to find my hosts, who were in the garage. With a blanket wrapped around her shoulders, Alison was directing Paul to boxes of Christmas decorations stored on high shelves.

"Afternoon, Elle." Paul noticed me first as he tugged a jingling box and lowered it to Alison's waiting arms.

"We're a few days behind since we usually do this before the leftover turkey has been eaten, but this is the first chance we've had." Alison's eyes were lit up like a child's at the idea of decorating for Christmas. Paul simply looked like a dutiful husband indulging his wife's whims as he stacked box after box on the floor at the base of the ladder.

"I always wonder where all this stuff is going to go, but every year she makes it work." He shook his head, but I could tell he was good-natured about it.

"Well, I'm heading out. I'm not sure exactly how long I'll be, but if you need me to pick anything up on my way back, please call or text. I'll be glad to grab dinner or anything else you may need from the store."

Alison shooed me off. "Of course not. We have everything we need, don't we, dear?" She didn't wait for an answer from Paul, and he didn't bother with one. "You know where you're going, right? I'm sure you can find it with your phone. We'll be praying it goes well! Your mom would be so proud of how you managed everything."

I had starting backing away, but her last comment stopped me. I'd hoped many times my mom would have approved of how I was handling her affairs. Alison's words cemented for me that her piano, and now her house, had both been passed on. Her car was the final item needing a new home.

It was the end of an era.

Vicky Miller was waiting for me in the lobby. She had deep red hair, definitely not her natural shade, but as vivid as her personality. Her briefcase, heels, and bold glasses underwhelmed my simple manila envelope holding the sheaf of paperwork and the ankle booties keeping my feet from freezing.

She greeted me with a careful hug that directed her meticulously applied lipstick away from my cheek. "Here we are, about to wrap all this up. How are you? I'm sure this is an emotional time."

"In a way, it is. I can't imagine how I would have ever done this without you. Especially from all the way in Tennessee! Thank you so much for all you've done."

"Anything for my friend Catherine—and anything for you." She switched to all business then, verifying I remembered my portion of the closing costs, copies of the death certificate and trust documents, and the house keys to pass along.

The closing went smoothly. The couple who purchased the house had twin daughters only a few years younger than me who were still in college. They regarded me with compassion when I presented the death certificate. My stack of paperwork was much smaller than theirs, and I was able to leave after signing the first several documents. My early escape allowed me to run by Lane's Bakery to pick up some Kringle, a Danish pastry famous in Wisconsin. Choosing between the various fruit, nut, and chocolate varieties was a challenge. I left with half a dozen, intending to give two each to Mae and the Spencers and take two back home with me.

When I pulled up in front of Mae and Tom's, it was disquieting to park in their driveway and not my mother's. The 'sold' sign had been removed by the Dales' real estate agent when they did the walk-through that morning, and the house was officially no longer my second home. Selecting the Cherry Cheese and Chocolate Fudge flavors that had been boxed together, I carried them to the front door and rang the bell.

I didn't stay long, as Mae and Tom weren't expecting me and were about to sit down for dinner. They were thrilled with the treat, and Mae playfully smacked Tom's hand when he tried to open the box right away. "Dessert, Thomas! You must wait until after supper!"

"It'll be great for breakfast, too." Tom grinned gleefully, and although I wasn't sure if he remembered me, he was noticeably pleased I'd stopped in. With one last hug for Mae and a handshake for her husband, I left with a promise to add them to my Christmas card list.

The sun was almost set, and the yellow Kia was just starting to blow tepid air again when I pulled up to the Spencers' home. Carrying the remaining four pastries, I picked my way up the steep drive.

Not wanting to startle anyone, I knocked softly on the door before trying the knob, which turned freely. Paul was in his leather chair, thick book in hand, and reading glasses perched on the end of his nose. I remembered then that Alison was at her book club.

"Hello, I'm back." Here was an opportunity to talk more about my mom with him, but now I wasn't sure I had the nerve. I unwound the scarf from my neck and stepped out of my boots, shuffling awkwardly at the edge of the living room rug.

"Hi, Elle. Ali says her book club ends at five, but you know her. She always sits around to gab much longer than that. If you're hungry, please help yourself to anything in the kitchen, but she says she'll be home to make dinner."

I lifted the Kringle boxes to draw his attention. "I'm not sure if you like these or have a preference of flavor, but I picked up a couple for you and Alison and a couple to take home. I have Pecan, Apple, Pumpkin, and Raspberry Cheese to choose from."

After laying them on the kitchen counter, I called out that I was going to change clothes. Micah and I had exchanged a few texts during the closing, and I now let him know I was in for the rest of the night. I smiled at his message saying he missed me as I pulled on jeans and a sweater.

Paul was in the kitchen when I went back downstairs, and he sheepishly let on that while he was making us an hors d'oeuvres platter, the Apple Kringle had tempted him. "Is it alright I picked this flavor? We could split it if you wanted it for yourself."

I waved off his apology and filled a glass with water. Together, we arranged pretzels and cubes of cheese on a tray with three more slivers of the Kringle he was relishing. "Don't worry. I won't tell your wife!"

He chuckled at my co-conspiracy and carried the tray to the family room. "How was the closing? Any hitches?"

"Nope, not a one. I think the new family will take good care of Mom's home. They were excited about moving closer to their daughters, who both attend UW-Madison."

Paul helped himself to another piece of pastry, scootching back into his recliner after lifting his book from the seat. To continue the small talk, I asked what he was reading.

"This old tome about World War II—a little light reading," he joked. "I think I've been staring at the same page for the last half hour. These short days make me tired earlier and earlier."

"Not to mention all your hard work carrying in Christmas decorations!" I'd counted at least eight stacked boxes tucked into the dining room when I came downstairs.

He shook his head. "Every year, it seems like there's more stuff than the one before. She knows how to talk me into pretty much anything."

I didn't respond at first. My opening was here somewhere if I could figure out how to take it. After a minute with only the sound of pretzels snapping, I took a small sip of my water. "May I ask you something? Something about my mom?"

He sensed my earnest tone and wiped his fingertips and mouth with a napkin. "Of course. I was wondering if our talk yesterday had sparked any questions."

I couldn't meet his eyes, now more unsure than ever of the propriety of asking this man—in his own home, with his wife due back at any time—why he hadn't tried harder to stay with my mother.

I had to bite the bullet. "Did you truly love my mom? Why didn't you fight for her? Was I that big of a deterrent? Did she never tell you how much she loved you?"

"Whoa, whoa." He pushed his chair out of its reclined position, resting his socked feet on the thick rug. "You said you knew a little about my relationship with her before yesterday. What did she tell you about me?"

I explained about the journals, and he listened without reproof. I even gave him the copy of the photo I'd found of the two of them with her trademark lipstick print on his cheek. When he asked what my impression had been of my mom's feelings for him, I didn't hold back. "It was clear to me she loved you. She genuinely loved you. And if you'd tried harder, she wanted to marry you. It sounds like you took her hesitation as a lack of interest, and I don't think that was the case. She had a difficult time with you marrying... someone else."

I felt like a complete traitor suddenly, having this conversation when Alison had been nothing but gracious toward me. And I wasn't sure why I needed to hear the answers to these questions. What would it change?

He spoke softly, and I had to lean forward to catch what he was saying. "I loved your mom. Very much so. I hope she believed that. And a part of me has had to live with some regrets. No—not regrets. That's an awful word to use. More so, 'what ifs.' Could I have made Catherine happy? I'd like to think so. I would have done my best to be a respectable father-figure to you. It wasn't that I didn't want to try, because I did. But I also wanted to honor her wishes. She knew best what was right for the two of you. And, at the time, she was adamant it wasn't me."

I understood then that Catherine had hurt him, too. There didn't seem to be anything else to say. A moment later, the blustery wind blew Alison in, and all seemed right in their world.

Some things simply are what they are.

Chapter Twenty-nine

I attended an afternoon showcase on my first day back but didn't hear any artists who won me over. I stayed for a few hours, alternately researching other open mic events, and trying to listen for the type of sound Raul and Sarah had encouraged me to seek out.

Something unique, not necessarily perfect, but unforgettable.

An attitude of swagger yet humility.

A marketable look.

The directions made sense in the office but applying them to a series of unfamiliar faces in an unfamiliar setting was like walking on uneven and shifting sand. As the third hour wrapped up, the empty seats and tables around me filled, and I began to feel uncomfortable. The bar was a draw for after-work drinks, and although there'd be more live music starting up, the artists were locally well-known and it was time to head out.

Friday night was the concert Micah had gotten us tickets for as my anniversary gift. With the V.I.P. access he'd scored, we didn't need to rush. We were able to park in the front lot and enter through the short lines right before being escorted to our private section. The evening reminded me of when we were dating. I was dazzled by the seats and star-struck when security led us backstage to meet the singer whose posters had once decorated my bedroom walls.

Driving home afterward, still riding on the high of loud music and the rare date night, I joked with Micah. "Perhaps I'll discover a rising star one of these days. After all, someone heard the magic in Taylor first."

"You're right. Whoever it is, they are just waiting for their big break. Just keep looking."

I wanted to spend some time over the weekend perusing a list of music blogs and *TikTok* videos to suss out what was on the horizon in the industry. Micah offhandedly suggested, "You know, I can help expand your connections."

I nodded. "The next party you invite me to, I'll be there." In this case, his extroversion could definitely come in handy.

On Sunday, we went to church without Josh and Carrie. She'd had four weeks of radiation, and it had worn her down, so Josh stayed with her most of the weekend. We slid into our, by now, regular row with Josh's friends Will and Celia a few minutes before the service began.

The sermon was based on Deuteronomy 6:5. "The NIV translation commands us to love God with all our heart, with all our soul, and with all our strength. The King James Version uses the word 'might' instead of strength. When I try to imagine what this would look like in the literal sense, I think about how I love my spouse. That's a suitable place to start since most of us can relate in some way. Whether it's a lifelong, everlasting love like ours," Pastor Tony grinned at the round of applause, "or a first intense crush. You know the kind: 'I just *can't* live without him!'" Everyone chortled at his impersonation of a dramatic teenage girl.

"When you meet 'the one,' they are all you think about. Have you been there before? You wake up thinking about them. You fall asleep thinking about them. Every time anything happens, you want to tell them first. You want to tell everyone all about them. They have your heart, your entire heart. You 'neeeed' them!" He drew it out, using his teenage girl impression again. Micah and I side-eyed each other. He winked, and my lips twitched.

"But what does it mean to love them with all your strength, or with all your 'might'? For a long time, that word mixed in with the heart and soul part for me. But, I promise, the inspired Word of God doesn't throw any words in for the heck of it."

"The original word has been translated to 'might' or 'strength,' but in Hebrew, the word is 'much' or, as a noun, 'muchness.' I don't know about you, but when I hear the word 'muchness' I think about Alice in Wonderland. There's a quote attributed to Lewis Carroll's character, The Mad Hatter. He says, 'You're not the same as you were before. You were much more … muchier … you've lost your muchness.'"

"So, strength and might—or muchness—is simply this: Everything you have at your disposal. Everything God has given you. Your possessions. Your talents. Your energy. Your attention. What you devote yourself and all your muchness to reflects what you are all about."

What did this say about me? I'd chosen my job over my marriage. I'd chosen my pride over my relationship with my mother. Oh, how I wished I could rewind time.

"I want to take it a step farther. How you interact with the resources in your life—be it money, your job, your free time, your relationships with others—should reflect your focus and intent for your life."

Micah shifted in his seat and rested his elbows on his knees, leaning forward.

"Let's say I, twenty-four, seven, devote everything I have to loving and honoring Millie. I base every decision on what will make her happy. My focus and intent are to love this woman the best I can. I'm not saying I'll always do a perfect job, but my capacity to love is all going toward her. I might surprise her with Chinese food for supper, not knowing she had Chinese food for lunch. The point isn't for me to be perfect, but that my muchness is all about her."

"Then, I get distracted. Maybe it's been a great six months, but now football season has rolled around, and my devotion is a little split between the Titans and the *other* love of my life. Maybe my fantasy football team is kicking butt. I'm less attentive to her on Sundays, Mondays, and Thursdays. She says, 'Tony, I feel like you used to be much more … muchier. You've lost your muchness.'"

"The Titans don't make it into the play-offs, and my fantasy bracket is falling apart. Or, here I am at almost fifty, playing a game of backyard football, and I wrench my back. Now I have time for Millie. Or, if I hurt myself, I *neeeed* Millie." Laughter erupted at the return of the dramatic teenage girl's voice.

"God is commanding us to love him with all our heart, all our soul, and all our muchness. Our career isn't a distraction from Him—its purpose is to bring Him honor. Our possessions are to be used to show Him love, and one way to do that is to use them to show love to others. Our relationships with family and friends and neighbors and strangers are part of our muchness. Taking all we have been given and looking for a way to help others and show our devotion to God is what this verse is about."

Later, coiling my scarf around my neck, we waved goodbyes to familiar faces as we walked with the Harts through the foyer. We were getting to know them better and had learned two weeks earlier that Josh's girlfriend from high school had been their daughter. She'd tragically died after being severely injured in a car accident following graduation. Celia's eyes shimmered while her husband summed up why they considered Josh to be family.

Micah and I hurried through the chilly air toward his truck. Before going home, we stopped by Carrie's to check on her and take photographs of my mom's CR-V, which I was ready to sell. The previous day, Micah had run it through the carwash in preparation for the anticipated sunny weather this afternoon, and I got some great shots for the ad.

Josh jumped up from his seat by the window to let us in before we could knock. He slipped a finger between the pages of the latest Tim Tebow book as he whispered a greeting. "Carrie's finally falling asleep. She had a rough morning."

"I'll be quiet. We picked up lunch for you both. Let me leave it in the kitchen." I stopped to tuck the blankets around Carrie when I passed the couch, and as I stood, I saw Josh nod while handing his copy of *Mission Possible* to Micah.

"I'll get another copy, man! It's a great time for you to read it too, I think. You know, with both of us in this transitional period. It's helping me take notice of the doors God is opening in my life," Josh whispered while glancing over at Carrie, who remained oblivious to our presence.

At home later, I did some research on the CR-V and was pleasantly surprised at the Kelly Blue Book value. My mom had purchased it three years before when it was only a year old, and the mileage was still low. Glancing out of the kitchen window in the twilight at my own older model in the drive, I wondered if I should reconsider putting the banana-yellow vehicle up for sale.

Shaking my head at the idea of keeping the CR-V for myself, I began creating a post. As it turned out, checking items off a list was easy. But letting go of my mother was proving to be a much different story. There was no schedule for that.

Oh, Mom. What I wouldn't give for one more day with you.

Chapter Thirty

Christmas was only ten days away, and I had just a few presents left to buy. We had driven to the tree farm two nights before and chosen a stately white fir that filled the corner of the living room nearest the large window at the front of the house. Because we hadn't bothered to decorate the previous Christmas, we were both going overboard to prove everything was different this time.

I was hyperaware Micah would be heading back out with the new year, gone every Thursday through Sunday for the short stint with the country duo. Following would be lengthier absences on the next tour Joe had promised him. In the meantime, he was occasionally able to join me when I went out scouting, and his presence provided comfort as I tried to embrace my new role.

Unfortunately, the two new artists I'd been excited about had slipped through my sweaty palms. A young man whose bashfulness resulted in a technically imperfect performance at a hole-in-the-wall showcase nevertheless demonstrated smooth aplomb in a series of videos he'd uploaded to *YouTube*. The second was a wall-flowery young woman. Her petite stature and too-long fringe of bangs concealed a powerhouse soprano and innate stage presence. Her voice stopped me in my tracks as I'd started to give up my seat for the burgeoning after-work crowd.

And I'd watched as they were both approached by other scouts before they'd made it off the stage. I'd flicked my business card between my carefully polished nails as I read their lips.

"You've got exactly what I need."

"I hope you're ready. Everyone's going to know your name!"

"I was just about to give up but you're worth all the mediocrity I've had to sift through."

Okay, maybe that's not exactly what they said, but whatever it was, I'd blown it. I needed to grow a backbone, or I'd never bring anyone back to Raul.

Carrie's last day of radiation was the coming Friday. She was still listless and losing weight, and the baby hairs had stopped growing due to her poor nutrition. But we were in the home stretch and eager to spend Christmas and New Year's with her and Josh, even if we needed to keep it low-key.

We unpacked the decorations for our tree, and the shoeboxes of ornaments from my mother's attic waited to the side. Micah stood on a stepladder, winding lights around the narrow top of the tree before squeezing between the wall and the window to help me pass the strand around the ever-widening boughs. Carols played from my phone through a Bluetooth speaker, and we sipped hot wassail while adding shiny gold, bronze, and silver balls. We only had a few real ornaments we'd accumulated as a couple: the obligatory 'Our First Christmas' with the year carved onto a banner and a cartoony version of us in a wreath, a Wisconsin 'squeaky cheese' ornament my mom had gifted Micah during our first year together, and another we had picked up ourselves of the logo for UNC Greensboro—Micah's alma mater—when we'd gone to visit his parents our first year as husband and wife.

Finally opening a box from my mother's, I grew quiet. I'd resisted confronting my emotions about this first Christmas since her death. The guilt of canceling the previous one with her, never imagining what I was indelibly giving up, coursed through my veins. My heart thudded, then began to race. My hands and face grow hot as shudders coursed through my body, shaking me to the point that Micah withdrew the box from my hands.

Looped over my index finger and clutched in my palm was a hideous felt gingerbread man, stitched at the sides with red yarn that barely held in the escaping twenty-year-old cotton balls. I'd brought it home from kindergarten, and she'd proudly hung it at the front of the tree, low enough for my three-and-a-half-foot-tall body to point it out. Obligingly, she moved it up as I grew each year, adding a popsicle stick snowman, a yarn-wrapped Rudolph, and a tissue-paper stained-glass star. She made a huge deal at the new decorations crafted from scraps, carefully preserving them year after year.

After a few minutes, I pulled myself together. Micah passed my mother's collection of crystal angels and a miniature ceramic nativity scene. Then, my parents' own 'Our First Christmas' with the banner proclaiming 'est. 1993' and 'John and Cathy' across the top. She'd once told me she'd been supremely irritated about it at the time. The man who personalized it hadn't been able to fit her full name, so he made an executive decision to shorten it. She'd smiled in a way that hadn't quite reached her eyes when she confessed that every Christmas they were married, she complained to my dad when it was time to hang it. Then she said after she lost him, that ornament was a reminder to keep things in perspective. To recognize the difference between an annoyance and a true catastrophe.

When the decorating was complete, we turned off the lamps and plugged in the tree. The twinkling bulbs woven between the ornaments joined my past and present, and they finally released the tears, not in gut-wrenching sobs but in quiet ribbons that reflected their light.

On Christmas Eve, we went to church with Josh and a peaked but cheerful Carrie, and on Christmas Day, we gathered at Carrie's home. She and I stayed cozy in coordinating flannel pajama sets I'd purchased for us, even though the guys refused to keep theirs on after posing for a photo to commemorate the day.

Despite my scolding, Carrie gave me a hand with the heat-and-serve lunch that included ham and all the trimmings. Her low energy and both of our disappointment over not having family to spend the holiday with cast a slight shadow, but we enjoyed ourselves. We watched movies, played board games, and took turns video chatting with family and friends. Aunt Jan, Uncle Jack, and Jonah, their son, made us promise to visit during the following year. Micah's parents and brother belatedly told us we should have come to North Carolina for Christmas, and we took the invitation for what it was. Josh FaceTimed Will and Celia, who were visiting their son's family in California, and we all chatted with them. He quietly excused himself afterward to call his own parents and rejoined us within a few minutes. I wondered if he ever talked to Carrie about them, but Josh never brought them up in my presence.

When the guys took the recycling out, Carrie and I discussed New Year's Eve. We reluctantly opted to forgo the downtown fireworks display and keep the gathering simple with homemade sushi rolls at my house. I held out my hand, admiring the bracelet Carrie had made of my mother's signature, copied from an old birthday card Micah had snuck to her.

The mix of print and cursive gleamed daintily in white gold across my wrist: *I love you, Mom.*

I peered over the screen of my MacBook, watching Micah fold jeans, pullovers, and boxer shorts into his duffle. I was stalking video-sharing apps to seek out promising talent, but discouragement had wormed its way into my headspace. I knew this job would be a challenge, but I didn't expect to be so bad at it. No one I'd brought to Raul's attention had made it past his pursed lips. It seemed everything worth doing had been done. Or, I simply didn't know how to recognize raw talent.

When I came across a possibility, I turned my AirPods off to play samples for Micah. After a few misses, we stumbled upon two interesting bands, and I made plans to see one of them locally while Micah was away in Georgia and South Carolina for the next three days. The second band was touring on their own in Illinois, and I was trying to nail down a convenient time to fly up and catch one of their performances.

"I emailed you a link to our schedule for the next two months. That way, you can see any changes as they happen. If tickets aren't selling in a particular area, I might have to move things around. But with all the PR I've done, I don't expect any duds." Micah's expression changed to a frown as he looked around the bed and across his dresser before snapping his fingers and disappearing to the hall bath for a moment. He reappeared with his Dopp kit, nestling it next to his basketball shoes. "Luckily, both of the guys shoot hoops, so I'll always have someone to play against if we can find some time and a court."

I smiled, relieved to see him making the best of the situation. Before he zipped the bag, he reached into his nightstand drawer and retrieved the book Josh had loaned him. I'd noticed he had been reading it several mornings when he'd gotten up before me, and the book was marked two-thirds of the way in.

It was a Thursday afternoon, and I'd escaped my office at lunchtime to see him before he left. The new band didn't fly to their gigs; they didn't even have an actual tour bus. Instead, they traveled by van and needed to give themselves plenty of time to make it to the first of their three bookings. They'd be by to pick Micah up from our house within the next hour, and I expected him back on Sunday evening.

Before long, a distant rumble grew louder. Concern flickered across my face at the sound. It must be Micah's ride. "Is it just me, or is their muffler going out?"

I sent him off with a kiss, my misgivings amplifying when I spied the chipped paint and license plate that hung askew on the conversion van where he'd be spending the next two months of weekends. As they reversed out of the driveway, a flannel-clad arm waved from the driver's window, and the two strangers absconded with my husband.

Our schedule became routine after a couple of weeks. I met the guys—Todd and Mack—when they dropped Micah off after the first trip. They appreciated Micah's efforts to make their tour profitable, joking about the plethora of sandwiches and cheap motels they would have to get used to. Every Thursday, they'd leave to reach the venue in time to set up, and each Sunday, they'd arrive home after eight to ten hours of driving. They replaced the muffler only to deal with a flat tire on their third excursion between Charlotte and Wilmington.

I'd gotten into my own pattern, working long hours when Micah was traveling but coming home on time when he wasn't to make sure we had dinner together, with rare exceptions. He conceded after several Sundays that he missed our church services and began watching the live-streams as they made their way back to Nashville. "Todd and Mack asked about it, and I don't even wear my earbuds now. And they barely talk over it."

My ad for the CR-V had been online for over a month, and although I'd gotten some calls, it hadn't sold. Eventually, I'd brought it back home and left my Toyota at Carrie's. I thought if I drove it around town with a 'For Sale' sign in the window, I might have better luck. Still, the only offer had been for considerably less than it was worth, and I couldn't accept.

A week later, Micah's tour schedule was cut short by a small fire at the venue they'd booked for Saturday. The van rolled up to our house late that night, and I waved to Mack and Todd from the porch as they pulled away, their faces morose through the windshield.

After a long hug, Micah excused himself to go shower, and I switched off the porch light and living room lamp and went to wait for him in bed. I was nodding off when the sheets rustled as he climbed in next to me. They'd spent fifteen hours traveling that day. No one at the dive bar thought to let him know about the fire before they'd driven from Raleigh to Virginia Beach. With a sigh, Micah mumbled, "Wake me for church in the morning." Before I could answer, he'd fallen asleep.

Chapter Thirty-one

*J*osh, Carrie, and the Harts were pleasantly surprised to see Micah with me when we ran into them in the lobby before the service. "Fortunately, no one was hurt." Micah explained, "Someone dumped hot ashes from the wood-burning oven into a bin by the back door before everyone left for the night on Friday."

Will Hart clapped Micah on the back. "I guess God wanted you here! Let's go see what Pastor Tony has to say today."

The worship band began with a version of Cory Asbury's "Reckless Love", one of my favorites. As I meditated on the words I was singing, Micah's tenor joined in. The lyrics express the sentiment that God will go to any lengths, no matter how inexplicable, to show us how much He wants us. He didn't merely present us with His word and leave us to choose to accept it or not; He unrelentingly chases after us. He never gives up, even as we are busy filling our lives with all that the world around us deems paramount. As the music faded into a different song, Micah reached over and squeezed my hand.

Pastor Tony walked toward the podium, the screen above it displaying a photo of a young Millie and him. She was cradling a bump the size of a watermelon, and he kept her from tipping over by placing his hands on her shoulders as they leaned forward to kiss. It dissolved into a new photo of Millie with damp hair plastered to her reddened cheeks, obviously in labor. The 'awws' from the congregation at the first photo likewise dissolved into embarrassed groans at seeing their friend in such an undignified and painful moment in time. The third photo was of their son, swaddled in a blue blanket, face in repose as though he had not a care in the world, and the 'awws' renewed.

"Ah, the birth process. My memories of that day are probably a little different from Millie's. I remember her water broke while I was at the grocery store at eleven o'clock at night because she just *had* to have a microwavable burrito." Millie, in the front row, must have made a face because Tony pointed at her and blew a kiss. "I came back to find her frantically dragging her overnight case down the hallway to the front door between contractions. The burrito was still on the floor, all thawed and gushy, when we came home three days later."

The guys chuckled at our turned up noses.

"I'm going to be talking about birth today, I should warn you squeamish folks. Trust me—I almost changed my mind when I started researching what birth entails. You don't get from the first photo you saw up on the screen to the last one without a lot going on in between."

"We talk about spiritual rebirth, or being 'born again.' What comes to mind when you hear that expression? In John chapter three, verses three through six, Nicodemus is confused about being reborn. Jesus answers: *'Truly, truly, I say unto you, unless one is born of water and the Spirit, he cannot enter the kingdom of God.'*"

"So, imagine being baptized. We start out standing in the water. We profess our belief. We are dipped under the water and emerge a new creation, literally washed and figuratively cleansed of our previous ways. It's a process, of course, but you may think the hardest part is making the decision that leads up to it. In fact, baptism itself is pure symbolism: biblical and important, yes, but it isn't the act of being baptized that changes us."

A new picture filled the screen above Pastor Tony's head. It was a newborn, perhaps their son, but virtually unrecognizable as the same cherub-faced baby from the previous slide.

"This isn't Gabe," Pastor Tony began. Amusement tittered across the congregation. "I was too busy being a loving and supportive husband and father to take pictures the moment Gabe was born. But I'll tell you: This wrinkled, pointy-headed, purple-faced, covered in goo, and probably in a bit of pain newborn is a better example of what our lives go through when we are brought out of our sin-filled existence and into new life. When we pray to God to change us, we better mean it. When we ask Him to make us a new creation, it means the old us passes away. Jesus tells Nicodemus it isn't about being born of the flesh but being born of the Spirit."

"While He does save us the moment we ask Him to, Millie argued against my comparison that rebirth is instant. She reminded me that sixteen hours of labor isn't anything to disregard." He waited for the murmurs of agreement from all the mothers in the room to die down before he continued. "So, my point is, it *is* a progression, a messy transformation. When God takes us from a life of sin to life as His child, He accepts us *as we are* but He doesn't leave us that way. Culling out the sin of our old nature is painful. It's life-changing, but it's not like accepting a Publisher's Clearing House check that's going to buy us everything we've ever wanted. We're talking about a fundamental change of who we are from the inside out—giving up our human heart and becoming someone with different desires. It's exchanging our priorities for what moves God's heart. Turn to Ephesians chapter four, verse twenty...."

I followed along, holding my mother's heavily annotated Bible so that Micah could see the scripture also. As I read, a conviction rolled through me that, despite my beliefs, I didn't feel fundamentally changed. That my new self, created to be like God, couldn't be put on like a sweater when I needed comfort. Human nature can't be simply covered up with salvation.

"... The decision isn't an easy one; not making it nor sticking with it. The life of a Christian isn't comfortable. It's giving yourself up every minute of every day. Believing He actually still wants us, especially when we continue to mess up time after time, isn't always easy. But He will never stop chasing after you with His reckless love. It might not be easy, but you'll never regret it."

The worship band had quietly assembled behind him and were meditatively singing the bridge of "Reckless Love". My heart swelled and I dropped to my knees. The magnitude of God's longing for me crushed my pride while reminding me who I was meant to be.

Beloved child of the King. Pursued not because of who I was but because of who He is. Unworthy but valued.

I reached for Micah's hand. By the intensity of his expression, the sermon had impacted him as well. The voices of the worship team faded into quiet emotional praise, and the pastor stepped back to the podium.

"If you are ready to take this step, if the Spirit is pressing on you to accept Him, please pray with me, and believe I will be with you through this transition." He bowed his head. "Dear Heavenly Father..."

As it turned out, both Micah and I were ready.

That day at church led to a more surprising and pragmatic development as well. Micah and I stood in line waiting to speak to

Pastor Tony to introduce ourselves and tell him of our momentous acceptance of forgiveness and new life. The balled-up tissue in my hand was rendered useless by the fresh tears welling in my eyes each time they met my husband's. When the pastor realized why we wanted to speak, he pulled us out of the line to a somewhat private corner. There, he prayed over us and discussed the next steps, including suggesting we join a weekly small group.

As we were thanking him, a gangly young man bounced impatiently on his toes nearby, eager to speak to the pastor.

"Well, this is the infamous Gabe," Pastor Tony nudged the teen. "Seventeen now, and a full head taller than his mother." He turned to his son, not quite dismissing Micah and me. "What's up, kiddo?"

"Can I please use the car to go to lunch with Peter? I can drop Mom and Anna off at home first, and she can come back to pick you up later, or…" His voice trailed off, but his eyes continued to plead with raised brows.

"We have got to think about getting you a car!" His dad's tone was humorous, but I could tell this was not a new discussion between them. "Give me a minute, and we'll go find your mom to ask what her plans are."

As Gabe scampered away while calling Peter's name across the lobby, Micah leaned down to whisper in my ear.

My eyes brightened. "Pastor Tony, it just so happens that we have a Toyota Corolla for sale!"

On Monday, Micah and I received an email from a couple who led a Wednesday night Bible study tailored for new believers. Eager to join, we promised to see them two days later. They lived not far up highway 31, so Micah and I easily rendezvoused at home after work to ride together. We could tell immediately being in the group would help our marriage and our fledgling faith.

Gabe and his parents met me at Carrie's the following Saturday to take my Corolla out for a test drive. He was chattering excitedly as he emerged with his dad after circling the neighborhood.

Carrie and I were standing on the front porch with Millie. "I'm so glad we met you when we did. Of course, mostly because of the decision you and Micah took in your walk with the Lord." Millie blushed. "But the timing was such a provision. It's been difficult to share two cars between the three of us. I wasn't sure we could go much longer without getting Gabe his own transportation."

After the deal was made and Gabe backed out in his new Corolla, I took Carrie out to eat with a portion of the profits as thanks for letting me use her driveway for so long. We hadn't spent much time together, just the two of us, in ages. With Micah gone most weekends, I busied myself with showcases at bars or clubs, only going out with her and Josh after church on Sunday afternoons.

We chose a Thai fusion restaurant we had discovered in our college days. Over Tom Kha soup and chicken eggrolls, Carrie and I felt the stresses of adulthood disappear into the lemongrass and ginger-spiced air.

"How are you and Micah doing?" Carrie asked.

"So much better. I'm amazed by what praying together has done for us, individually and as a couple. We are connecting in ways we never had before. The level of trust and vulnerability we have with each other now…"

My sentence trailed off when a throaty cackle caught my attention. The woman's back was to me, but the thick blue hair rippling down it was as familiar as my own. I'd had nightmares about that cackle and that hair and everything else about this woman.

Carrie turned, along with half of the other patrons, most of whom recognized Martine as the face of Still Waters. Unfortunately, just then Martine decided to switch seats with her date, undoubtedly to present herself to the crowd *en masse*.

As she glanced around to make sure she had everyone's attention, her gaze landed upon mine. I shouldn't have been so astonished. Nashville really can be a small town. A splotch of crimson crept up her neck, replacing her usual smugness. Ostensibly forgetting she wanted to draw everyone's attention to herself, she held her menu in front of her face, forcing the server to lean down to catch her order.

I went back to my meal, thoughts swirling. While continuing the conversation with Carrie, my eyes kept darting to Martine, who conspicuously refused to look in my direction again. As I paid the bill and slipped my card back into my wallet, conviction flooded my spirit.

"Carr, will you wait here? I feel like I need to talk to her."

The man's voice registered over the din in the restaurant as I came up behind him. "It's getting harder for him to hide it. She's not as stupid as he thinks, anyway. He came up with some ridiculous reason to sell the cabin in Aspen—hey!"

Martine's dinner partner stopped speaking and grabbed the shin she had just kicked. Glancing up, he noticed me. The look that passed between Martine and me must have clued him in that I hadn't stopped by for an autograph.

"Mal, can you give us a minute?" If she thought a showdown was coming, she didn't want him to witness it.

With a raised brow, he excused himself and wound between tables toward the restrooms.

Martine was holding a martini glass to her lips when I slid into the seat across from her. She put the glass down, her lip curling like she'd swallowed sour milk, and the beverage sloshed over the rim. As she wiped her hand on a napkin, I attempted a joke. "I think martini glasses are designed to spill."

"What do you want?" The coldness in her eyes would have intimidated me once, but tonight I looked closer. I wondered what it was concealing.

"Martine." I paused, wary of this compassion that was trespassing on my bitterness. "I want to tell you I was sorry to hear about your contract being canceled. It was a messy situation, but you and the band are so talented. I'm sure you'll find another management agency."

Her biting laugh made me flinch. "The last thing I need are your platitudes. In fact, I should be the one feeling sorry for you and your pitiful marriage. You think Micah is happy? Do you even know what he wants?"

Whatever sympathy I'd started to feel dissolved. "What would you know about what my husband wants? We are doing just fine. Great, as a matter of fact. So, yes, he is happy. We both are!"

"Are you ready to give him a child? Or are you still stalling?"

Of all things, why would Martine bring up children? Micah and I were in agreement—we were building a firm financial foundation before starting a family. We'd laughed over the alliteration. How did Martine know anything about our plans? I was speechless.

"Yeah, that's what I thought. You didn't know he talked to *me* about how badly he wants to be a dad, did you?"

Martine stabbed her veggie burger with her butter knife. The threat would have been laughable if it hadn't been for the smirk. And the fact that Micah had assured me that his intimacy with Martine had only been physical. But he'd shared something this personal about us—our marriage—with her?

I stood as her date returned. Carrie immediately appeared at my elbow with my coat and handbag draped over her arm. "Excuse me," I murmured to the well-dressed man. I needed to get some air.

What else had Micah not told me?

Chapter Thirty-two

"Elle, this is Jennie from small group. I hope you don't mind that Karina gave me your number."

I took me a moment to put a face to the name. The call had come in while I was sitting in the grocery store parking lot, replaying my argument with Micah.

"Jennie, of course I don't mind. What's going on?"

Jennie Hughes was the only single female in our Wednesday night Bible study. A young woman in her mid-twenties with a mocha complexion and a thoughtful countenance, she'd revealed enough for us to know she'd lived a rough life before accepting Christ. She self-consciously tugged at the cuffs of her long-sleeved shirt, but I had detected scars at her wrists when she allowed them to ride up once or twice.

"I'm sorry it's so last minute, but I was talking to Karina about doing something different for small group this week. I'd like to invite everyone to an event where I'm performing. It's a fundraiser for a homeless assistance program I..." She hesitated before finishing, "...I used to benefit from when I was younger."

I could envision the way she must have closed her eyes and had an inner dialogue before choosing to trust me with that admission. She used the same maneuver in Bible study when she revealed she'd run away from the foster care system.

"That sounds wonderful! We would be honored to attend." I tried to convey encouragement, knowing it wouldn't be easy for Jennie to explain this repeatedly as she called everyone in our group. I hoped she didn't sense the unshed tears thickening my voice.

After asking her to text me the details, I continued to stare out of my car window at the shoppers coming and going, pushing their carts—holding their children's hands.

"Why would you tell Martine anything—anything at all—about our family planning?"

"It wasn't like that, Elle! It was just a passing comment. That day in New York—the day I told you about. We were watching kids skating at Rockefeller."

"Were you daydreaming about having a child? With her? Micah, that's just...just..."

"No! She was watching this little girl with her mom, and she starting crying. She said they were happy tears—that seeing them just made her miss her family in Colorado. We weren't talking about anything personal. Then, suddenly, we were. She asked if I wanted to be a dad. I said I did. I don't know, Elle. I must have just said something like you weren't ready—WE weren't ready yet..." Micah's story trailed. He sounded confused.

"Micah, I can't take anymore of this. I can't. Martine continues to make me the fool."

"Elle, there's no reason for you to feel that way..."

"Don't tell me how to feel, Micah!"

The fight had been terrible. One of our worst. And, when we were finally too exhausted to keep going, there was only one last thing I wondered.

Was a baby a good idea, or would we just be trying to fix the mistrust that kept rearing its ugly head?

On Wednesday evening, Micah and I were running behind schedule to leave for the charity event. My temper had cooled but we were still on edge. I needed space, which the cab of his truck didn't provide. The traffic was atrocious, and we were unable to veer off the highway at the exit we needed. His phone was slow to reroute us, and digging for my own to help caused me to drop one of my earrings into the irretrievable space between my seat and the center console. By the time we arrived, we were uptight and cranky with each other and certainly not in a charitable mood.

Our small group had saved us seats at a table in the back. The tension between Micah and me flashed like a neon sign, and I began to wish we hadn't come. I made stilted conversation with Karina, who graciously pretended nothing was amiss. A red-headed woman at the podium narrated a series of photos on a screen showing teams in blue and white t-shirts handing out meals, blankets, and clothing to long lines of people experiencing homelessness.

"Last year, through the generosity of many of you, we were able to assist thirty percent more people in our community than we did the year before. In fact, we expanded our programs to include portable showers, tutoring for the youth, and five additional temporary housing facilities!"

The image of the never-ending line of men, women, and children waiting for something as simple as a sandwich and a bottle of water made my throat tighten. I'd entered this space with my heart hardened by a traffic jam and a lost cubic zirconia stud, and God was certainly humbling me.

When Jennie approached the piano angled at the edge of the stage, I whispered to Micah that I was moving closer to take a video of her performance. Abandoning my plate of baked chicken and a half-eaten roll, I unobtrusively slid as near as I could without distracting her or the rest of the guests.

There was a moment of staticky feedback in the microphone as Jennie adjusted it. She had transformed from her usual appearance of dark clothing and braids. Tonight, she wore her hair in its natural afro and a pink sleeveless dress. The pale streaks at her wrists flashed occasionally as she played a hauntingly beautiful melody I'd never heard before.

Listening closely to the lyrics, I realized they were about battling rejection and depression. The words echoed the stories she had shared about her own life. As her aching alto crescendoed into the chorus, the sorrow transformed to hopefulness as she sang about finding new life.

My camera was still recording, but I was transfixed by the radiance that shone from her face as the notes faded away. The entire ballroom had gone silent, with no clinking of silver against dishes. Jennie had mesmerized everyone with her passion and talent, but even more so with her openness. It was a story only she could tell.

A story of how our mess can become our message.

Raul leaned back in his chair and let out his breath in a rush. I'd never seen him speechless before, and I hoped it was a promising sign. "Wow." That was it. Then, "Wow!" again.

"Right? The thing is, she doesn't know I'm showing this to you. Even when we were telling her how blown-away we were by her performance, she never said anything to indicate she's trying to break into the business. But she writes all her own songs, and she performed half a dozen last night that are all as gripping as this one."

In fact, I'd recorded three more before my phone died. I wanted to talk to Jennie more after the benefit, but she'd been surrounded. Halfway through, she'd shared some of her back-story with the crowd, including how she had been aided by the organization. By the end of the night, if the atmosphere in the ballroom was any indication, this event was the most successful fundraiser the charity had ever had.

Now, I could see Raul's wheels churning. After a minute of silence with me biting my lip, Raul began writing on a pad while simultaneously barking instructions. "We need to sign her now. Her look is perfect. Her sound is perfect. She has it all. Her contract will stipulate that she records her own stuff. Get her in here to meet with me, and also with Frank and Deb—within the next two weeks!"

I had no idea if Jennie would be interested in a recording contract. I'd finally found an artist who impressed Raul, and she might turn me down. I took the sheet of paper he'd ripped from his pad and headed back to my office. I still had her number. I just had to figure out what to say.

Micah was gone for his shows with Todd and Mack, so I couldn't talk it over with him. They were driving to Little Rock for a gig, then working their way back with bookings in St. Louis and Owensboro, Kentucky. The two bands I'd been con-templating hadn't worked out, and I was desperate for a success. But more than that, I believed Jennie needed to be heard. She was an inspiration. Raul was impressed by her look and sound, but her raw vulnerability was the hook. No one else had her life story and the ability to touch people in the same way.

I decided to call rather than text her. Shutting my office door, I prayed, *Not my will, but yours, Lord.*

"Jennie? Hey, it's Elle Reed from church. I had to call and tell you how amazing you were last night..."

By the time I hung up, Jennie had agreed to see me on Friday night, although she wouldn't commit to meeting Raul or coming to our studio to record a demo. I scrapped the showcase I'd been planning to attend and sent texts to the other scouts in my group in case they wanted to check it out.

Clearing my desk of everything but the paper Raul had scribbled on, I began researching other Christian artists who had signed with Starship. There were surprisingly few. Raul had surely known that, but he hadn't hesitated to say yes to Jennie before even she was on board.

This scenario was backward from the others. During my brief conversation with Jennie, I could tell she would need convincing. She was currently working at a children's hospital overnight while taking classes for a nursing degree. Her schedule was so full she'd been hesitant to wiggle me into her Friday. We were meeting for coffee at the shop near her job before she had to go in that night.

A thought my mom had written in one of her journals came to me suddenly. The verse was in Proverbs, and I remembered looking it up.

"Many are the plans in a person's heart, but it is the Lord's purpose that prevails. Proverbs 19:21."

How reassuring it is to know I am not powerful enough to mess up God's plan for my life!

After a lifetime of trying to force God's will to align with mine, the burden of trying to regulate every outcome was being lifted. The reasoning of a seven-year-old deduced that my father didn't come back because I'd done something wrong, and my narrow shoulders had born a weight that had shaped the next twenty years of my life. But I was never meant to carry it, and it was time to set it down. I could finally give control to the One who'd had it all along.

If it was God's will that Jennie pursued this with me, nothing I could say would stop it. And if not, nothing I could say would change that either.

Chapter Thirty-three

J was waiting at a bistro-style table in the café when Jennie came in, stomping the snow off her tennis shoes. It was rare for snow to stick here, but I'd woken up this morning to the big, fat flakes that reminded me of Wisconsin, and specifically of Mom. The blanket that had formed over the course of the day was somehow comforting.

I'd waited to order until she arrived, and we both asked for mugs of peppermint hot cocoa. "You'd think I'd be surviving my crazy schedule with lots of coffee, but I try not to indulge in anything addictive, even caffeine." Jennie wrapped her hands gratefully around the hot ceramic mug as we settled in at the high tabletop.

I smiled but knew her remark wasn't a joke. "I definitely don't need coffee at this time of night myself. How hard is it for you to stay awake overnight for work?"

"I've had this schedule for about eight months now, and I don't think I'll ever get used to it. It doesn't help that I leave here and go directly to class on Tuesdays and Thursdays. It's kind of a brutal routine," she admitted with a slow nod of her head.

"So," I took a deep breath, "what are your plans right now? You're in school. How long until your program is finished?"

"I'm taking pre-requisites now," Jennie began. "I didn't graduate high school when I should have, so I only got my

G.E.D. two years ago. I kept trying, but, you know, life gets in the way sometimes. And I had no idea what I wanted to be 'when I grew up,' so I wasted a lot of time."

I grinned at her use of air quotes. So far, I hadn't found much in the way of common ground between her life and my own. I needed a springboard to launch my idea.

"Well, I'm not sure you appreciate what an extraordinary talent you are. Your lyrics and your voice are unique, and honestly, there's nothing I want more than for you to focus on your music and let me be the one to help you." Her cheeks colored at the compliment, and I took it as a sign to forge ahead. "This might not necessarily fit in well with your current schedule, but I would be happy to help however I can to make this work. Jennie, your story, your background... it's your testimony. And I think it could make a real impact on people."

I wasn't trying to use her new faith as our common ground, and I hoped she wouldn't take it as a ploy. If she said this wasn't for her right now, I'd accept it, or so I told myself. But I knew even as the words lingered between us that this wasn't about finding the next big thing or anything I'd gain personally. I was serious when I said her testimony needed to be shared because it could help people.

I sat quietly, letting her deliberate. I could see her weighing the possibilities against her current obligations. Finally, the corner of her mouth lifted. "I wouldn't mind coming in to talk to your boss. And I'm working on something new I could record a demo of. If you still want me after that, we can figure out where I'll find extra hours in my week."

Relieved that I could give Raul the good news, I asked her for some days and times she could be available to try to match up with his schedule. Watching her hurry across the street toward the hospital for her shift, I shivered with excitement while swiping the accumulated snow from my windshield.

Micah had one more weekend out with Mack and Todd. Joe had hooked him up, as promised. The new job with an established band was slated for nine months, and Micah was already prepping their tour. He would be home for the first half of March before the new schedule would keep him away for weeks at a time. I resigned myself to it, but I didn't have to like it. However, music was his career, and our life together would always be unpredictable fits and spurts of time together.

We were sharing the leather couch having a casual dinner. My bare feet were wedged under his leg while he balanced a plate piled high with spaghetti on his knees. It was a Tuesday night, and we had the news on in the background. The meteorologist was giving the forecast for the remainder of the week. Cold, cold, and more cold. When her calendar expanded to the ten-day outlook, we both perked up at her mention of possible warmer temperatures. "It's too soon to say, but we may see some spring-like weather by the beginning of March, so stay tuned as we get a little closer. Luke, back to you!"

"Hallelujah," I cheered. "I am so ready for spring dresses after this winter!"

"Yeah." Micah glanced at the television. "Would be nice."

I went back to filling him in on the progress Jennie was making. By then, she'd met with Raul, Frank, and Deb. She'd recorded a song she'd written called "I'm Safe," and even Lorna had shown up in the control booth to listen in. I was sure a tear rolled down her face before she dashed her knuckle across her cheek and slipped back out as the music ended.

"She truly is phenomenal. I've never seen anyone before or since with such ability to make you forget everything else you were doing, and just listen to her. Not just listen, but *connect*. I can't believe she fell into my lap like this. I would have never found her if we didn't join that Bible study!"

Micah grinned, the dimple in his cheek as charming as it had been on day one. "I'm so happy for you both. And I'm glad she has people in her corner who only want the best for her. From what she's said, this may be one of the few times she's had that in her life."

I nodded somberly. I'd learned more about her in the time we'd spent together: from being raised within the foster care system, which had failed her more than it had nurtured her, to eventually running away when she was only fourteen. We were nearly the same age, but her upbringing was light years from my own. During the phase when I thought I was cool for vaping, she was having drugs like Molly and cocaine pushed at her. While I argued with my mom over too-short skirts and too-strict curfews, she was living out of a trash bag and sleeping under overpasses. And when I was watching my mom fall apart over losing my dad, her parents had long before left her alone in a hospital waiting room wearing not much more than a dirty diaper.

Jennie's journey to finding Jesus and believing in His love for her had taken her through incomprehensible valleys. She had also stunned me with stories of others who'd lived on the streets with her in Memphis. She'd hightailed it to Nashville when she was eighteen, arriving on a bus late one night with five hundred dollars under the insoles of her shoes and one aspiration: to stay out of trouble. By then, she'd tried every means of survival on the street, and she professed the grace of God as the only explanation for where she was now. She'd been found months later, out of money and almost out of time, with her wrists slashed as she laid on a park bench waiting to bleed out. She never knew her rescuer, but she'd awoken in a hospital room.

The woman who started the homeless assistance program that held the fundraiser had been called in by one of the nurses. This nurse's impact on Jennie led her, all these years later, to pursue a career in the medical field. Part of me felt guilty for trying to lure Jennie away from this goal, but we had prayed about it together. Jennie wasn't changing her mind about that career but decided to put it on hold. Regardless, she had signed a recording contract last week, and we hoped to have a finished EP by summer.

Micah left again that Thursday for the last of Mack and Todd's gigs. They had done well for this first run and were planning to go back on the road again soon. Micah had told them that as pleased as he was with their success, they'd need a new manager for the future, and they begrudgingly accepted the news.

They got back in town Sunday evening, the two-month tour having sapped them. After all, none of them were young men. I'd offered to have them stay for celebratory steak and lobster after their diet of sandwiches and gas station snacks. By the time they left, my ears were ringing from their raucous reveling as they bragged about all the trouble they'd gotten into on the road, which, according to Micah, was greatly exaggerated.

In two weeks, Micah would be heading out with the new band. Money had been tight while he'd toured with Todd and Mack, but we'd made it through. He'd earn a lot more with this new tour, but our sacrifice was time apart.

Thankfully, we had our faith to connect us.

Chapter Thirty-four

The weather did indeed warm up. On Wednesday, as we drove home from Bible study, the radio deejay confirmed the weekend called for temperatures near seventy degrees during the day. Grinning impishly, Micah asked, "Any chance you can cancel whatever you had planned for Saturday afternoon?"

"I didn't have anything planned for Saturday, just Sunday with Josh and Carrie, as usual. Why? What's up?"

"I'm actually not going to tell you." His dimple flashed when he winked. "But don't wear heels and be ready to go somewhere around, hmm, let's say noon."

On Saturday morning, I stepped outside at eleven to check the weather. There was a slight nip in the air, but the sun was bright and golden, and I went back inside to slip into a sundress covered in daisies. Micah had left on a mysterious errand and promised to be back to pick me up by twelve. His secrecy took me back to when we were young and new at love.

So much had happened in the short span of our relationship. We had grown up, and in a way, we were different people than we'd been when we'd first met. By my count, it had been four years and one month. And a lifetime to go.

I was checking my reflection when his truck pulled into the drive. I'd left my hair curly and realized that I liked this wild side. Perhaps perfection was overrated.

Waiting to hear him come in, I went to the closet to grab sneakers and a cardigan. "Micah?" I called out, waiting for a reply. I received none.

The chime of the doorbell startled me, then made me giggle when I cracked open the door. Micah stood on the porch holding a bunch of wildflowers, which he presented with a gallant flourish of his arm. "Elle, thank you for agreeing to a date with me. I'm sorry if I'm late. It's difficult to find wildflowers in March."

"Micah! What are you doing?"

"You're breaking my heart! I'm here for our date, of course. Did you forget?"

"These are lovely, thank you! Um, let me grab a vase."

A few minutes later, still not knowing where we were going, I pranced out to his truck. We were on an adventure that could be the start of something beautiful. He flirtatiously swatted my hand when I tried to peek under the lumpy blanket on the backseat.

"Maybe you need a blindfold. Yeah, I think we'd better…" Micah reached across me toward the glove compartment.

"No, I promise I'll behave. I won't peek!"

He relented with a dramatic sigh. "Ok, fine. But I still think you should keep your eyes closed."

"Let's at least get out of the neighborhood first. I don't think that part is a surprise." I couldn't stop laughing, and neither could he. I didn't want to admit I had detected the fragrance of food coming from the backseat, but I still didn't know what he had up his sleeve.

Our route didn't take us to the highway. As we drove through the familiar Five Points area, Micah commanded, "Keep your eyes closed until I turn the truck off." The bouncing movement of the truck, the hilly terrain, and the occasional lane change gave me slight vertigo, but I didn't want to complain. With my eyes closed, I quickly lost all sense of direction, but it was only a few minutes later when the engine turned off.

"Okay. You can look."

"Are you sure? I mean, do you want to lead me out of the truck or anything?" I teased.

"The last thing I need is you twisting an ankle, so no, I think you'll figure it out pretty easily now."

I opened my eyes to an unfamiliar sight. We were in a parking lot, facing a row of mostly barren trees. I searched for a clue, seeing walking paths and finally a large sign with a map. I could tell it was a park, but I didn't recognize it.

Micah waited, enjoying my bewilderment. He finally hopped out, mystifying me with no further clues. I turned when he opened the back door of the truck, and as my eyes lighted on the picnic basket he'd now uncovered, I understood the significance of the wildflowers.

"It's the grotto! We're going to the hidden spring grotto!"

It was our first date. Micah had said he wanted to take me somewhere I'd never been before, which I'd insisted was presumptuous of him. But the spring grotto at Shelby Park was a best-kept secret, and I hadn't even heard of it.

We were atop a hill in a lot that led to the park. With the picnic basket on his arm and the blanket folded underneath mine, we walked down the hill toward the lake, following the path to the hidden spring. We chose a spot where sunlight dappled the ground around us, laying out the blanket and settling into the marvelously balmy spring air. Micah's basket contained all our favorites from Caviar and Bananas, a gourmet market we'd discovered after moving to our new neighborhood.

On our first date, our picnic had consisted of an assortment of vegetable sticks and blocks of cheese he'd picked up from the local grocer. As we unpackaged today's offerings, I was impressed at the variety of olives, cheeses, nuts, and salads he'd selected. Our deconstructed charcuterie board took up most of the picnic blanket.

"One more way you've made me a better man," Micah gestured. "There was a time I didn't know the word 'charcuterie.' Now look at me!"

As we nibbled on lunch, our conversation drifted between Carrie and Josh, church, work, and trying to make plans for the next few months on the occasions when he'd be home for more than a day. His schedule was so unpredictable it was impossible to plan anything definitively, and it was more like daydreaming.

He gave me a side-eye and cleared his throat.

"What?"

"Um. I was wondering if you knew anything about Still Waters breaking up."

It was the first time either of us had brought anything even tangentially related to Martine since the baby conversation, and I didn't want to mess this up. This would be the test to see if we could talk without fighting. "What?! No, I didn't hear that. What happened?"

He raised his brows, then said, "I don't know the details, but I think it was mutual between all of them. The guys are starting a band with a new singer—a young man this time. And I have no idea what's going on with Martine, but she's keeping things low-key these days. Joe told me yesterday, but I'm sure by now the news has made its way halfway around town."

"Micah, I never told you this," I began. It felt silly, but it wasn't. It was maybe the most important thing I could share. "The last time I saw Martine, the reason I walked over to talk to her—it was to forgive her."

Yeah, Micah looked pretty skeptical. "Of course, as soon as I started to tell her that, she turned it all around," I scoffed and rolled my eyes. "She used the one thing she had left to hurt me, and then forgiveness was the last thing on my mind."

Micah reached for my hand. "It was still good of you. To want to try. I know that couldn't have been easy." He sighed. "None of this was easy for you."

"Forgiveness isn't easy. Loving the unlovable sure isn't easy." Aunt Jan's words at my mom's funeral swirled with my dear friend Carrie's urging, and I murmured, "But maybe that's why we're here. To pour love into those who don't have enough."

We grew silent, each of us escaping into our own thoughts. I found myself silently praying for Martine. I didn't know her background or what made her who she was. My time with Jennie, and even my recent knowledge of Carrie's childhood experiences, had taught me there are all kinds of traumas, and all kinds of responses. And we never really know what experiences shape other people's behaviors.

But I was profoundly grateful for the life my mother had made for me, keeping me protected and safe in her love.

Chapter Thirty-five

June 9

It's Elle's birthday. I called her first thing, same as I do every year. I wasn't sure if Micah was home or if I'd be interrupting any early morning birthday celebrations, but she was still in bed, and he was on the road, she said. That must be a hard lifestyle for them to maintain, with him gone so often.

She sounded sad, sort of lost. She's like that a lot lately, at least with me. There's been so much hurt between us these last months. I want to talk about our disagreement in January, but I'm afraid telling her about the babies I lost will only make her feel worse. It's too much heartbreak to put onto my child, even if she's an adult now. Maybe she's right, in a way. That's what I need to tell her. Perhaps I have looked to her to fulfill the emptiness I've lived with. A wonderful marriage and a family with a lifelong partner-that was taken from me far too soon, and then I gave up on having it with Paul.

I have an amazing life, full of blessings. But no one to share it with.... Something I regret to this day. I was 40 when I met Paul. Can that be? Twelve years already! Anyway, he'd never married or had children. He said work kept him too busy for pursuing anyone when he was a young man, and he'd eventually settled into bachelorhood. I was so flattered when he said I made him feel like he was missing out on something more in life. But I assumed if being a father hadn't been important to him before, he wouldn't want to become one now, especially to a teenager who was trying so hard to find herself. He was 46 when he married Alison. She was married before, she told me once-but her husband left her for a younger woman. She said he was frustrated she'd never gotten pregnant, but, as it turned out, the difficulty lay with him, as he discovered with his new wife. By the time she married Paul, it was too late in the game for them to try.

Hearing her story made me even more thankful for Elle. I wonder if she'll ever understand how very much I love her. Perhaps one day, when-if-she has a child of her own. She'll learn that when she hurts, I hurt. I tried so hard to always do what was best for her, but I know I let her down. She needed her father, even in memories. In the beginning, it was so hard to talk about him. So very hard. Losing John was traumatic and left my heart closed off. I found myself, as time went by, filling my days with projects to distract myself from thoughts of what I wished could be. Elle gets that from me-trying so hard to distract herself from heartache with work. What if, instead, I'd kept John's memory alive for Elle's sake? I thought I was protecting her from the pain of losing him, but she deserved to keep as many pieces of him as she could. The next time she's here, I will bring the boxes of his things down from the attic. I haven't opened them in forever. Thinking of him inevitably leads to thinking of Brianne and then my other two, and it snowballs into a deep pit that's so hard to crawl out of. But Elle and I should share these memories. They were her family too.

For a long time after John, I couldn't imagine loving anyone else. I may have even still used Elle as an excuse, rather than the real reason I wasn't able to commit to Paul. She is the light of my life, but those early teen years were difficult. She needed to know she could count on me being there for her, even when she pushed me away. Bringing a new man into the picture at that time-she would have thought my focus was split. She would have taken it personally, like she was losing another parent instead of gaining...not a replacement, of course, but Paul could have helped hold me up, taken some of the weight off. Maybe, in turn, that would have allowed me to be an even better mom. Still, everything I did, or didn't *do, was for her. She fulfilled my dreams of motherhood, and I pray I've been the best mother I could be, despite all the time I had to spend away from her.*

Losing her three siblings was devastation on a whole new level. I feel so guilty saying it, but I don't know how I would have managed being a single mom to four children. I would have done whatever it took, of course! I am afraid that part of the reason I never bared everything to Elle is that she'd have seen some sort of relief in me that I didn't have to figure out how to manage. Yet, it wouldn't have been up to me to figure it out. Isn't that the lesson that I've learned, over and over? I don't have to work any of it out myself. I know God always has a plan. Was His plan to call Brianne and my other babies home so I wouldn't struggle even more? That's a terrible thought, and I will never fully understand, but I know He has a reason, and as bad as the pain of losing them was and still is, I wouldn't have wished them out of existence. I wouldn't have been me without each of them. He redeems every situation, and we always have the opportunity to let it be used in our lives to bring Him glory.

My greatest blessing, outside of Elle, is knowing I've helped other families through the trauma of losing someone to violence. Every one of them is a reminder of how precious life is.

I have felt "less than" so often in my life. I hated when people would ask if Elle was my only child. Asked out of innocence, I know, but even in this day and age, people don't realize that can be such a touchy and personal subject. Most people probably assumed I had Elle out of wedlock and judged me for it.

I have Jan, and I know she wants to help. But she's busy with her life and her career and her family. She has it all. All the things that keep me a few steps behind, trotting after her like I did when we were children. She'd be with her cool older friends or her boyfriend or studying for her 'examinations,' as she said (trying to sound all sophisticated- when I found out three years later that was just a fancy word for a regular test). Regardless, as much as I love her, she's always stayed a few steps ahead of me. I wonder if she realizes how lucky she is. She made the choice to stop after one child to "keep her career on track," she said. I couldn't understand it. She's a good mother with a wonderful son, but she wasn't interested in having more.

Anyway, what does it matter? I love the kids at the grief support center. Tyler was so broken and angry when he first came, and now he runs to me every time he hears me coming. JD was so shy, unwilling to talk to anyone. Discovering his talent for drawing and seeing him connect with Matthew over their shared love of art was one of my favorite experiences. And Anya was afraid to go back home, even though her father was no longer there. Thankfully, we were able to help her not fall behind in school. I sometimes forget the impact I've been able to have is perhaps even more important than meeting the world's expectations for success.

Now I sound like Elle. She accused me of forcing an 'outdated itinerary' on her. Even in my quest for the best for her, I managed to drive this wedge between us. It's clear she and Micah are having difficulties. She won't talk to me about it, but a mother knows. I'm afraid she has always had that streak that demands learning lessons the hard way. I know she and Micah love each other, but a marriage without God's protection isn't barricaded well against the sin in this world.

I still wonder if John was tempted to find someone easier to deal with when I lost myself after the first miscarriage. After the second, thankfully, I leaned on him instead of shutting him out. Even in my anger, God brought us together, and that experience was somewhat made easier by sharing the burden. I should have trusted him after we lost our first baby instead of walling myself off to deal with the pain on my own. He needed me, too. We aren't meant to shoulder such *heartache alone. God provided me with a helpmate, and I rejected John and God Himself in my lowest valley.*

Only by grace did my heart eventually open, and our marriage became even better. Quite honestly, if it wasn't for the trials John and I endured together, we might not have had as strong a relationship. Edwin Markham says, "Defeat may serve as well as victory to shake the soul and let the glory out." I understand what that means now, although ironically, I had to learn the hard way.

But it's not about what we've done in life; it's who we become.

The entry in her final, pale gray journal spread over almost two weeks of the previous June, as if she'd been mulling over her life and adding to this train of thought in her spare moments each night. The ink was deceptively bright blue, like it had flowed recently from a new pen rather than seeping into pages that waited expectantly on her nightstand before making its way to my closet shelf, and now finally being read nine months later.

I reflected on all the years I'd had with my mother, and further back—before I was even a twinkle in my father's eye. My whole life, I'd been catching glimpses of a stranger's rolled-up newspaper, leaving me privy to only partial sentences. Now it was spread wide, exposing the missing chunks of the story.

I remembered that birthday phone call. She'd lingered, trying to draw me out. I was upset about Micah, rehashing the previous evening's argument in my head. Still angry, yet irritated that my first phone call today hadn't been from him. I shared just

Jessica Stone

enough with Mom during that call to satisfy her. I glossed over her queries about Micah; instead, expounding intricately upon my plans with Carrie for a day of shopping followed by dinner to draw the conversation out to an acceptable length. I sighed with relief when Mom told me she needed to be on her way to church.

I flipped back and read the pages again, slowly this time, trying to put myself into my mother's shoes. She'd wanted to tell me about the other miscarriages, but stopped in her desire to protect me. Everything she'd done was for me. She'd held back defending herself against my cruel accusations to shelter me from the pain of those losses.

She'd been lonely. Husbandless, on her own, without the partner she'd adored. She'd tried so hard to be both mother and father to me, to fill my days with so much activity that there was no room in my memory for anything else. The dreams at night of my dad came more frequently after reading about him in earlier journals and getting lost many evenings in the photo albums I'd made room for on the small bookcase in the living room. I had smothered the sadness of my childhood loss for so long, in my mind, our family had not seemed incomplete.

For my mother, it wasn't the same. She longed for that missing piece, right up until the end. She'd been torn apart by the death of her husband, then left heart-wrenched as she watched Paul devote his life to someone else. She hadn't said it in so many words, but she hadn't ever really gotten over Paul. My mother, full of love, had only wanted the right man to share it with. She'd given him up for my sake. And all she'd asked was that I not take my own marriage for granted. As much as I hurt reading these pages, I knew how happy Mom would be about Micah and me dedicating our lives and our marriage to God.

My mother's guilt-ridden thoughts on what raising my three siblings along with me would have required of her brought tears

278

to my eyes. Here and there, her tears had splashed on the page, blossoming the cobalt ink into starbursts and leaving me peering at the script to decipher the words. This paragraph left me feeling my mother would have never expected another person to read these journals. The words were honest, but I understood my mom's heart enough to know that the thoughts behind them must have been darker. She professed faith that God would have seen her through, but as she referred to His plan, I imagined the struggle of wondering why he'd allowed her pregnancies, only to lose the precious lives her body was tasked with keeping safe.

There were no scriptures quoted or verses referenced on any of these pages. The words were all her own—raw and revealing a lifetime of disappointments and blessings. Her hurt feelings over not fitting in, watching her sister gain and, in her eyes, perhaps not fully appreciate, the gifts she herself had hoped for. Eventually, finding some sense of fulfillment through the families she helped support through tragedies of their own.

Seeing my marriage through her eyes, my attitude toward becoming a mother myself brought back my biggest regret. I could have, should have, trusted her with the truth about the problems Micah and I were experiencing. The end of this section of the journal ended with the Edwin Markham quote. I hadn't heard it before, and I sat quietly contemplating it now. God uses all kinds of circumstances to bring about His glory. If Micah hadn't gotten involved with Martine, we could have plodded along for who knows how long in our complacent marriage. Neither of us had been willing to confront the dissatisfaction we were feeling head-on. Martine had unwittingly forced us to communicate, and we had eventually sought the Lord together, now keeping His will at the center of our love for each other.

It's not what we've done in life; it's who we become.

Epilogue

Micah left on tour yesterday. This is a huge opportunity for him, and we are so thankful Joe made it happen. Leaving him at the airport was hard. It'll be three weeks before he's back, and even then, only for two days. I have plenty to keep myself busy, though. Josh proposed to Carrie! I'm sure I'll be spending all my free time with her. She's back to practicing with her orchestra, preparing for their summer concert schedule. My favorite time of year is here, and spring flowers are starting to bloom. I know the time will go quickly, but I already miss Micah.

Jennie is busy recording. We are planning to release "I'm Safe" as her first single. Her name is already buzzing in Music City circles, but we're still searching for the right manager to handle her publicity and image and eventual tour.

I love working in A&R now. Every day is new, and I never know when I'm going to meet someone whose dreams I can help make come true. I'm learning a lot about myself. I think Mom would be proud of me.

I decided to start journaling, obviously. It helps me to focus on the good things, the blessings. Romans 12:2 says: "Do not conform to the pattern of this world, but be transformed by the renewing of your mind. Then you will be able to test and approve what God's will is—his good, pleasing, and perfect will." I am so

grateful for this season and excited about the future. I am learning
that no matter what circumstance I find myself in, as long as I
wake up every morning willing to let God use me, He'll make a
way for His plan and purpose.

Micah came home once in early April, twice in May, and again in the middle of June. By then, Jennie's album was recorded, and the first single had an amazing reception. She had radio interviews and appearances lined up, but we still hadn't found a tour manager.

Micah's June visit lasted four days. During that time, he talked with Joe and told him that as much as he appreciated the work, he wasn't willing to endorse the drug use, profanity, and promiscuity he was being exposed to by working with this band. Joe didn't get it. The money was great, and they were selling out venues. What did a little debauchery matter? Micah said he hadn't expected Joe to understand; nevertheless, he'd have to find a replacement.

Jennie needed an all-around manager who could put together a tour, and Micah was suddenly available. He said he was using his "muchness" for God. He wanted his life to reflect what he was all about. And I had no qualms sending my handsome husband out on tour with this mocha-skinned beauty I had grown to love. Prayer doesn't change God. Prayer changes us.

It must have been during that four-day visit in June when we conceived. Catherine Anne was born one day early, on March 19th of the following year. It was the first day of spring.

As the nurse handed her to us, we both caught sight of the bright pink 'stork bite' birthmark across her forehead. It looked just like the smears of lipstick my mother used to leave behind.

Micah laughed so loudly it startled our baby girl. "Well, I see you met your grandma!"

Acknowledgements

This book has been in the works for longer than you'd ever believe, and I am so grateful for each person who helped make this story and this series a reality.

To my parents, who introduced me to the joy of books and nurtured my love for them and my dream of one day doing this exact thing. Thank you for reading (and rereading and rereading) the many version of my half-written manuscripts. But you haven't read this version yet, so enjoy!

To Kaylee, who barely reads anything I write. One day maybe I can get you to sit still long enough to finish a book. Maybe it'll even be this one! (How long was *Rory's* reading list?) Seriously, thank you for being my Nashville travel buddy over the years. Together, we discovered so many of the places mentioned in this series. I'm grateful for the memories we made and continue to make, and how having you for a daughter inspires me every day.

To my husband, who never doubted this day would come. Thank you for supporting me as I pursue my passion for storytelling. Thank you for indulging me when excitement and frustration and new ideas and changes have me talking your ears off. Thank you for loving me.

To Kaelynn, thank you for letting me borrow your middle name for my villain-who-isn't-always-going-to-be-the-villain.

Thank you for letting me borrow your song for a working title and mood music, and for letting me use your band's name. Thank you for working so hard to help conceptualize the cover (and for the many iterations of it). It's time to hang my painting in my office, by the way!

To Chris Aloi and Penny Lauricella for their real estate insight, and to David Mullen for his input on the music industry. Thanks for helping me get the details right!

To Betsy St. Amant and Tara Johnson for your helpful edits and encouragement. I appreciate you both so much.

To my agent, Barb Roose, who took a chance on an unpolished story and a writer who didn't have a clue. Your belief in me and patience as I reworked (and reworked and reworked) this manuscript is so appreciated. And you were right about the changes. All of them.

To Jill Kemerer and Janet Grant and Story Architect, I believe this is the beginning of a long and beautiful journey. You have no idea how much I appreciate you.

To my readers—I hope you love the sweetness interwoven in this story, and I hope you stick around to see what becomes of Carrie and Josh, to hear Martine tell her side of the story, and to watch Jennie's beautiful journey. *(Don't tell the others, but she's becoming my favorite!)* And I'd love for you to visit my website and catch another glimpse of Lorna and Donovan. Like me, and no doubt you as well, none of these characters are without their stories of redemption.

Finally, to my Savior and my Lord—thank you for blessing me with this gift and love for storytelling, thank you for surrounding me with such encouragement, and thank you for redeeming my own messy story.

About the Author

*J*essica and her husband, Jeff, reside just outside of Raleigh, North Carolina, near her parents and other family. This story—and her confidence to write it—were inspired by her own *Gilmore Girls-esque* relationship with her daughter, Kaylee, who is living out her dreams as a fashion designer in Paris.

Whether at home pushing one of her cats off her keyboard or while sipping espresso in a Parisian café, you'll usually find Jessica writing contemporary faith-based women's fiction and cleverly thought-provoking romantic comedies that point to

Jesus. Because she simply loves telling stories about life and love … and He authored the greatest love story of all!

> Follow @jessicastonestoryteller on Instagram/Threads
> @jessicastone—storyteller on Facebook
> Free stories and more at *jessicastonestories.com*
> Contact: *jessica@jessicastonestories.com*

JESSICA STONE

Telling stories about life and love.

A Thornbush and Juniper Story